A crack rent the air

The unexpected noise came from behind the Executioner. He turned his head quickly to witness the black canopy opening, then checked the altimeter on his right wrist.

The parachute was deploying too early.

An invisible hand grabbed Bolan by his neck and jerked him into an upright position, his head snapping backward. His hands flew automatically to the risers that would enable him to gain some semblance of control in his descent. They weren't there, and his terminal velocity hadn't significantly decreased.

Bolan looked up and cursed. The black parachute, all three hundred and seventy square feet of it, had collapsed and become entangled in itself. Bolan plummeted toward the ground.

Completely out of control.

DON PENDLETON'S MACK BOLAN®

ARMED RESPONSE

A GOLD EAGLE BOOK FROM
WⓄRLDWIDE®

TORONTO • NEW YORK • LONDON
AMSTERDAM • PARIS • SYDNEY • HAMBURG
STOCKHOLM • ATHENS • TOKYO • MILAN
MADRID • WARSAW • BUDAPEST • AUCKLAND

Recycling programs
for this product may
not exist in your area.

First edition April 2015

ISBN-13: 978-0-373-61576-6

Special thanks and acknowledgment to
Glenn D Williams for his contribution to this work.

Armed Response

Printed in U.S.A.

Though I walk in the midst of trouble, you preserve my life; you stretch out your hand against the wrath of my enemies, and your right hand delivers me.

—*Psalms* 138:7

Threaten the innocent, and I will threaten you. Take an innocent life, and I will take yours. Steal what is not yours, I will reclaim it. No place is dark enough to hide from my wrath.

—Mack Bolan

Dedicated to members of the Red Cross,
who leave their homes and families at a moment's notice
to assist those who have lost everything

CHAPTER ONE

Djibouti City, Djibouti,
Horn of Africa

Air-conditioning.

Peter Douglas stood in the foyer of the Waverley Hotel and breathed deeply, ignoring the chaos around him along with the dust and dirt that stuck to his sweat-stained face. The temperature outside was already at an unbearable level, while the foyer was an oasis of comfort.

Douglas listened to his partner coughing next to him, trying to adjust to the temperature difference as quickly as possible. Yes, air-conditioning had to be one of man's greatest inventions and he briefly wondered how the hotel kept it running during these troubled times. But only briefly, only out of curiosity. In reality he didn't want to know and vowed to return to the Waverley as often as possible.

This day, however, it was business and information that brought the two CIA agents to the uptown hotel on the edge of the Plateau de Serpent, the more luxurious end of Djibouti City, if one could say that living in a famine- and drought-stricken region could in any way be luxurious. Douglas took another deep breath, removed his sunglasses and surveyed his surroundings, wondering if his newly assigned partner, Peter Davies, was doing the same. What a joke that was. Somebody at Langley had to have been having a laugh at the time. Peter and Peter, the washed-out, veteran has-been and the rookie. Let's put them together in the hellhole of the Horn of Africa and see what happens. Assholes.

The hotel foyer was a chaotic jumble of humanity and equipment. Sports bags and other paraphernalia were piled up against the wall as aid workers and journalists milled around, waiting for rides out of the city to the refugee camps. People were shouting at one another and at the staff behind the reception desk, demanding to know where they were supposed to go. Didn't the staff know who they were?

Douglas recognized one of the people, a journalist from CNN who thought that Douglas worked for the US Consulate as an aid adviser. He gave a quick nod to the journalist before moving on to survey the rest of the people. Beside him Davies was still busy brushing the dust out of his loose-fitting white shirt and beige cargo pants, besides running his fingers through his hair, mumbling about the heat and how hot it was and how unfair it was that they had to stand in line and be searched, not once but twice. The first search by the Djiboutian military who manned the checkpoint outside, supposedly to protect the hotel and foreigners and then by the facility's private security, who didn't trust the military as far as they could throw them. That had taken more than an hour, an hour standing in the searing sun at ten in the morning. Douglas was grateful for the bottle of water that he had brought with him, a bottle that one of the soldiers had wanted to confiscate, but instead had chosen to accept the dollar bills in Douglas's hand. Dollars could buy food for the family; a bottle of water would go only so far. So, they had passed through both checkpoints and now stood in the beehive of activity. Douglas figured that many of the aid workers were new on the ground, having arrived maybe yesterday, hence all the baggage scattered around. They would be moving out shortly, into the heat, the desperation, the misery of a dying population.

Many people had moved closer to the city from the outlying country. The large US Marine and naval base at Camp Lemonnier had been locked down so that the masses couldn't storm the gates in search of the food and water they knew the American military had to have. The adjoining Djibouti-Ambouli International Airport was also closed and guarded by the Marines. Only international aid and military flights were coming in and out, but that didn't stop the desperate from wanting to stow away and find somewhere safer to live. A memory flashed by of a story he had heard about six refugees who were found dead on a flight after it landed in Germany. The cargo hold hadn't been pressurized, so the six had perished. Douglas shook the morbid thought from his head and returned to the present. Their contact would be waiting for them in the dining room.

He began to work his way through the people and toward the hotel's dining room, aware that Davies was following him, still brushing dust off his clothes and seemingly paying little attention to his surroundings. Douglas hoped that the rookie was staying alert, that Langley still arranged to have basic field craft taught back home. So far Douglas hadn't been impressed with Davies. The kid—Douglas couldn't help but think that of him; the kid was twenty years younger, athletic and talked about computer games all the time—had moaned about everything since he'd arrived a week earlier.

They were not based at Lemonnier; that would have been too obvious. Instead they had a small safehouse not far from the airport. That way it was hoped that they would "blend in," as if such a thing were possible in the height of the drought. Americans always looked well fed while everyone around them was emaciated. The idea of blending in baffled Douglas. Instead he maintained his cover and did what he could to assist various aid agencies while keeping his ear to the ground for rumors of potential jihadists that wanted to stir things up and drive the Americans out of Djibouti altogether.

"Shit, it's already hotter than New Mexico out there," Davies said to him above the general hubbub.

Douglas stopped, turned to the younger man and prodded him in the chest with his index finger.

"Listen, Peter, a French friend of mine wants to meet with me, and we're here to find out why. You will sit down, keep quiet and learn something. Whatever you do, do not interrupt."

"Hey! What did I do?" Davies protested.

"Nothing yet. That's what worries me. Come on, we're already late."

The dining room was as busy as the lobby. Douglas craned his neck to look over the top of the crowd. Yes, there he was, sitting in the corner with his back to the wall, keeping an eye on all the movement, besides watching the military checkpoint that was no more than ten yards from the big bay windows. If he saw Douglas, he gave no sign. The CIA agent, with Davies following, threaded his way through the tables toward his contact.

In his late sixties, with a head full of white hair and dressed in a tan suit, Pierre Saint-Verran was immaculately groomed. The man watched Douglas as he neared the table and gave a slight nod in greeting. Then he focused on Davies.

"Who is this, Peter?" The Frenchman spoke English with a slight French accent.

"Pierre, this is Peter Davies, a colleague. I have to show him the ropes, so to speak."

Davies leaned past Douglas and held out his hand. The Frenchman looked at it for an instant as if it were something distasteful, then reluctantly grasped it. "I'm Peter Davies," he gushed, shaking hands vigorously.

Douglas pulled out a chair and sat down. Davies released Saint-Verran's hand and did the same.

"Pierre Saint-Verran," the Frenchman announced, then ignored Davies, who was already beckoning to a server, and regarded Douglas. "Peter, I do not have much time. I have a very important meeting with several companies later, so I will keep this short." He broke off as a smiling but harried server appeared and began taking their orders.

Douglas waited until the server had departed. "What's wrong? You seemed quite worried when you phoned last night."

"Not worried, no. More concerned. We have known each other for a while now, and I know what it is that you do for your embassy."

"Hey." Davies suddenly felt the need to jump in. "We just work for the ambassador."

"For pity's sake, shut up! What did I say to you before we came in?" Douglas kept his voice quiet but was unable to hide the exasperation that he felt.

Saint-Verran raised a hand and smiled faintly. "Of course you do. But I am sure the information that I have will be of interest to the ambassador, as well."

"Please, Pierre, ignore my young and impertinent friend here. What's concerning you?" Douglas was already troubled himself. Saint-Verran had lived in Djibouti a long time, working freelance as a security consultant for various companies and aid agencies. As a former counterintelligence agent, Saint-Verran knew almost every important person in the country, including the senior officers of the French Foreign Legion stationed here.

"A few months ago—" Saint-Verran paused as the server returned with their drinks. "A few months ago I was approached by a US oil company wishing to explore the north Obcock region. I advised against it, not only because of the bandit raids but also because of the increased tensions between Eritrea and Ethiopia. Many of the people in Obcock originate from those two countries, and ethnic tension is always present. But the two men of the company insisted, so I reluctantly provided them with guides and saw to it that they had the means to get out of the area in a hurry. Ten days later they returned, paid up and left. My guides claimed that the oilmen seemed quite excited when they were up in the mountains." Saint-Verran took a sip of his coffee.

"What was this company called, and did they find oil?" Douglas asked.

"They told me they worked for a company called

Trenchard Oil Industries. I researched the company, and they do appear to be a legitimate business, if a bit small compared to their rivals. As for finding oil, I do not think so. Total, ExxonMobil, Royal Dutch Shell, they have all scoured the country and never found a single drop." Saint-Verran smiled into his coffee cup, seemingly lost in thought.

"However," Saint-Verran continued, "that is not why I asked you here. A few days ago I heard a rumor from a source that gave me two, no, three pieces of information. First it seems some sort of military camp has been set up in the same area. It is possibly Eritrean. Some of their people have been looking for a place to train out of the sight of Ethiopia. My contacts within the Djiboutian army know nothing about it, and with the current tension in the city, they have no interest in investigating it. Second, it seems that there are two groups of white men also in the same area. The first group seems to be the Trenchard men, looking around again. Who knows, perhaps they did find something. However, the second group of men is why I called you here. They seem to be mercenaries, training and teaching in that military camp."

Douglas sat back in his chair and took a sip of water while he analyzed the information. It could mean almost anything. Africa was full of mercenaries. Maybe they were training Eritreans, or any other group for that matter. They could also be training jihadists or pirates, and that would be a concern. Djibouti was of great strategic importance. The Marine and naval base, Lemonnier, was the only one of its kind in Africa, and its proximity to Yemen and the rest of the Middle East increased its value tenfold.

"Have you any idea as to the nationality of the mercs? Are these oil guys in any danger?" Douglas asked.

Saint-Verran smiled again, this time a little sadly as if to say that his intel wasn't quite up to scratch. "I am afraid that I have no idea who these mercenaries are. The Trenchard men—if it is them—did not return to me for my services. Nor did they approach my competitors. They have not reapplied for visas to enter the country, unless they changed their nationality to French. It is possible that they are in danger, so my answer is yes. If rebels or jihadists find them, then they would be killed or taken hostage. You know how your television loves it when Americans are taken hostage."

Douglas groaned, and even Davies looked worried at that thought. If these men were Americans working for Trenchard Oil Industries or any other company, and if they were captured or killed, the fallout would be huge. Then he would come under the scrutiny of the company and the ambassador, both wanting to know why he hadn't acted sooner. This was just what his career needed, another disaster in the making.

Pierre Saint-Verran rose from his chair. "I am afraid that I can offer you no further information at this time, my friend. I am sure that you will be able to learn something for yourselves. Many of my clients are oil companies, and I am sure they will be very surprised to learn of oil being discovered in Obcock. The drinks are my treat." He smiled at Douglas, nodded curtly at Davies and walked over to the bar to settle the bill.

"What now?" Davies asked. He had already finished his cola and seemed to be wondering if there was time for another before they trekked back outside into the blistering heat.

"We make a report and have these Trenchard guys checked out. The idiots. They probably think this is a backward hick country, where visas don't apply. Unless they're French nationals. Then they wouldn't need a visa. And we have mercs running around. God only knows who they are or what they're doing. We'd better get back and see what we can find out. Maybe we can get some of our guys to fly a drone up there. Jesus, what a mess."

Douglas and Davies waited for a few minutes until Saint-Verran had departed. They didn't want to be too obvious by leaving with him, although Douglas reflected that meeting in such a busy and public room was hardly unobtrusive. Standing up, they observed a white Mercedes-Benz car, its windows blacked out, pull up to the main doors. They watched as Saint-Verran climbed into the back, the hotel's doorman closing the car door behind him.

"Can he be trusted?" Davies asked, indicating the car.

"About as much as I would trust anyone around here. He knows a lot of what goes on in Djibouti, so, yeah, I think that we can trust him for now. He can be as slippery as an eel and almost certainly has his own motives for passing this intel on to us. He's probably hoping that we make a mess of things, get the Trenchard men killed and then he can sell the oil information to somebody else. Come on, let's go." Douglas began to work his way toward the dining room door, past the bar, Davies in tow.

Peter Douglas had no true recollection of what happened next.

There was a bright flash, followed by an almighty bang.

The bay windows of the dining room imploded, sending thousands of shards of glass into the hotel on a wave of superheated air.

The shock wave hit him hard, sending him up and over the bar. The mirror above the bar, along with the bottles of alcohol and all the drinking glasses, simply shattered, cascading onto the floor.

Douglas hit the ground facedown with a thump, his head slamming violently against the wooden floor. He wasn't aware of it hurting. A heavy weight landed on top of him, which knocked the remaining air from his lungs. He was partly aware of being wet, wetter than he should be. He moved his right hand along the floor, instinctively jerking it back as a large sliver of glass cut deeply into his palm. Blood flowed from the wound, mixing with the cocktail of whiskey and vodka.

Douglas tried to move, tried to raise himself up but couldn't. He couldn't move. His vision was swimming. Were his legs broken? His back? He moved his head to the left and saw that his third hand wasn't moving. His third *black* hand. He tried to make it twitch, to make it respond but it wouldn't. His inner voice was trying to say something, but he couldn't hear it. He gritted his teeth and listened. Listened intently. The voice, his common sense told him that it wasn't his hand. It belonged to someone else.

He began to struggle out from under the deadweight, trying to avoid the broken glass. After moments, minutes, hours, he was free of the load. Still lying on his stomach, he slowly turned his head to see who had been on top of him.

The sightless eyes of the dead bartender stared back.

Douglas gradually moved into a sitting position. The world wobbled. He was soaking wet. There had been a flash. Where was the rain coming from? He raised his head and stared directly into the fire sprinkler on the ceiling. As he watched, it stopped, the flow of water ending. Had there been a fire? Where was he?

He realized that he couldn't hear anything. There was a lot of smoke and a lot of glass. He was covered in it. He raised his hand and caught the edge of the bar and began to lever himself up. His feet went out from under him, and he landed on his buttocks. Again he tried, this time with two hands. He managed to get to his feet, his legs wobbling under him. Using the bar for support, he looked around, trying to comprehend what he was seeing.

He cursed in horror as his memory began to return.

The dining room of the Waverley was gone. The bay windows shattered. Outside the hotel was a smoking crater, where what appeared to be the remains of a white car were burning. Through the smoke he thought he could see what was left of the military checkpoint. Inside the hotel was a scene of carnage and total devastation. Chairs, tables, people had been flung like confetti around the room. Everything was soaked. Nobody was moving.

There was no sound. None.

Douglas raised his cut and bleeding right hand to touch his ear. It was still there; he hadn't lost it. It dawned on him that he was deaf, hopefully only temporarily. He'd be retired from the CIA if it was permanent. The CIA! Shit! He was with someone. Davies! Douglas heaved himself up and over the scratched and splintered mahogany counter, falling to the other side when his feet failed to keep up with him. Pain returned to his hand in an instant, and he thought he might have yelled from the shock of it. Davies, where was Davies? He had been following right behind him… There! There were his beige cargo pants. Douglas crawled over and found the kid intact. No arms and legs seemed to be missing. The kid was facedown, unmoving. Douglas rolled him over and felt for a pulse. Could he feel one? Were his fingers still working? Then he thought he felt something. As if in confirmation, Davies moved slightly. The kid was still alive.

Douglas coughed and heaved a sigh of relief simultaneously. The kid was still alive. Then he remembered seeing the torn wreckage of a white car burning outside the hotel. Saint-Verran. It had to be Saint-Verran. A car bomb? How had it gotten past the checkpoints? Who had planted it? The mercenaries in the north? Somebody else? It didn't make sense. Douglas held the kid in his arms and felt rather than heard movement behind him. He craned his neck and saw people entering the room, looks of horror on their faces. He raised his left hand and waved slowly at them.

"Over here," he yelled. Then all thoughts disappeared as a dark wave overtook him and he fell back onto the drenched floor, unconscious.

CHAPTER TWO

Above Southern Yemen

Loadmaster Terrence Smith almost tumbled from the ladder as he emerged from the flight deck of the Lockheed Martin C130J Hercules C5. He caught himself in time and slid down the ladder into the main cargo hold of the massive aircraft. The noise of the four turboprop Rolls-Royce Allison engines was overwhelming, and he was thankful for his military-grade ear mufflers. The aircraft was currently at fifteen thousand feet, making three hundred knots. That would be changing very shortly. They were about to make their approach to Aden International Airport.

Smith squeezed past pallets of rice, tents and other humanitarian aid, all destined for the Horn of Africa and parts of Yemen. The drought covered vast areas of Africa. Great Britain, along with many other nations, had flown in extraordinary amounts of emergency supplies using a squadron of semiretired Royal Air Force—RAF—transport planes. Aden was often used as a staging point for the aid, where the pallets would be split up and redistributed to various agencies. It was a routine flight. Everything was normal and on schedule.

Almost everything.

There was one anomaly.

The Hercules had a mysterious passenger, a last-minute addition during the refuel in Naples. The orders were specific. The man didn't exist. He was never on the aircraft, and Smith was not allowed to remember him. He didn't know who the passenger was or even what nationality he might be, but Smith knew enough to know what the man represented. Special Forces. His ice-blue eyes made Smith shiver. Even from several yards away, the stranger emitted a presence that spelled danger.

The man looked up, pinning Smith to the spot with his gaze. It was impossible to hear anything over the thunder of the engines, yet the commando had heard Smith approach. In the ten minutes that Smith had been away from him, the unknown soldier had applied combat cosmetics to his hands and face; he had also changed into a pure black jumpsuit. The man removed his gaze from the loadmaster and resumed preparing himself. A parachute was already strapped to his back, and a long black gear bag was lying next to his feet. Smith decided this was one guy he wouldn't want to encounter in a dark alley, even if he was a friendly.

"Two minutes to the drop zone. You had better get ready." Smith had to yell in the man's ear to be heard.

The soldier merely nodded. Smith watched as the man ran his hands over the buckles and straps of his parachute harness, leaving nothing to chance. Together the two men walked over the vibrating deck to the side cargo door. The jump light was still red, but that would change within the next minute. The man secured himself to the aircraft frame to prevent himself from falling out. There was no need to worry about decompression or specialist breathing equipment, as they were not flying high enough. He reached out and pushed a button on a control panel and plunged the cargo hold into darkness.

Smith heard him punch another button. There was a hiss and a thunk as the side door opened. The noise level increased tenfold. The freezing night air rushed in, whipping around them.

Twenty seconds more.

Loadmaster Smith reached out and grabbed a metal strut for extra support. He disliked parachute jumps and being a parachute dispatcher. The height didn't bother him. The sensation of falling did. But serving in the RAF meant standard parachute training, and he had managed to conquer his fears. The old anxiety, though, was always there.

Ten seconds.

Smith was glad that he was not jumping this night. A nighttime parachute jump was a terrifying experience for those who had never attempted it. A nighttime jump over the desert would only increase the tension. On a moonlit night the sand would appear as water, giving a false illusion as to exactly how high the jumper was, making him misjudge his landing and break limbs on impact. However, for a highly experienced soldier, one equipped with all the latest gadgets, it should be a walk in the park. And he could tell that the stranger was no novice.

Zero seconds.

The jump light changed from red to green.

The stranger exited the aircraft.

In a blink the man was gone, leaving only empty space and howling wind behind him. Smith didn't bother peering out into the void. There was no point. The soldier would already be lost to sight.

Smith pushed another button that closed the door. He shivered in the cold. The aircraft's interior lights came back on. He released his safety belt and walked toward the flight deck to report that the passenger had departed. The big man in black, whoever he was, was off to war.

And Smith wished him well.

PITCH BLACK.

Mack Bolan, aka the Executioner, plunged through the night on the latest mission of his War Everlasting. The noise from the Hercules was already lost, replaced by the sound of cold air roaring past his head, his suit and gloves keeping his body reasonably warm in the ice-cold air. Bolan didn't bother trying to locate the aircraft, concentrating instead on his trajectory in what was called military free fall. He lay horizontal to the earth, chest out, back arched, steering with his outstretched hands. His gear bag was tight between his knees. The parachute, a standard MT1-XS fitted with an automatic opening device, had been borrowed from a US Navy SEALs unit that was on exercise in southern Italy. The parachute would automatically open at three thousand feet, giving Bolan plenty of time to glide the canopy to his designated landing zone. The parachute, like everything else on this mission, had been hastily arranged. The target was just too important for Bolan to be allowed to slip away.

The target was one Zaid abu Qutaiba. Bolan's mind quickly ran through the known facts and conjectures as he plummeted to the ground. Qutaiba had been on

Stony Man's most-wanted list for some time. At one time the man had been a captain in the Iraqi Republican Guard. Now he claimed responsibility for the destruction of an embassy in Kenya, the attempted shooting down of a US commercial aircraft and several assassinations of liberal politicians in Pakistan, Iraq and Afghanistan. It was also believed that he was behind several car bomb attacks in Israel.

These atrocities were more than enough to bring him to the attention of the antiterrorist unit at Stony Man Farm.

Qutaiba had been spotted before, not only by Stony Man but also by several key law-enforcement agencies around the world. Yet Qutaiba had managed to avoid capture through the use of disguises and false names, despite all the technology and all the human resources brought to bear. The report had come in less than twelve hours earlier from the CIA. An agent had followed Qutaiba and his entourage to an abandoned village that was probably being used as a transit point on the southern shores of Yemen. The window of opportunity was slim. Bolan had been in Italy at the time, accepting a mission to free a hostage, a mission that was scrubbed by the time he arrived, the hostage already freed by the Carabinieri. So he was hastily pressed into a new operation and was now jumping out of an aircraft at ten thousand feet.

The mission was simple.

Locate the terrorist transit camp.

Identify Qutaiba.

Termination with extreme prejudice by drone strike.

Although Mack Bolan carried enough firepower to take on a small army, his task this time was one of pure surveillance: make sure that it really was Qutaiba, then contact the Farm. They in turn would relay the message to the Pentagon, who in turn would contact the pilot of a remote drone that was orbiting high overhead. The White House had made it clear to all parties involved. No mistakes. No civilian casualties. Make sure it really was a terrorist camp. Make sure that Qutaiba was at the location. Then and only then would the order be given to destroy the terrorists. All of this would require boots on the ground, and those boots belonged to the Executioner.

Bolan had to give the terrorists credit. Not a light showed anywhere. The camp was under observation from an orbiting Keyhole KH-12 satellite, which would be using infrared and thermal imaging. It would show the observers back home how many warm bodies there were.

Crack!

The unexpected noise came from behind the soldier. He turned his head quickly to witness the black canopy opening, then checked the altimeter on his right wrist.

The parachute was deploying too early.

The automatic activation device fitted to the chute had to have been faulty. Bolan hadn't had the time to thoroughly check all of the equipment himself, and when he had preset the required height, he hadn't noticed anything unusual.

An invisible hand grabbed Bolan by his neck and jerked him into an upright position, his head snapping backward. His hands flew automatically to the risers, which would enable him to have some semblance of control over his descent. They were not there, and his terminal velocity had not significantly decreased.

Bolan looked up and cursed. The black parachute, all 370 square feet of it, had collapsed and become entangled on itself.

Bolan plummeted toward the ground completely out of control.

He had only seconds to react. The gear bag had slipped from between his knees and was now hanging by its quick-release cord. The weight of the equipment in it was causing him to gyroscope, spinning him to the left in ever-quickening circles. Soon it would be impossible to maneuver. The centrifugal forces would prevent him from moving his arms. He forced his right hand slowly down to his belt, fighting the gravitational force. He fumbled for several seconds, unable to locate the emergency-release cord.

Suddenly it was in his hand and he tugged hard. Immediately the gear bag dropped away, disappearing into the darkness. With the loss of ballast, Bolan began to spin slightly slower. His fingers were throbbing, his head felt as if it were about to pop from the blood being forced into his extremities. Gritting his teeth, he found the emergency release for the parachute with his left hand and depressed it.

There was a snap as the faulty parachute let loose.

Bolan was once again in free fall.

Instinct told him that his time was almost up. He curled in a ball, rolled over and threw his limbs out in a star formation. He pushed aggressively down with his right arm and leg, and the spin quickly was brought to a halt. Reaching down, he tugged on the cord for the reserve chute.

Once again there was a crack, and Bolan was grabbed from behind into an upright position. Above him the black canopy of the reserve chute opened to the familiar rectangular shape, its 270 square feet fully spread. Bolan's unchecked descent slowed.

He reached for the risers and checked his altimeter.

He was a mere two hundred feet above the ground. Swiftly he pulled them to further slacken his speed and braced for impact. He began running as he landed on the soft sand, which absorbed the shock. His left foot went out from under him, and he fell down the side of a dune, dragging the parachute with him. Bolan rolled several times before coming to a stop. He was now wrapped up in the collapsed parachute.

Could anything else go wrong?

Bolan released the straps and cut through the cords and material with his Cold Steel Tanto fighting knife. Once free he quickly crawled away from the landing site, all the time listening for sounds that somebody had spotted his parachute, that they were coming to investigate.

There was no movement. The desert was silent.

Stony Man Farm, Virginia

BARBARA PRICE, mission controller at Stony Man Farm, felt her heart thud as she watched the thermal image of Bolan falling out of control on one of the digital screens in the Computer Room. She and Aaron "the Bear" Kurtzman, head of the Farm's cyberteam, quickly surmised that there was a problem when Bolan's body began to windmill. What exactly was happening was impossible to say. They couldn't see what the situation was with the parachute or the gear bag.

But for several long seconds they watched as Bolan plunged through the sky.

"How high is he?" Price asked Kurtzman, a slight tremor in her voice.

"Not high enough" was the muted reply.

"What went wrong?"

"I have no idea."

They could only observe the imminent death of the Executioner, a man they had known, admired and supported through the years, a man who was Price's occasional lover.

It was a huge relief when they saw the falling man resume a normal position in the air, then suddenly slow. They watched as the figure rolled and tumbled on the ground. He was down and very much alive.

Kurtzman turned back to his computer, tapping at the keys. After several seconds he looked up at Price, his expression grave.

"There is a slight problem."

Price looked away from the screen, shifting her focus to her friend and colleague. "What?"

"Striker is here," he said, pointing at the main screen, "but his equipment, including the transmission gear, is here." The image on the main screen zoomed out. "He must have dropped it when he lost control during the free fall. The problem is these two guys."

On the screen they could clearly see two shapes advancing toward the gear bag. The bag contained not only Bolan's long-range weapons but also the transmission equipment needed to contact base. The two men were believed to be a foot patrol, one of several that monitored the area.

"When they open it and find the guns, they'll run

all the way back home and show their treasure to the boss. If it is Qutaiba, then he'll disappear, and a hunting party will be looking for Striker."

"And there's no way we can contact Striker to have him intercept the patrol."

"No way at all," Kurtzman confirmed.

"Inform our contact in Yemen that there's a problem. See what assistance he can offer," Price ordered.

Kurtzman nodded and immediately got to work.

Southern Yemen

MACK BOLAN STAYED at the landing site for ten minutes, waiting, watching, ignoring the cold night air. Nobody came. He had quickly regained his breath; he had hundreds of hours of experience with parachute jumps and had been extensively trained in what to do when things went wrong, but even so, an uncontrolled free fall was something to be avoided. It wasn't his first bad experience during a jump, and most likely it wouldn't be his last.

His biggest worry now was the loss of his specialist weapons and equipment. The electronics would be smashed, the guns damaged beyond use. He was now only armed with two pistols, a .50-caliber Desert Eagle and a Beretta 93-R, with its custom sound suppressor. Two hand grenades hung from his combat webbing. He also had a garrote, the knife he cut the chute with, a small map and compass, a tiny flashlight and two hundred US dollars along with several spare magazines of ammunition in various pouches and pockets. Everything else was gone.

Bolan considered the situation for a moment. The

mission objectives hadn't really changed. He would be able to find the terrorist camp from the map; he would still be able to locate and identify Qutaiba. The only difference was his inability to communicate with the Farm. They would in all likelihood still have him under observation via the drone. If he could find a way to signal them, then the mission was still a go. And if he was unable to do so, then he would find a way to remove Qutaiba himself. Then get out of Dodge, avoid the Yemeni army should they show up, rendezvous with the contact and leave Yemen as fast as possible.

Yes, the mission was definitely still a go.

A thousand things could yet go wrong. The drone might have been called off. The powers that be might decide to fire the drone's Hellfire missiles despite Bolan being unable to report in. His main parachute might be discovered, alerting the terrorists. And who knew where his gear bag had landed. The mission could go to hell in an instant, but the soldier had been in tight spots before and knew exactly how to get out of them. This time would be no different.

Bolan buried his reserve parachute in a shallow hole that he dug with his bare hands. The warm jumpsuit joined the chute in its grave, unlikely to be seen ever again. Now dressed in his combat blacksuit, he quickly checked his weaponry for damage and for sand blockage, before withdrawing the map and compass. Using the miniature flashlight, he roughly worked out his position. Returning the navigation equipment to a pouch on his combat webbing, he straightened and started a slow jog across the loose sand in what he believed to be the correct direction.

The Executioner had a date with a terrorist.

CHAPTER THREE

The solitary candle flickered in the draft from the tiny open window, its flame creating and erasing shadowy images in an instant. The black cloth that covered the opening billowed slightly, held in place by four nails hammered hard into the surrounding wall. Zaid abu Qutaiba lay on his camp bed, his left arm tucked behind his head, using it as a pillow since there was no real one to be found. The arm had long since gone to sleep, and Qutaiba knew that it would hurt like hell when he did eventually move. For now he ignored it, lost in the imaginary world that the candlelight formed.

The dancing shadows shaped themselves into the face of a devil, before shifting to a flower, before reimaging into a racing cheetah. Qutaiba's eyes remained unfocused, seeing but not seeing. In his mind's eye he focused on only one image set against the backdrop of the yellow light—that of an old, long-lost photograph of his wife and young son smiling happily. It worried him that he was unable to recall their expressions, their mannerisms, their real faces. The only recall was of the photograph, which he had lost when Mossad had closed in on him in Tel Aviv, when he had been forced to dress as a woman to escape their clutches. The loss of the keepsake felt like a betrayal to their memory, and as punishment, it had made his memories of them decay.

Qutaiba could feel a wet line running from his eye to his ear, but ignored it. It was the Americans, of course, always the Americans. There were plenty of Shiite versus Sunni killings. Those were bad with their constant car bombings and suicide attacks, but the Americans had killed his beautiful wife and son; they were the ones who'd sprayed indiscriminate bullets around the marketplace in Kirkuk, not even sparing a backward glance when they left behind the torn bodies of the "insurgents," including a five-year-old boy and his mother.

Qutaiba had not been there. Having survived the American-led invasion as a captain in the Republican Guard, he had thrown away his uniform and joined the newly reformed police force instead. He'd never cared for Saddam or his warped sons and wanted so much to help rebuild Iraq, even if it meant cooperating with the American occupiers. They would leave eventually, he had reassured his wife, Aya. But they didn't leave soon enough. A new phenomenon appeared in American warfare—private armies. Supposedly hired to guard diplomats and protect foreign workers, some of these men took their duties too far and saw Iraq as a free-for-all. Anything could be done. No repercussions.

When a patrol of these private mercenaries had stones thrown at them in the marketplace by disenchanted youths, they had retaliated with extreme violence. The youths were gunned down, along with many other shoppers. When their magazines were dry, the mercenaries clambered back into their jeep and left. He could remember the call of the dispatcher over the scratched and battered radio, summoning all to the scene of the massacre. When he had arrived, he had been physically held back by colleagues, who had found the torn bodies of his family.

There was a blank after that, a large blank. Qutaiba imagined that he could remember the funerals the next day, but there was no definition, no clarity. There was a vague image of throwing away his police uniform, which he had been so proud of, but again that could also have been a fictional memory. What he did remember, like a searing pain, was that there had been no claim of responsibility from the Americans. Nothing. No mention of it anywhere. It was just gone, denied as if Aya and his son, Ajmi, had never existed. He'd felt his faith die along with his family. Revenge, vengeance, hate, it all became the same.

He'd sought out the company of the rebels; he'd known who they were and where to find them from his police days. At first they'd been skeptical, but Qutaiba had showed them what he was made of, leading a devastating attack on the Iraqi offices of the private soldiers responsible for the deaths of those he most valued. He'd slaughtered the men inside, shooting the corpses in their faces until all identity had been erased.

The insurgents had been impressed, but Qutaiba had wanted more. He was hungry for it. He'd vowed to kill Americans and their allies wherever they were to be found. He began kidnapping Western soldiers and civilians, making bargains with them in front of the rebels: if they could kill him in single combat with a knife, then they could go free. The prisoner was given a choice of fighting knife. One kidnapped diplomat had cut himself before the fight even started, so Qutaiba promptly had helped the fool by cutting his throat. All of the corpses had been dumped in a prominent part of the city where patrolling soldiers could find them.

He'd come to the attention of al Qaeda, who had taken him under its wing, faith or no faith, molding him into what he was today. He'd discovered a talent for leading and planning, one that the Mullahs, the mad, hypocritical Mullahs, encouraged. Qutaiba felt he was using them as much as they used him and didn't care if they knew it.

Afghanistan, Pakistan, Iraq, Israel, Kenya—all had suffered from his wrath. But still he felt empty; nothing filled the void that he dragged around with him. Maybe, just maybe, the emptiness would go within a day or two, for then would come his greatest attack, one so simple that the Americans would have no time to respond, just as Aya and Ajmi had had no time to respond.

Qutaiba shook himself out of his reverie, closing the door on the ghosts. Blinking, he sat up on the camp bed, cursing as the pain of pins and needles surged through his sleeping left arm. Reaching over to the bedside table, he grabbed the half-filled plastic cup of cheap red wine and took a sip. Not being a devout Muslim had its advantages. He grimaced. The wine had warmed. Awful. Scraping his tongue against his teeth to remove the foulness of the warm wine, he replaced the glass next to a notebook, which he knew he should not have. But there were certain details of the operation that he needed to be reminded of and the notebook was invaluable.

The wooden door opened, and the candle almost

gutted itself as an imposing figure stepped into the room. The door slammed shut behind him, the figure neither caring about noise or the intrusion. Qutaiba didn't need to look up from his position to know who it was. Only Hakim Haddad would enter so, only Haddad lacked the manners and the sensibility to knock first. Only Haddad could repulse him more than all the Americans and Israelis put together. The man was a complete animal, and Qutaiba had to wonder if Haddad had finally come to kill him. Qutaiba's AK-47 was propped against the wall next to the door, now out of reach. He tried and failed to suppress the shudder that ran through him. To hide it, he reached out for the wine, preferring its foulness over the presence of the Afghan visitor. He heard Haddad's sharp intake of breath and smiled slightly, noting once again how easy it was to rile the fanatic.

"What do you want, Hakim?" The tiredness in his voice came as a surprise.

"The first group has arrived at the destination. They will begin their attack at the correct time. The rest of our group will arrive shortly. The men are eager for battle. They wish to bathe in the blood of infidels." Haddad's voice was a growl, and Qutaiba wondered if Haddad wanted to bathe in his blood, as well. The man certainly viewed him as an infidel, and only the orders of the Mullahs had kept the two men apart. Qutaiba finally turned to look up at the towering Taliban dressed in traditional Perahan Tunban clothing. Whereas Qutaiba grieved the loss of his child every moment, Haddad had actively murdered his own daughter in an honor killing, never blinking, never mourning. The very thought revolted Qutaiba. He wanted the monster gone, out of his single mud-brick room.

"Anything else?"

"I sent extra patrols out. Some men saw something fall out of the sky. They went to look."

"Fall out of the sky? A bird?"

Haddad glowered. The man was a powder keg; the slightest perceived insult would provoke him. Qutaiba tried to keep his mocking tone in check.

"Perhaps. Or it was a spy or a robot drone. I sent them to look."

"Yes, Hakim, you did well. Keep me informed."

Haddad's demeanor didn't change as he turned and left the hut. The hate stayed in his eyes. Qutaiba closed his own eyes. It was so debilitating to work with these people, but it was a necessary evil. They were nothing more than cannon fodder. They would all be dead and gone within the next few days; maybe even he would be dead. There was an escape plan, one the pawns did not know about, but Qutaiba didn't know if he wanted to use it. That empty aching void was dragging him down. The plan would kick into action soon, an attack against the hated enemy, one that would not be forgotten. And during that attack, he would make his peace with Aya and Ajmi, begging their forgiveness as he rushed to join them. It would happen soon.

Nothing could stop it.

MACK BOLAN, LYING on his stomach, observed the comings and goings of the terrorists from his vantage point atop a large sand dune. Even in the predawn gloom he could clearly see that the men were no normal villagers. Armed with AK-47s, they kept up a loose, sloppy guard. These were men not expecting trouble. They seemed more excited about something than keeping an observant lookout. Bolan could occasionally hear their enthusiastic conversation, even from three hundred yards away, the words too indistinct to discern. He had found this outpost an hour earlier and been in position ever since. It was obvious from the ground that this was no true village. Not one of the mud-brick buildings had been finished, there was no main road leading anywhere, and there were no animals of any kind, not even a chicken.

Situated as it was between the hills and sand dunes, Bolan could conclude that the village had been constructed for only one reason: a hiding place for terrorists. They would know that drones regularly flew overhead, so hiding out in the open made perfect sense. But this place wasn't yet completed, and that ruined the illusion. Plus, the buildings were too uniform, ten in total, five facing five, with a dirt track between them. No, the village wasn't complete. They should have waited before occupying the buildings. Yet they didn't wait, which meant to Bolan that an operation was being planned.

He had counted ten men so far, but no doubt there were more. He managed to identify the barracks building. It was the largest at the end away from him, and most of the activity was focused there. Qutaiba would not be there, being too important too mingle with the common troops. The building opposite was equally large, designed to house vehicles. There was a slight glow emanating out of the darkness, the only unnatural light to be seen. The soldier thought that he could make out a fender of one vehicle but was too far away too be sure. The other buildings were much smaller; the smallest was closest to him. It could contain only a single room, and he had just witnessed a large man enter for a few moments before leaving again. An outhouse, maybe?

Dawn was approaching. He needed to quickly scout out the village, a quick in and out before the morning sun truly arrived. The activity down below seemed to be increasing, and Bolan suspected that the enemy would move out soon, assigned missions to kill and destroy. Time to pay them a visit.

Bolan waited for the two-man patrol to return. In the darkness they had passed him, supposedly on duty but in reality discussing a whorehouse in Aden. He had learned rudimentary Arabic some time ago as part of his ongoing war against terror, and while tough local dialects were hard to follow, these two had spoken clearly enough to be understood.

They were fast approaching, eager to return to the barracks, discussing something about boats and trucks and laughing quietly to themselves. Bolan pushed himself back into the sand as he quietly raised his Beretta 93-R. Once again they passed by Bolan, paying him no heed. He couldn't wait much longer. In seconds they would be in sight of the village.

With the Italian pistol cupped in both hands, he settled himself on his elbows. Using the luminous dots painted onto the iron sights, he pointed and fired, once, twice, a quiet sneezing of the sound-suppressed weapon that would be inaudible in the village. A red hole appeared in the first man's head, followed by a hole in his partner's. There was barely time for a look of surprise before both terrorists collapsed onto the sand, dead.

Bolan waited a moment to see if the sound of the dying men had been heard. It hadn't. He holstered the pistol, crawling over to the two corpses. Both had stopped twitching. He quickly removed the two AK-47s, examined them, checked the corpses for extra magazines. One rifle was scratched, pitted, uncared for, and Bolan discarded it after removing the banana-shaped magazine. The other weapon was better. One corpse gave up a single, half-full magazine. The other had nothing.

Seventy-five rounds. Not enough to kill a terrorist group with.

But enough to make a start.

The second of the two corpses was the larger of the two, and Bolan began to strip the dead man of his clothing, intending to masquerade as an Arab in the predawn gloom. His appearance might survive a glance, but if somebody stared for more than a few seconds, the flimsy cover would be blown. Bolan pulled the long garment over his head, only to find it was too tight in several places.

Using his knife, he cut several large holes along the seams, under the arms and down around his legs. When it came to combat, the robe would have to be quickly discarded. Replacing the knife in its sheath and slinging the AK-47, Bolan slouched as he made his way down to the village, hopefully looking like a sentry who was bored and tired to anyone who happened to glance his way. The sand shifted under his feet as he trudged down the side of the dune. Would they notice his combat boots under the robe? One of the dead terrorists wore running shoes, while the other had on flip-flops.

His plan of action was foolhardy in the extreme, but he wanted to know if Qutaiba was there. The drone's Hellfire missiles would blow the place to kingdom come, and if there was no body left to identify, then Qutaiba could very well be elsewhere. Besides, Bolan was also more than a little curious about what the terrorists were plotting.

He fully intended to find out. The hard way if necessary.

CHAPTER FOUR

Stony Man Farm, Virginia

It was ten o'clock in the evening when Barbara Price returned to the Computer Room in the Annex. Other business had taken her to the farmhouse. She found Hal Brognola—liaison between Stony Man and the White House and joint founder of the Farm—sitting next to Aaron Kurtzman, peering bleary-eyed at the cyberwizard's monitor. The drone's-eye view showed Bolan's location in real time.

Brognola looked up and gave Price a weary nod. She handed him a weak, tired smile before sitting. Kurtzman transferred the image to the main wall screen.

"Status?" Price queried.

"While you were away, Striker eliminated a two-man patrol and is now circling the village. My guess is that he's making his way toward this building." Kurtzman used a laser pointer to indicate which building it was. "We believe that it's a vehicle pool. Striker probably intends to disable anything he finds there."

"How much longer can the Reaper drone stay in the area?"

"It will stay as long as needed," Brognola stated. "The President has given this op special consideration—

the pilots at Cannon are aware of that." The Reaper's pilot was operating the drone out of Cannon Air Force Base near Clovis, New Mexico.

"I sense a *but*," Price said. "A big one."

The men looked at each other briefly before looking back at Price. "Striker may be in a lot of trouble within the next few minutes." Kurtzman sighed. "We've been monitoring this patrol hurrying back to the village. We believe that they've found the lost bag."

"So security will be suddenly increased. That will be awkward. And?"

"And two trucks are rapidly approaching the area. One is full of warm bodies. The other less so."

"More troops and increased awareness. Can we take out the trucks?"

"The drone could do it, but the explosion will alert the camp. Cannon is on hold, waiting for instructions. There is an Air Force colonel itching to take the place out, man on the ground or not."

Price grimaced. The military was always looking to fire its guns at anything that moved. She eyed the situation, watching as the figure believed to be Bolan slipped into the largest building.

"The Yemeni army?"

"Is on standby, just outside Aden. The government has been protesting being kept in the dark about foreign incursions on their sovereign soil," Brognola stated.

Price grimaced again. There were elements in the Yemeni army that would love to send a warning to their terrorist friends. So far the Yemenis had been told nothing, only to keep a focus on a certain direction, the opposite from which Bolan now operated.

She watched the large screen as the terrorist patrol entered the village, the sudden gathering of men around them, of Bolan slipping out of the building, working his way around the back to the smallest hut, stopping, moving in, waiting…then a bright flash where the group of terrorists were. Flickers of light, probably muzzle-flashes from Bolan's position.

Engagement!

"Instruct Cannon to take out the truck with the most terrorists. Hold back on the other Hellfire missile. Striker might need it later."

Kurtzman hurriedly relayed the orders; hopefully a pilot would be able to engage the truck in time. Then all three watched as the Executioner went to war, fighting overwhelming odds. Again.

Yemen

FIRST LIGHT.

The garage was to be his first destination. Bolan decided to disable all the vehicles, bar one, which he would commandeer for his extraction.

The soldier had surreptitiously worked his way around the village, avoiding the men who would shoot him on sight. None of them were Qutaiba, of that he was almost certain. None of the terrorists showed any deference to a leader. They seemed satisfied with talking among themselves. Bolan was now content that this was a transit camp. There was no litter, no animal dung, nothing to suggest previous habitation. When the drone strike came, no civilians would be injured or killed.

The soldier worked his way around the back of the

mud-brick buildings, crouching, head down. He passed through a narrow alley, more of a gap, between the fourth structure and the garage, taking in the main street, two clusters of men, the closest twenty feet away. Bolan slipped into the garage unobserved.

He found three 4x4 vehicles, all identical. One was parked slightly forward of the rest, its fender protruding slightly outside the building. All three were dark green UAZ-3151 all-terrain vehicles, sometimes referred to as GAZ-69, former Soviet Union. Bolan hadn't seen this type of vehicle for a while. The UAZ, like the AK-47 rifle, was known for its easy maintenance and reliability. With the collapse of the USSR years earlier, many had been sold off. It was the perfect transport for the terrorists: old enough not to be noticed and reliable enough to get them quickly around the desert. All three showed their age, both inside and out, but that did not bother Bolan. What did interest him was the ignition key in the first vehicle's slot. Bolan smiled grimly. At least something would go right on this mission. The only question was would the vehicle start?

Bolan turned sharply at a sudden noise that emanated from the rear of the building. Somebody was moving around by the third UAZ. Bolan drew the silenced Beretta and crept forward. He could now see a faded light beneath the vehicle, a flashlight whose batteries were all but finished. A man was working his way from under the UAZ, yawning. The Executioner moved fast, stepping over to the terrorist. The man saw him, mistook his identity due to the poor light and opened his mouth to say something. Bolan fired a single Parabellum round. The guy's head snapped against the concrete, the bullet ricocheting out the exit wound in the back of his head. The terrorist died without making a sound.

Bolan ducked behind the second 4x4, waiting for someone to respond to the noise. Nobody did. He rose slowly, weapon ready, expecting trouble. Nobody was waiting for him to appear, no shouts of alarm. Bolan turned his attention back to the UAZs. He pocketed the keys from the first vehicle before approaching the second two. He worked his way around both 4x4s, removing the ignition keys and flinging them as far as he could into the sand.

To counter the chance that somebody would have a reserve set, he returned to the corpse. Placing his AK-47 on the floor, Bolan removed his knife and began cutting chunks of cloth out of the mechanic's clothing. Then he rolled the cloth into balls, which he stuffed into the tailpipes of the UAZs, pushing each in hard with the tip of his knife. He repeated the procedure several times for both vehicles, wanting to be sure that the engines would choke out on the built-up gases in the event that somebody did manage to start both 4x4s.

The Executioner glanced up from his work and realized that he was out of time. It was now light enough to see by, the sun having risen fast. He finished sabotaging the two vehicles and stood, quickly cutting away the robe. The garment would only hinder him now. He ducked as two terrorists entered the barracks opposite the garage. They paid no interest to the motor pool. Bolan crouch-walked to the entrance and peeked around the corner. Very little had changed in the time that he'd been busy. There were still two groups of terrorists, and it appeared that neither contained Qutaiba. He exited the garage quickly, silently, back up the way that he had come. The sound of raucous laughter reached his ears. The men were too preoccupied to notice anything amiss; all was working to Bolan's advantage. He reached the space between the second unfinished building and the outhouse, its door facing the opposite building's wall.

He was about to move between the two buildings when he heard raised voices, recognizing several words.

American! Intruder!

The silent probe was over. It was all about to get noisy. Bolan raised his AK-47, moved to the corner of the second building, observing what the terrorists were doing.

Two new men had arrived, hurrying into the village, talking excitedly, clasping something large between them. The largest knot of men had stood back, allowing the patrol to present their findings to a large, bearded thug. Bolan recognized the type, a man who used his intimidating presence to bully others, killing those who were not in awe of him. The men moved around, trying to get a better look at the discovery, and for a second Bolan saw it, as well.

It was his gear bag, which he had cut loose during the parachute jump.

Bolan cursed softly to himself. He slipped a hand grenade from his web harness, watching as the bearded thug upended the gear bag, tipping the contents onto the sand. There was consternation from the men, then the Beard began shouting orders, pointing in different directions. Bolan pulled the pin on the grenade and let the bomb fly, aiming for the pile of equipment at the Beard's feet. Bolan ducked behind the corner of the building, counting off the seconds. There were shouts and screams as the terrorists recognized the grenade.

The bomb detonated, a loud crump among the yells. Bolan spun out of his hiding place, his liberated rifle raised to his shoulder. Several men, including the Beard, were on the ground, dead or getting there fast. More were picking themselves up or standing still in shock. Bolan opened fire, the AK-47 on full-auto. Years of experience helped him keep the bucking rifle under control; the muzzle rising only slightly, Bolan swept it from left to right. Men screamed and died as a storm of metal cut through them, sending them to join the Beard in whatever hell awaited them.

Chips of mud brick exploded above Bolan's head as a terrorist from farther back along the street attempted to return fire. In his excitement his aim was off by at least a foot. There would be no second chances for the man. Bolan fired a quick burst, on target, the shooter shuddering as the high-velocity ammunition cut through him, throwing him onto his back. The soldier released the magazine from his weapon, unsure of how many rounds were left, slammed another one in, arming the rifle even as a group of terrorists tumbled out of the barracks, weapons at the ready, looking for something to shoot. Bolan supplied them with a target as he opened up, delivering a greeting card of death. The three screamed and shook as they were cut down, not having a chance to respond. A fourth man stood in the doorway, clearly seeing Bolan's position, then ducked back into the barracks. The soldier fired several shots into the open door, wanting to discourage any resistance. A rifle muzzle poked around the base of the frame, firing in his general direction, no hope of hitting anything. Bolan dodged back, preparing to retreat to the motor pool, where he would be able to lob his final grenade into the building.

The firefight had lasted all of ten seconds so far. Bolan had taken only two steps when a muffled boom brought him up short. Somewhere in the distance there had been an explosion, a large one. He paused for a second, briefly considering what it was before focusing on priorities. Another step. The door of the outbuilding opened. Qutaiba stood there, his AK-47 pointing directly at Bolan's head.

THE ACHE RETURNED a few moments after Hakim Haddad had left his room, the constant nagging ache. Qutaiba did his best to ignore it, blinking away the image of the lost photograph. He picked up the notebook, hoping to hide away in the grand plan, wanting to hide anywhere. He flicked through the pages, not really seeing the words or occasional diagram. He should burn the notebook. He would do so in a moment. The trucks would arrive, they would leave in a convoy, reach their destination, take control and use it against the Americans. A thousand things could go wrong, but Qutaiba and the Mullahs had prepared for most eventualities. He considered the class of militants that was supplied to be a liability, but the Mullahs assured him that the men would perform well when the time came, that they would all be welcomed into heaven with open arms. Qutaiba hadn't believed a word.

And now the time was here. A lasting, painful strike against America. A major target. An act of revenge for those two lives taken from him. He blinked, knowing that he was slipping away again. "Focus," he snapped out loud. The attempt might fail, he knew, but it would be noted and reported. It would make news around the world. And that would be success enough.

Qutaiba had to have drifted off, because the next thing he heard was excited shouting coming from outside. The thick walls muted what was being said, but it sounded as if the men had found something. Maybe Haddad's mysterious falling bird. Qutaiba rose to his feet and walked to the door.

Chaos had erupted.

A muffled crump was followed by screams, followed by a lot of shooting.

They had been discovered.

Qutaiba froze for several seconds, unable to believe that the plan was about to fail. Not now. Maybe some of the men were shooting at shadows. No, there was too much chaos. He picked up his AK-47, checked that the safety was off and that the weapon was armed. He opened the door, ready to fire.

A black-clad stranger stood in front of him. Rage engulfed Qutaiba in an instant. The man was the very type of commando who had murdered his family, his dreams. He brought the rifle into play, raising it to his shoulder, pointing it at the intruder's head, pointing it where the intruder's head had been a split second before. The commando had dropped to his knees. Qutaiba fired too late, bullets smacking into the wall. He began to adjust his aim, fighting the recoil. Too late. Too slow. He didn't have time to scream his frustrations. The commando had whipped around his own AK-47, holding it one-handed, firing at Qutaiba's chest...

BOLAN FIRED HIS KALASHNIKOV, the first four rounds slamming into Qutaiba's chest, three more missing altogether. The terrorist flew backward, arms outstretched, his weapon fallen from his hands. Bolan rose to his knees, approached his enemy, his weapon pointing at the terrorist's head. Qutaiba shuddered as life went out of him. Bolan checked vital signs, making sure he really was dead, then scooped up the fallen AK-47. His own was virtually depleted; Qutaiba's most likely had a nearly full magazine. He didn't have time to search the room that Qutaiba had been inhabiting. He could hear an engine in the distance, rapidly approaching. Reinforcements? A small blue notebook on the table caught his eye. Bolan glanced quickly around, making sure that no one was bringing him into target acquisition. He saw nothing, took the chance, darted into the room, snatched up the notebook and stuffed it into one of the side pockets on his combat suit.

Time to go.

He quickly reloaded the AK-47 with his final full magazine; the partially loaded one he tucked back into his combat webbing. Stepping over the corpse, he brought up his gun, ready to fire at anybody standing outside. Nobody was around. He returned to his original position of attack, to see if anyone there was pursuing him, to see if the barracks had disgorged more men. Bodies lay everywhere, none moving. His gear bag lay on the ground, surrounded by the dead, its contents spread around. Bolan would gather it later if he got a chance.

At the top of the village road he observed a truck stopping, braking hard. Three men jumped out of the cab, yelling incoherently, waving their arms in panic. They stopped dead when they spotted the carnage of their fallen friends. Their silence lasted a second, no more. Bolan was bringing his sights to bear when the three split off in different directions. He cursed as he saw one plunge into the garage. He would now have to hunt the three plus the other survivors cowering in the barracks. Bolan ducked back into cover, quickly retracing his steps around the back of the building, passing Qutaiba's tiny building again. He spun around the corner, rifle ready, only to slam into two terrorists creeping up on his rear.

The two terrorists barreled into him, their mouths open in shock. Bolan reacted without thinking, without allowing surprise to distract him. The Executioner dropped his AK-47, stepped in close, grabbed the left guy by the throat and head butted him full force. The man's nose collapsed, spraying blood. The guy screamed, hands reaching for his face even as Bolan was swatting away the barrel of the second terrorist's weapon. With his hand still around the throat of Broken Nose, the soldier brought up his right foot, then slammed the sole of his combat boot down on the knee of the second terrorist. The guy joined his screaming friend as his kneecap shattered. The terrorist fell, all the fight going out of him as he was overwhelmed by pain.

However, Broken Nose wasn't finished. As he

clawed for his holstered handgun, Bolan drew his Desert Eagle. He pushed the barrel into his adversary's chest, squeezing the trigger, simultaneously releasing his stranglehold on the man's throat. The gun fired at point-blank range, the muzzle velocity throwing the terrorist through the air, an exit hole the size of an orange in his back. Satisfied that the kneecapped terrorist was no immediate threat, Bolan holstered the Desert Eagle and snatched up the dropped AK-47. He had no time to check the dead for ammunition. The thunder of the .50 Desert Eagle would have advertised his position to everyone in the area.

With his AK-47 leading the way, Bolan walked to the end of the village, to the final building, the motor pool. He could hear shouting, panicked voices encouraging one another to seek out the enemy. There were several shots, nothing remotely aimed in Bolan's direction. They were firing at shadows, hoping to provoke some sort of response from their invisible attackers. Bolan worked his way down to the edge of the edifice, quickly scouting out the situation. The truck was parked in the middle of the street, between the barracks and the garage, blocking his view of the enemy.

Bolan dropped to his belly and peered under the truck. As he suspected, two terrorists were hiding beneath the cab, calling out to the others, one of whom replied from the barracks. When they believed that there was nothing to fear, they would emerge from their hiding places. But Bolan didn't want to wait that long. The clock was counting down in his head. It was only a matter of time before somebody in America

gave the order to destroy the village. Bolan wanted to
be long gone before then. He drew the Beretta, holding it two-handed, resting on his elbows, pointing it
at the back of one of the terrorists' heads.

CHAPTER FIVE

Stony Man Farm, Virginia

"Mr. President, that isn't enough time. Striker is still on the ground…Yes, sir…I understand that, but we need more time. The target still has not been confirmed…A firefight does indicate the presence of militants, yes, but…Yes, sir, I'll inform them."

Brognola broke the connection to the White House. He looked up at Price and Kurtzman. "The President has been convinced by the Joint Chiefs and other advisers that they need to strike now. The Hellfire missile is going to be fired. The remaining truck will be the target. Striker has less than five minutes remaining." The big Fed turned his attention to the large screen. "How many terrorists are left?"

"Five," Kurtzman said. "Five and a half. We've been tracking this guy here." With a laser pointer, he indicated a figure moving slowly around the rear of the buildings toward Bolan's position. "I think that he's severely wounded by the way that he moves. I doubt that he will be much of a threat to Striker."

"Where is Striker now?"

"Under the truck," Price replied.

"Oh, God in heaven! Get out of there, Striker, get out now!"

Yemen

He twitched. He groaned.

Pain washed over him in waves. Pain unlike anything he had ever experienced. A tiny voice told him that he was injured, that a hand grenade had exploded, that he was dead unless he moved.

Hakim Haddad groaned again and attempted to open his eyes. He was blind! He couldn't see! He panicked; his hand shot up to his face. His fingers found his left open eye by accident, causing more pain as he poked it too hard. Wincing, he felt for his right eye. There was nothing there. A hollow space. Gone.

Haddad screamed in terror and frustration. Before he realized it, he had rolled onto his front. His mouth filled with sand and dirt. He stopped screaming and started to gag. Choking, fighting the horror, Haddad forced himself to calm down, take deep ragged breaths.

The infidels had taken his eye!

Trying to remember what had happened took an age. The agony was everywhere. He blinked, finally seeing some light through his left eye. He could see his blackened fingers covered in sand. Sanity was returning. There had been a bag, a soldier's bag. They had emptied it, turning it upside down. Military equipment had spilled out. Weapons. There had been a clatter, which he had heard above the excited chattering of his men. He watched the grenade roll, thinking at first it had fallen from the bag. But he saw that it had no pin and realized that it had been thrown. He pushed the man closest to him toward the grenade, turning…

Haddad praised Allah for placing an unworthy soul next to him, an inconsequential soldier who should have been glad to sacrifice himself to save his leader. The man had taken the full brunt of the explosion, his body shredding in slow motion, the velocity of the steel ball bearings in the grenade vastly decreasing as they passed through his body and then struck Haddad. He knew nothing after that.

He understood that Allah had saved him, had guided his actions. That soldier would now be feasting in paradise. Hakim muttered a quick prayer. It wasn't his place to understand what Allah wanted, he knew. But he could guess. Vengeance. Destruction of the attacking infidels.

He closed his eyes—his eye—breathing, just breathing. He attempted to rise. The pain flooded back and Haddad fell onto his face. He pushed himself up onto his knees, rocking back and forth, waves of nausea washing over him. Eye closed, he listened. There was shooting, a lot of it, close by. The infidels were still here. His men were brave, resisting. He would join them. Lead them. Set an example.

Qutaiba.

The name popped into his mind. That man was their true leader. And an infidel with his alcohol-drinking ways. He meant to kill Qutaiba. He had been waiting for the right moment—now it had arrived. Kill the man and blame it on the ambushers. The great Mullahs would understand what had happened and expect him to lead. Except he didn't know the details of the attack. Only Qutaiba did. But he had a book, a little blue book. He had to find it before the enemy did.

Hakim opened his eye. He could now focus. He turned his head slowly, painfully to the left to see the bodies of his men lying on the ground, ripped apart by the grenade. He got to his feet with difficulty. He saw stars, staggered forward and found a warm mudbrick wall to lean against. He gasped. More nausea. He needed a weapon, something to kill Qutaiba with. He didn't want to bend to pick up a fallen weapon. If he did, he might stumble and fall, never to regain his feet. His right hand moved down his robes, feeling, patting. Somewhere...yes, there. He withdrew an old Russian pistol his father had taken off the body of a Soviet soldier. He stood upright, breathed deeply, then turned and reeled toward Qutaiba's building.

He tripped several times but didn't fall, keeping his balance, windmilling his arms. He stopped outside the hut, at first not comprehending what he was seeing. Qutaiba lay there, red holes in his chest. The attackers had already been here. Good. The Mullahs could not blame him for this. Where was the book, the little blue book? Haddad lurched into the room, standing on Qutaiba's bullet-riddled chest. Blood oozed out, covering his boots. Hakim didn't notice. The book had been on the table, next to the devil's drink. It was gone. Rage filled him. He had to find the book! It was important. He didn't know exactly what Qutaiba had written in there, but it had to have been important. He had to get it back.

Outside he teetered to the back of the buildings, inadvertently following Bolan's path. There lay two more soldiers, one man's chest soaked in crimson. The other Hakim recognized but was unable to recall the man's name. He seemed to be alive, but one leg was covered with blood. They had been a patrol that he had sent out. Was he the only man alive, the only man able to challenge the intruders? There was shooting somewhere, as if to remind him that there were other survivors, waiting for his leadership. He looked up and saw a shadow, a man in black, duck behind the end building. Haddad knew that this was the man that he was destined to kill, the reason why Allah had spared him. He moved forward, one foot in front of the other, the pistol heavy in his right hand, using his left for support against the walls of the buildings.

He finally reached the end of the row. He swung around the corner, pistol raised, fully expecting to find his target cowering and begging for mercy. Nothing. Only empty space. There was more shooting close by, panicked yelling. An explosion. He fell backward two steps. Out of the corner of his eye he saw the black-clad commando dart up between the garage and middle building, run back down the way Haddad had just come, then duck into another alleyway. The devil was fast. Haddad staggered after his enemy, feeling more and more light-headed. Pain seared where his right eye had been.

For a second, sanity returned. He was pursuing a single man. A single man had done all this? Had taken down his handpicked soldiers, men who he had trained himself? Impossible. The enemy could not be that good!

Haddad reached the alley between two buildings. There was the enemy commando, kneeling, waiting to fire. Haddad grinned. He would get close, raise his pistol, witness the fear in the demon's eyes, then pull the trigger, sending the evil into oblivion. He crept, swaying, down the alley. Up ahead he saw one of his men run straight into the enemy's gun sights. The infidel showed no mercy, gunning the brave soldier down. The man's weapon locked on empty. Haddad had him; now would be his chance. He raised his pistol, trying to bring the shaking in his arm under control. The commando in black stood, turned to face him. He dropped the rifle and reached for a sidearm. Haddad pulled the trigger.

Nothing.

There was a strong mechanical resistance. He tried again. Then it dawned on him that he had neglected to release the safety. He had failed. Completely.

As Haddad's enemy raised his own pistol, the terrorist hoped that Allah would still welcome him with open arms.

MACK BOLAN SQUEEZED the trigger of the Beretta, its muffled shot hidden behind the firing of another terrorist's AK-47. The target jerked, all life exiting in an instant. His friend didn't notice, as he was too busy shooting at shadows. Bolan introduced him to real shadows with his second silenced shot. The village went quiet, the silence broken only by the ticking of the cooling truck engine. Bolan wormed his way backward, out from under the truck, regained his feet and his AK-47.

Frenzied calling erupted, coming from the barracks. Another voice joined in. Bolan was certain that there was still another man in the area, the one he had seen jump out of the truck. But which two had he just shot? Had the two in the barracks been joined by a third or was the third man hiding somewhere else?

Bolan decided to check out the garage quickly before lobbing a grenade into the barracks. The men in the barracks opened up, their Kalashnikovs spraying bullets in full-auto mode. Several slammed into the truck, glass shattering. Bolan ducked, not believing that they knew his position. Again they were just firing for effect. He crouch-walked into the garage, peering under the vehicles. Nothing, only the body of the mechanic. Bolan nodded, satisfied. Then he worked his way down to the front of the truck, noting that he had enough space to drive the UAZ out of the garage.

Two terrorists poked their rifle barrels out of an open window, looking for something to shoot. Hidden behind the front wheel, Bolan removed his final grenade from his combat webbing. He pulled the pin, waited all of a second, then spun out from hiding, lobbing the grenade in a perfect arc through the open window. He ducked back behind the wheel, hearing the screams of the two terrorists, feeling the loud crump as the bomb detonated. The screaming stopped. Quiet returned.

Bolan poked his head around the truck, eyeing the village. Had he taken them all out? A barrage of bullets gave him his answer, the rounds hammering into the truck just above him, the headlight and light cluster shattering, the front tire detonating from the sudden release of air pressure. The soldier moved, fast. He rocketed away from the truck, down the alley between the garage and the fourth building, autofire tearing chunks out of the walls as he passed. Sprinting, he tore around the corner, then right, up the next alley. He slowed as he approached the end, dropping to his knees, his AK-47 up and searching.

The remaining terrorist was somewhere on the other side of the street. Where? The man stepped out of a building opposite, eyes fixed on Bolan's last-known position by the truck, then took off down the street, screaming wildly. Bolan opened fire, stitching the man with a burst of fire. The terrorist staggered a few more steps and fell face forward. Bolan's rifle locked on empty.

He was regaining his feet when he heard shuffling behind him. Dropping his empty AK-47, the Executioner spun, right hand reaching for his Desert Eagle. He was too late. The apparition behind him, covered in blood, an eye missing from its socket, had already raised a Makarov pistol. The barrel was wavering, the guy unable to hold it straight. Bolan briefly recognized him as the big thug who had emptied the gear bag onto the street. Bolan's Desert Eagle cleared its holster. He brought the weapon into target acquisition and fired, the .50-caliber round all but decapitating the half-blind man. The corpse fell backward, the pistol falling from nerveless fingers.

That had been close. Bolan reloaded the Desert Eagle and waited, crouching, ready to fire. There was no more movement. All resistance had been neutralized. After several moments he rose to his feet and walked slowly into the street. Death was everywhere. The barracks were on fire; soon it would consume the interior of the building. Bolan moved cautiously toward the garage.

How many men had he killed in the last five minutes? He had no idea, and didn't bother with a count. Killing was something he would never get used to. His only respite from remorse was knowing that for every enemy he killed at least one innocent life had been saved somewhere. He reached the building without incident. Climbing into the UAZ, he adjusted the seat to fit his six-foot-three frame and inserted the ignition key. The engine turned over once, twice, then fired. Bolan shifted into First and slowly accelerated out of the garage and around the truck. He stopped the vehicle by the ruins of his gear bag and climbed out, leaving the engine running, gearshift in Neutral. Bolan stepped around the corpses of the fallen terrorists and began to retrieve the damaged equipment, not wanting to leave it behind for somebody else to find and then accuse the United States of interference. As he heaved the contents into the back of the jeep, the reserve satellite phone began to buzz. Bolan grabbed it, opening the connection.

"Striker..."

"Get out! Get out now! Run!" Kurtzman yelled.

Bolan dropped the phone to the ground, jumped into the vehicle and threw it into gear. He stamped the accelerator, the driver's door open, flapping as the vehicle shot away from the village. Behind him, in his rearview mirror, the truck at the end of the village turned into a fireball as the Hellfire missile struck, rendering it only twisted metal. The garage, the burning barracks and several neighboring buildings turned to rubble in a blinding flash. The shock wave shook the UAZ. Bolan fought hard to keep it under control.

The soldier stopped to observe the village when he was sufficiently far away. The buildings that hadn't collapsed were burning fiercely. Thick smoke rose into the sky from the garage and truck wreckage. He knew that the Yemeni army would be on its way, ready to clean up and take credit for his actions.

It was time to make his way to the rendezvous point, to meet his contact and to get out of Yemen before anybody realized that he was there.

CHAPTER SIX

It was destined to be another scorching day in Yemen. The sun was already high, the sky bright blue, not a cloud in sight. Nelson Thompson pushed his shades back up his sweaty nose and took a sip of warm water from the plastic bottle. The contact was late. Thompson would give him a few more minutes before relocating to another position a couple of miles away and waiting there for a short while. If the contact still didn't show up, then it was time to report in and retreat back to Aden.

Thompson tried to ignore the large column of thick smoke behind him to the east, searching instead to the west where another column of black smoke, this one much thinner, was attracting the attention of several Yemeni army helicopters.

Thompson shifted uncomfortably. He had been born in Phoenix, Arizona, so the desert heat didn't really bother him. He grimaced as the familiar ache shot through his right leg, a leg he no longer had. He shifted his weight to his left, cursing the phantom pains in his artificial limb.

His official profession was that of freelance journalist, keeping tabs on the political situation in Yemen for several big newspapers back home. Unofficially he was to keep an eye out for terrorist activity and feed the information back to a contact in the Justice Department.

Several years ago he had been a Ranger and loved every minute of it. The training, the assignments, the various wars in foreign countries—it all fulfilled him in a way that life back home in Arizona could not. Then it all changed. He had been at Fort Benning when orders had come in specifically for him. A new assignment, a special job, nobody had known what it was or where he was being sent. The only thing he'd discovered was that an unknown somebody had recommended him.

A week later he'd been standing in a field in the Blue Ridge Mountains, dressed in civilian clothes and armed with a submachine gun and instructed by his new CO, one Buck Greene, to guard a farmhouse with his life. He had been rotated into a team of professional guards known only as blacksuits. Welcome to Stony Man Farm.

He threw himself into his six-month assignment, knowing that the oath he'd sworn would not allow him to discuss the six months with his fellow Rangers back at Benning.

Three months into his rotation he and a small team of blacksuits had accompanied a five-man team on a mission to Central America. Thompson had stepped on a Claymore and lost most of his right leg. That had ended his stint with both the blacksuits and the Rangers.

While in the hospital, a government type had visited him and told him that the blacksuits looked after their own and offered to cover all expenses for any retraining Thompson needed.

Thompson had recovered, accepted the offer and had become a journalist. With a helping hand from his Justice Department contact, he was employed by a national newspaper. Due to his combat experience, he was often sent to war zones. In exchange for the assistance, Thompson had agreed to keep an eye out for anything that might be of interest, particularly terrorist activities in whatever country he was visiting. Never once had he queried why his contact was from Justice and not State.

The previous day he had been leaving Aden International Airport after covering a story about international aid when he had spotted a known terrorist. After sending a text message over his phone using a special number, he'd followed the man at a discreet distance. Once in the desert, when he could no longer follow his quarry, he'd texted that, as well. A reply had come through a few minutes later. The target was being tracked. Meet a man at specific coordinates in the morning and assist him with exfiltration. Nothing more.

Thompson took another sip of water. Still waiting. The game of spies was deadly dull. Apart from the helicopters, apart from the distant long-gone sounds of a car, there had been nothing. No sign of life anywhere. He turned his attention to the larger column of smoke coming from Aden.

As he did so, he felt the cold muzzle of a pistol being pressed behind his left ear. Thompson knew in that dreadful moment that either his skills had deteriorated so much that he deserved to be shot or the guy holding the pistol was the stealthiest bastard he would ever come across. He tensed, waiting for the bullet.

"Six Alpha Green." It was the sound of a chilling graveyard whisper.

"Alpha Deep Six" was his response. The gun was lowered and Thompson breathed out. He raised his hands cautiously into the air. "May I turn around now?"

"Yeah. But do it slowly and put your hands down."

Thompson did as instructed and turned to face an apparition from hell. The man was covered in dried blood, sand and combat cosmetics—his face, his hands, as well as the all-too-familiar blacksuit. The man stared back, his ice-blue eyes penetrating deep, inadvertently causing Thompson to flinch. It took the African-American several seconds to find his voice, during which the man holstered his Beretta.

"Shit! You sure know how to make a guy turn white. I must be slipping to have allowed you to sneak up on me like that." Thompson caught himself babbling and reddened, feeling unprofessional. He tried again. "Hey, um, I recognize you. You used to train with us sometimes. Buck called you Striker. Damn, you were good."

"You're making me blush. Where's your car?"

"Just down the slope, on the other side of the road. I brought some water so you can wash, and a change of clothes. When you're finished, we can head out to the safehouse. But I have no idea how to get you out of the country quickly. And what should I call you?"

"Cooper. What's the problem with the evac?"

"See for yourself." Thompson pointed in the direction of Aden, to the thick column of black smoke, which was now spreading across the sky.

MACK BOLAN HAD already seen the pillar of smoke. He turned to Thompson for an explanation.

"It's the airport. A passenger flight from Turkey crashed about an hour ago. From what I heard on the radio, it appears that there was a Mayday, a fire on board, and an emergency landing was attempted. Other than that..." He shrugged. "The city will be bogged down in traffic. The airport is more or less right in the middle of Aden. It will be closed for a quite a while. I'm missing one hell of a story."

Bolan gazed at him, wondering if Thompson was missing the point of the tragedy. People had died. People who had lives, dreams. It was more than just "a story."

"If it's a story you want, then I'll give you one," he said coldly, "but for now you have an unexpected guest who needs an alternative method of extraction. Return to your car. I'll join you in a few minutes with my vehicle. I need to transfer a few things over."

Thompson nodded and hobbled away, his artificial foot making scuff prints in the sand. Bolan watched him for a few moments before turning his attention to the distant, burning village on the far horizon. Shielding his eyes, he could just make out the two helicopters buzzing around, searching for survivors. The army troops would find the tracks of his UAZ once they got over the initial shock of finding so many bullet-riddled bodies. Time was of the essence.

He started to jog toward the dunes where the UAZ was hidden. The sun was searing.

It took him several minutes to reach the vehicle, start it and drive to where Thompson was waiting, the trunk of his white Peugeot car open. Bolan hopped out, opened the rear and prepared to transfer his equipment.

Thompson spoke up. "You do know that we have to

pass through several checkpoints before we can enter the city, don't you?"

Bolan closed his eyes, disappointed with himself. Of course he knew that. Lack of sleep had made him lax. He had been on the go for almost thirty-six hours. The catnap in the Hercules had done nothing to ease his weariness. He nodded. "We'll have to bury the equipment and burn the vehicle. My fingerprints are all over it. Just in case." He sighed, knowing that he had wasted precious time. He pulled an entrenching tool out of the UAZ and proceeded to dig a shallow hole at the side of the road. He chucked the ruined gear bag in along with the remains of his sniper rifle, several grenades and various other items for which he no longer had a use. He noticed that the sat phone was missing. He thought it had fallen into the back of the UAZ when Kurtzman had yelled at him, but now realized that it had been left behind in the village. Another mistake.

Kurtzman would be able to remotely erase any electronic footprints, but it was still careless to have left it behind. Too much was going wrong with this mission. He refilled the hole and scattered the remaining sand. "I'll drive your vehicle over the hill and burn it," Thompson said. "You really need to get yourself cleaned up. There's a small compartment under the passenger seat. You can stash the hardware there. It's also where your papers are hidden. They were rushed over to me during the night. You're now a freelance journalist like me. Water is in the trunk. Once the UAZ is burning, we'll have to move. Another smoke column will attract the choppers."

Bolan opened the hidden compartment as Thompson drove away. Inside he found a passport along with forged Yemeni travel documents. The name inside the passport was Mike Blanski. He smiled. That was one name he thought had been put to rest long ago. The passport looked a little tatty, and Bolan wondered where it had come from, where it had been stashed. A picture of his younger self stared back. How many miles had he traveled since he'd last held this?

He removed and reloaded his weapons before placing them in the compartment. The blue notebook of Qutaiba's joined the two guns. If anybody did a thorough search, then they would be quickly discovered. In the trunk he found a bowl to be used as a basin and a gallon of water in a large plastic bottle. A bar of soap had also been provided. A white shirt, a pair of jeans and a pair of casual training shoes, all cheap imitations of famous American makes, lay neatly inside.

Bolan stripped off his ripped bloodstained blacksuit and proceeded to wash himself all over. Within minutes he felt human again. He dressed, the clothes a perfect fit, then buried the blacksuit and his combat boots in the sand. Somewhere over the dune there was a muffled whump, the familiar sound of a gasoline explosion. A few moments later he saw Thompson working his way down to the car. Bolan poured the bowl of soapy water into the sand, slammed the trunk shut and waited.

Thompson grinned when he got close to Bolan.

"Wow, you sure look pretty enough to ask to the prom."

"Flattery will get you nowhere. Let's go before they see that." A column of smoke was working its way into the air.

"Yeah." Thompson got into the vehicle and turned

the engine over. The old car belched black exhaust fumes, coughed, then caught. Thompson grinned again at Bolan, who was climbing into the passenger seat. "Well, she ain't pretty, that's for sure, but I keep the engine fine-tuned, and she won't attract any undue attention. There are hundreds of them in Aden." He put the automatic transmission into Drive and accelerated away.

"Why haven't we seen any traffic on this road?" Bolan asked.

"It's a road that goes nowhere. I have no idea why it was built. But we'll be joining the main highway in a moment, and it'll get a little busier."

It did get busier on the main highway. As they traveled toward Aden, they encountered several troop trucks heading in the opposite direction.

"They're probably going to see where you were playing."

Bolan didn't reply.

"There's a camera on the backseat. Hang it around your neck. You'll look the part of a journalist to them."

Bolan leaned back and grabbed an old Nikon digital camera. "Does it work?"

"Sure does. I've even taken a few photos of the desert if they care to inspect it. They'll stop us at the checkpoints and ask us what we're up to. We'll say something about following the troop trucks for a story, got turned back and now we're on our way to the airport to cover that story. I have some money to slip into the passports, for administration purposes you understand. Say, are you going to tell me what happened back there? What happened to Qutaiba? It was Qutaiba, wasn't it?"

"Yeah."

"Damn, I knew it. Oh, this is going to be on the front page of the *New York Times.*" Thompson glanced at Bolan. "I can report this, can't I?"

"As long as all credit goes to the brave Yemeni army who tracked and engaged Qutaiba in a gun battle, killing all of his terrorist team while sustaining no casualties themselves. Something like that."

"Damn. And they won't even give you a medal for what you did."

"That's the way it goes." Bolan leaned back and closed his eyes. "I found a notebook of Qutaiba's. I haven't had time to look at it yet. We'll need to decipher it when we get to your place. How much farther is it?"

"Depends. Without checkpoints and disasters, about an hour. But this one wasn't here this morning, and it looks like they're checking all cars."

Bolan's eyes snapped open as Thompson brought the car to a halt behind a truck full of bleating goats. There were at least another four cars in front. The barricade was no more than a couple of military-style jeeps parked on either side of the road and two wooden barriers, which could be raised and lowered. Half a dozen soldiers milled around.

The Executioner closed his eyes again. There was no point in looking nervous. It was just another day for a freelance journalist with a job to do. Just another checkpoint. Thompson didn't seem nervous, either. The man had to pass through roadblocks every time he left the city. Three cars, then two, then one. It was the truck's turn. The driver chatted with the soldiers a few minutes before being waved through.

Thompson drove the car to the makeshift barrier, smiling at the soldiers. They didn't seem impressed, especially after spotting a white man in the passenger seat. Thompson was instructed to turn off his engine. A young soldier held his hand out for papers, never taking his eyes off Bolan or Thompson. The others stood back, hands on their AK-47s. The young soldier scanned the documents for a few seconds, discovered a small pile of US dollars hidden within and slid the money into his top pocket. He looked down at Thompson.

"Who this?" he asked in heavily accented English, indicating Bolan with his chin.

"Why, my new colleague!" Thompson said. "We came out looking for a story for our newspaper."

"How you find story in desert?"

"Well—" Thompson lowered his voice conspiratorially "—I have a friend in the glorious Yemeni army, quite high up, a colonel, and he told me that you guys had a big gunfight out here somewhere in the desert. So my friend and I, well, we came looking. But then some soldiers turned us back, saying they would shoot us if we didn't go away. So now we're going to the airport to see what story is there."

How much the soldier understood wasn't clear, but he seemed to get the gist of it. He continued to stare suspiciously at Bolan and Thompson before finally waving them through. Whether it was the bribe that convinced the soldier, the mention of knowing a colonel or a combination of both, Bolan didn't know. Thompson let out a breath, muttered something about good luck and drove away from the checkpoint at a cautious speed, apparently not wanting to raise further suspicion.

"The first of many," he said.

Bolan closed his eyes again. The sun beat down. Thompson turned his inefficient car cooling system to full. Warm air blasted into Bolan's face. He adjusted the vents so that they pointed toward his feet, then he dozed off.

They passed through another army checkpoint on the outskirts of the city. The situation was no different from the first: some money in one of the passports, answer a few questions about journalism, mention a nonexistent colonel and be waved through.

The city appeared in the distance. They passed the outlying buildings, billboards advertising cola, jeans, cars. Bolan asked for the cell phone, and Thompson passed it over. There was a strong signal. The soldier typed in a long number and waited for it to ring. The number was good for one call. Once used, the number would be reassigned by one of the phone companies, becoming a launderette or pizza parlor. The signal would pass through many cell phone providers and bounce off several satellites before being answered. The entire electronic journey took two seconds.

"Yes," a disembodied voice answered.

"Six Alpha Green," Bolan replied.

The phone clicked a few times, then Barbara Price came on the line.

"Striker?"

"Affirmative. The line is unsecure."

"Understood."

Bolan reached for the dashboard and turned the

car's roaring air system down in order to hear what was being said.

"Our friend was at the location, but had to depart quickly to meet his maker."

"Understood." There was slight relief in Price's voice at the confirmation that Qutaiba was confirmed dead.

"I'm now heading back I'll check in again at our other friend's house."

"Understood. Be advised that the boys in green have found a burning car in the desert. The local police have been informed."

"Roger that." Bolan broke the call and handed the cell phone back to Thompson.

"They found the burning UAZ," he said, "and have informed police."

"Yeah, I was afraid of that. The police won't be as easy to please."

"I could bail out and make my own way in."

"What would that achieve? If you get caught, then you'll have even more explaining to do. Stick together and we can give them the old dumb-Yankee-journalist routine."

Thompson had a point, and Bolan decided to go with it. The concealed weapons were the only problem. The Executioner spotted an industrial building with several large garbage containers outside. There wasn't much activity around the place.

"Pull over here."

Thompson complied, driving the car up to the containers. Bolan reached behind the seat, to the compartment, and removed the two weapons and the blue notebook. Working quickly he stripped the two pistols to their component parts, emptied the magazines of bullets, then spent several moments spreading the contents among the garbage, ensuring that no two pieces could be found together. The ammunition was similarly dealt with. Bolan climbed back into the car, and they left the scene without anybody taking any notice.

Bolan flicked through the pages of the notebook. Some of it was in English, but the car bounced too much for him to be able to read anything clearly. He looked up from the book when Thompson began to slow the car. A police checkpoint loomed ahead, consisting of several police cars and an armored vehicle. The police were stopping and searching every vehicle entering the city. They watched as an officer mounted the tailgate of a truck before clambering in among the goats and sheep. The animals could clearly be heard bleating in protest. The policeman jumped out, the truck was waved on and the procedure began again with the next car. And the next. After ten minutes it was finally Bolan and Thompson's turn.

The police officer who leaned into the vehicle was instantly suspicious. He held out his hand for their papers, while several armed colleagues moved up close. One began to check under the car. Bolan knew that if they had the equipment to check for traces of cordite, he would light up like a Christmas tree. The officer instructed them to get out. Bolan and Thompson complied. Bolan had tucked the blue notebook into his shirt's top pocket, where it was clearly visible, hiding in plain sight. They were ushered away from their car as several policemen began the search, popping the trunk, the hood and clambering inside. They found the empty compartment easily. The first officer finished examining the two men's papers and looked at them, staring coldly. Bolan knew he could easily stare back but didn't, knowing that the challenge could be construed the wrong way. Instead he wore the air of someone slightly cowed and intimidated. Thompson remained cool, smiling at the official.

"No problems?" Thompson asked.

The man continued to stare. Eventually he broke his silence. "Where have you been?" he asked. The question sounded like an accusation.

"Well," Thompson began, but the officer silenced him.

"I ask him," he said, pointing at Bolan. "Mr.... B-lan-ski."

Bolan gave the man a weak smile. "We were looking for a story. We were told that there was shooting in the desert. We followed the army out, but they turned us back at the checkpoint. They told us there was nothing to see. So now we are going to the airport to cover that story."

"Airport closed. Who told you about shooting?"

"Colonel Nissal," Thompson said. "He's a friend."

The policeman was unimpressed with the reference to an army colonel. He looked at one of his approaching officers, a black eyebrow raised in question. The other man shook his head, muttered something and then stared at Bolan and Thompson, obviously hoping to intimidate them more. The official in charge turned back to the two Americans.

"Why compartment under seat? You hide drugs?"

"No, no," Bolan protested. "No drugs. It is for this." He held up the camera hanging around his neck. "We hide it in the car—we don't want it stolen."

The officer seemed to find this answer acceptable. He examined the papers again, hoping to discover a discrepancy in the passport stamps, the work permits. Finding none, he reluctantly handed them back.

"You go now. Leave."

Bolan and Thompson thanked him and climbed back into the car. They left the checkpoint, the police still staring after them. Thompson let out a gasp of pent-up relief.

"That was tense. I'm sure glad I didn't slip in the customary bribe. I don't think that guy would have appreciated it."

"No, he was dedicated, I'll give him that. Colonel Nissal?"

"Guy in the army who I have tried to interview a few times. I think that he's on the take. Keeps turning me down. Maybe the police will check him out. Revenge is sweet."

Bolan chuckled. The city became more and more modern. Low houses gave way to towering apartment buildings, extremely white, and shining in the sun. The road was black and smooth, the cars driving on it far more modern than those outside the city. More billboards lined the road and hung on the sides of buildings. It barely seemed like the Middle East. Almost ringing the city was a long, unbroken chain of stone hills. Thompson caught him taking in the sights.

"You ever been here before?" he asked.

"I've passed through once or twice." Bolan said.

The buildings to his right vanished, offering a fantastic view of the bay and the sea beyond. Bolan could see all manner of oil tankers and freighters docked in the harbor, entering, leaving, all floating on a perfect blue surface. The whole vista was simply stunning. Thompson broke the spell by reminding him that the USS *Cole* had been attacked just down there, then the view was gone as the car turned to head up a hill, its diesel engine laboring. Traffic was heavier, the main roads blocked. The column of smoke from the nearby airport had all but dissipated. Bolan had a brief glimpse of the facility, of distant, flashing blue lights, before that, too, disappeared from sight, cut off as the car went around another corner and Thompson took them down a narrow alley.

"I live close to one of the abandoned Christian churches here in Aden," he said. He drove out of the alley onto another road, narrowly missing a minibus, its driver tooting angrily. "This area is called The Crater. The whole of Aden is built on a volcano. Don't worry. It hasn't erupted for thousands of years, or so they tell me. Did you know that Aden is a Free Trade Zone? That's why it's so affluent around here—plenty of money and goods passing through. Hell of a black market, let me tell you. The whole place was British, as well, right up until the late 1960s. They built the airport. Originally it was an RAF base. But Aden is ancient, man, ancient. Hey, local legend has it that Kane and Abel were buried here…"

Bolan tuned out the travelogue. He wanted nothing more than to check out the notebook, have something to eat and then bed down, leaving Thompson to sort out some sort of travel arrangements. He had a suspicion that getting a little shut-eye wasn't going to feature on his agenda.

Thompson had stopped his chatter and turned on the radio instead. An accented voice, speaking in English, stated that up to one hundred people had been on board the Turkish aircraft, that all were dead, that flights would be delayed all day and maybe the following day. Thompson turned off the radio. He pulled the car into a space on the side of the street and shut off the engine. He leaned over to Bolan.

"We're here," he said, before exiting the vehicle. Bolan climbed out and Thompson locked the car's doors. He followed his contact to the door of a two-story house. They entered the dim hallway, the temperature difference surprising Bolan. The house felt cold compared to outside. Thompson didn't seem to notice.

"I'm upstairs," he said. "A guy from the British Embassy has the downstairs apartment."

Bolan followed Thompson to the top. The journalist opened the door and led the way into a spacious white-walled living room. At one end was an immaculate kitchenette. At the other an L-shaped sofa faced a large flat-screen TV. A coffee table separated the two. Bolan's eyebrows rose.

"You have a maid?" he asked.

"No, man. I clean it myself. In case you're wondering, the television and all the Blu-ray paraphernalia I got from a guy who knows another guy. Like I told you, there's a hell of a black market here."

"Stolen goods."

"Nah, I was given to understand that a crate had been found floating in the harbor."

"Right. Where's the satellite hookup?"

"In here." Thompson showed Bolan into a bedroom. A single bed occupied one wall, while the opposite wall had a desk and several bookshelves packed with magazines, novels and nonfiction books. An all-in-one printer sat next to the computer monitor. Thompson shook the mouse to clear the screen saver and entered a password. Then he clicked an icon. A white pop-up appeared, asking for a number.

"The computer came from your guys. It's clean. Say, do you want a drink?"

Bolan nodded and followed Thompson to the kitchenette, where he was handed a glass of cold orange juice. He downed it and asked for another. Thompson obliged him.

"So, what can you tell me about the events of last night? I'll need to file some sort of story to keep the editors happy." Thompson took several eggs from the fridge and started preparing an omelet for breakfast.

Bolan thought for a moment before narrating what had happened, emphasizing that the Yemeni army did everything; he was never there.

"So let me get this straight. They sent you in to confirm that Qutaiba was on the ground. Instead you jump out of an airplane, without a functioning parachute, lose your guns on the way down, then decide you will take on a hundred bad guys using only your six-shooters and your fists, before strolling nonchalantly across the desert to rendezvous with me?"

Bolan nodded, a ghost of a smile touching his lips. "Yeah, that's just about it. Don't forget the bit about dueling with the kingpin."

Bolan finished his orange juice and plucked a cookie out of a nearby glass jar. He pulled the notebook out of his pocket.

Time to get down to business.

CHAPTER SEVEN

The pages still didn't make much sense. Bolan could read a little Arabic, but the words seemed disjointed, out of place. A few English words were scattered in between. Bolan looked up at Thompson. "Is there a place around here called Cape Faith?"

Thompson thought for a minute. "Can't say there is. Not a land feature, anyway. I'll check online." He left the omelet and went into the spare bedroom. Bolan could hear him clacking away at the keyboard. Thompson came back into the living room. "Nope, and there isn't a charity or church in the region with that name, either. Is it a target?"

"No idea. And it seems they wanted to buy a Ford. See what you make of this." Bolan handed the notebook to Thompson and finished off preparing the omelet. He was famished. The former blacksuit flicked through the pages as Bolan began to eat.

"This is gibberish," Thompson said. "These are real Arabic words, but in some form of code. I can't make anything out of it."

"Do you have a scanner? A method of uploading documents to your Justice contact?"

Thompson nodded.

"Then you can scan the book in, while I clean up."

"The bathroom is in there." Thompson pointed to a

door. "Plenty of towels, and I have an extra toothbrush in the cupboard. I'll get on with this."

Bolan went into the bathroom as Thompson began to scan in the pages. The images would be uploaded to a cloud host, no doubt, passing through several internet service providers and subject to scans by military servers, before being picked up by Hal Brognola, director of the Sensitive Operations Group. Untraceable. Thompson also sent an encrypted email to Brognola, alerting him to the fact that documents were on the way and needed deciphering. By the time he was finished, he heard his contact leave the bathroom. He found a clean and fresh-looking man in the living room.

"And now?"

"Now I check in and we wait to see what happens."

Bolan poured himself another glass of orange juice, then walked to the spare bedroom. He closed the door behind him and sat at the desk. The program asking him to type a phone number was still open. He typed in the digits, different from the ones he'd first used, and waited. The computer came equipped with a microphone headset. Bolan plugged the headset into the computer's jack socket.

"Yes."

"Six Alpha Green"

"One moment…"

Barbara Price came on the line. "Striker?"

"Don't you ever sleep?" he joked.

"Don't you? What's the status on your end?"

"I'm with our friend at his place. Images have been scanned in and sent to Hal."

"He forwarded them to us immediately and we're working on them now."

"The target is confirmed down. The notebook was his. This isn't over yet. He was up to something. I'll need that intel pronto because I have a feeling that there isn't much time. Also I might need an extraction. The airport is shut down. Oh, and the parachute I was given failed. Probably folded wrong. Somebody needs his ass handed to him for that. What's the status with the Yemeni army and police?" The information and questions were blunt and to the point. Bolan didn't want to spend too much time on the line.

"The State Department is praising the Yemenis for a job well-done. They don't know whether to accept the credit or protest over the drone strikes and incursion onto their soil. There's chatter that they're looking for a team of commandos that's suspected to have fled in a helicopter. You and our friend are in the clear. I'll pass on a memo about the parachute. My heart was in my mouth when I saw that happening."

"Where do you think mine was?"

"We understand that the airport will be closed all day. More than a hundred casualties. The aircraft was old. Many flights are canceled. You won't be leaving via Aden International. We'll look into it." There was a pause and Bolan could hear a muffled voice in the background. "Striker? I have to go. Able Team needs assistance. Stay put if possible. We'll be in contact about the book." The line was broken.

Thompson was sitting on the sofa, banging away at the keys of an old laptop. He stopped as Bolan opened the bedroom door.

"How's it looking?" Thompson inquired.

"Hurry up and wait" was Bolan's reply.

"Yeah, nothing changes. Just filing a quick scoop

on the Yemeni army. Seems everybody else around here is focusing on the crash."

"State is already congratulating the Yemeni government."

"Really? Then I had better include that, as well. Make yourself at home." He waved his hand in the direction of the kitchenette, the living room, the spare bedroom, before returning to his typing. Bolan nodded and turned, intending to make good use of the spare bed. Hurry up and wait indeed.

BOLAN WOKE TO a chirping from the computer. He estimated that he had slept for two hours. Fully awake he rolled off the bed and grabbed the headset, stabbing at the keyboard with his index finger.

"Striker."

"Striker, it's me." The voice was that of Aaron Kurtzman. "We have deciphered the code, which is quite simple. You need to be on your way, ASAP. We're making arrangements as we speak."

"What's the situation?"

"*Cape Faith* is a ship, a small freighter, currently docked in Aden Harbor. She is loading rice and other aid, bound for Djibouti. She sails in three hours. You're expected on board, a last-minute passenger."

"What are they up to?" Bolan asked.

"They aren't up to anything, as far as we can tell. However, Qutaiba had two groups, a two-pronged attack. You have removed one. The second intends to board the freighter midocean, making out as Somali pirates. Once in command they'll sail the ship to Djibouti and ram it into the side of the USS *Ford*, a frigate currently moored in Djibouti. The idea seems to be a suicide run. Cause as much damage as possible."

"The USS *Cole*, but on a larger scale," Bolan said.

"Exactly. We're in the process of alerting the USS *Ford*. We can put a Special Forces team on board fairly quickly—there are enough guys stationed in Djibouti—but we don't know when the pirates will be boarding. That information wasn't included. Qutaiba's group planned to seize a different freighter, one that is moored in New Aden. We believe that attack has been fully scuppered, but we are alerting the authorities to keep an eye on it."

"What do you want me to do?" Bolan asked, already suspecting but wanting confirmation.

Price's voice cut in, sounding tired. "We want you on board, as an observer and backup in case something goes wrong or terrorists are already among the crew. The ship will be monitored. The moment any small boats approach, US Navy helicopters from the USS *Ford* will move in to intercept."

"I'll need some hardware," Bolan said, "and a way to get it past customs."

"According to our records, our friend has a piece. We'll arrange something with customs. You're using a really old identity, I believe." Price said.

"Yeah."

"You'll be met at the harbor by a contact who will stamp your passport with the correct visa. It isn't a long voyage to Djibouti, about a day and a half. Once you arrive at Djibouti City, you'll be met by another contact who will escort you to Lemonnier, where you'll be expected. Then it's just a question of catching the next military flight out. We'll arrange all that from here."

"Roger that. Where can I find the *Cape Faith*?"

Aaron Kurtzman gave him the dock number, which Bolan memorized.

"Anything else?" Bolan asked.

"Yes, good luck," Price said.

"Go get some sleep. You sound like you need it," Bolan said softly, breaking the connection. He rejoined Thompson in the living room.

"We're leaving," Bolan announced.

"Where are we going?"

"You're taking me to a certain wharf in the harbor. There we will part company. But first I need to buy some clothes, preferably black, a sports bag and a decent-looking camera. Oh, and I want your gun."

"The clothes and stuff are easy," Thompson said. "There's a market down the road that sells all the best knockoffs. But my piece? How will I be able to shoot stray mad dogs without it?"

"Get a new one, or get a new hobby."

Thompson went into the master bedroom, returning with a shoebox. He withdrew a Beretta 92-F, a pistol similar to Bolan's preferred 93-R. He handed it over along with four magazines and a cleaning kit. Bolan quickly checked the immaculate weapon, armed it and tucked it behind his shirt. When he bought the sports bag he would hide it in there, among the clothes. He smiled at Thompson.

"Okay, soldier, let's move out."

RUST BUCKET.

Those were the only words that sprang into Bolan's mind as he gazed at the light blue sides of the small freighter. At least, it had once been blue. Now orange streaks of rust were prominent, overpowering the blue paint. The superstructure at the rear was equally shabby. A stained, blackened funnel was perched atop it, noxious fumes pouring out in waves. The Plimsoll mark of the small ship was barely visible, indicating a full load. As Bolan watched, a last pallet was hoisted into the sky by the ship's derrick, the job of the dockside stevedores all but done. He noticed that the ship's name had been changed several times. The name MV *Cape Faith* was now crudely painted on the vessel's side in letters of differentiating height.

Bolan shook his head. He had traveled all over the world on all manner of transportation, but seldom had he voyaged on such a dirty, rusty freighter as this.

It was just under three hours since he had spoken with Stony Man Farm. Thompson had first taken him to the market, where he had bought several T-shirts and pairs of pants in black, a baseball cap, a pair of sunglasses as well as sturdy walking boots, a sports bag and toiletry items. A Nikon camera had been last on the list. It all went into the bag. As Thompson had promised, all were first-class knockoffs. A cheap, burner cell phone joined the items. Bolan had no idea if he would need it, but not to have one and be searched would arouse suspicion in itself.

Then they headed to the massive natural harbor that was the source of all income in Aden. The main causeway that served the eastern half of the port ran past the runway where the aircraft wreckage was plain to see, surrounded by emergency vehicles. The road was jammed solid, north to south, with cars. It seemed that everybody wanted to rubberneck at the smashed remains of the passenger aircraft on the runway. Thompson was forced to take a road that ran around the back of the airport. Even that was busy.

Finally they were past and proceeded to the dock gates, where they parted company. Thompson waved as Bolan exited the battered Peugeot. Then he drove away, back to his normal life as a journalist.

As the white car left, an old man approached Bolan. A bearded, smiling Arab, he held out his hands, saying, "You need visa, sir? You need visa?"

Bolan proffered his passport and the man promptly stamped it then and there, in broad daylight. Still grinning, he handed it back to Bolan, pleased with his day's hard work. Bolan handed him a few US dollars, the expected tip. The Arab man bowed and faded back into the nearby building from which he'd emerged.

Bolan proceeded to walk to the wharf where the MV *Cape Faith* was tied up, his sports bag slung over his shoulder. With his baseball cap and dark sunglasses, he looked like any other sailor heading back to a ship. The docks were huge, and he was glad that he didn't have to cover a great distance in the sweltering heat. He passed several large container freighters, off-loading, loading, before he arrived at the *Cape Faith*, dwarfed between two other massive ships. Bolan stood and stared at the dirty little freighter, the target of suicide bombers who wanted to smash her into the hull of a US warship. Even if the ship could make only ten or twelve knots, the sheer mass of four thousand tons ramming the moored USS *Ford* would break the warship in two. Still, forewarned was forearmed. If the terrorists succeeded in boarding the *Cape Faith*, then US assets would sink or board the vessel at sea. She would never be allowed to get close to the *Ford.*

Mack Bolan approached the gangway. Several scruffy crew members and stevedores standing on the wharf eyed him suspiciously, but none tried to stop him or questioned his presence. At the top of the gangway he was approached by a dirty little man wearing a filthy yellow T-shirt and equally grimy blue shorts. Bolan took an instant dislike to him, more from the fact of extreme grubbiness than anything else. Grubby proudly exhibited his blackened teeth as he held out his hand to Bolan, who reluctantly shook it, then resisted the urge to wipe his own on his trouser leg. Grubby's hand stayed in place, as if he expected a bribe or tip.

"Permission to come aboard?" Bolan asked.

"Yes, yes. Come. You are Blanski passenger?" Grubby's English was broken and stilted.

"That I am," Bolan said, role-playing the part of a brash American journalist.

"Good. Good. You pay now." Grubby waved his open palm under Bolan's chin.

Bolan knew that Stony Man had already paid the ship's owners for his passage, making sure that an extra cut was passed on to the ship's master to ensure Bolan wasn't harassed by any busybody officials who enjoyed making life difficult for foreigners. The cut was more than generous. Yet here was this little guy, who was clearly not in charge of the freighter, demanding money. Bolan felt his irritation rise, joining his tiredness and frustration at the heat. The deck plates were burning holes through the soles of his cheap running shoes.

He removed the sunglasses and glared down at

Grubby, his ice-blue eyes, which had intimidated so many gangsters and criminals throughout the world, pinning Grubby to the spot. The man wilted, his crooked grin fading away. His outstretched arm fell to his side.

"Are you the captain?" Bolan's voice was chilling.

"Er, no, I, er..." Grubby was tongue-tied. Then to Bolan's amusement, a lightbulb lit up behind the little man's eyes, the running cogs almost visible inside Grubby's skull. His grimy palm once again shot up, occupying the space under Bolan's chin.

"Captain send me here," he said, "for money." He again waved his empty hand. Several crew members stood in the background, observing the confrontation, wondering which way the discussion would go. Bolan left them in no doubt. He bent forward, leaning into the man's personal space, his eyes inches away from Grubby's widening dark brown ones.

"No," Bolan stated. "You are not the captain, and he did not send you here. Take me to him now, or I'll find him myself and tell him how you tried to rob me."

The man's face fell. Bolan could see the hate slowly rising in the brown eyes and knew that he had just made an enemy. The watching crewmen chortled at Grubby's humiliation. He glared at them and shouted something unintelligible. Still laughing, they turned their backs and got back to work, securing the main hatches. Bolan followed Grubby across the vibrating deck and up an open stairway to the cramped bridge.

Three men were on the bridge, one of whom was yelling into a telephone receiver. Grubby stood next to telephone man and waited. The phone was slammed down hard. Grubby started to address telephone man in a language that Bolan was surprisingly unfamiliar with. All heads turned, and Bolan felt the hostile stares of the bridge crew on him.

Telephone man crossed the bridge, pointing an angry finger at Bolan's face. He was taller than Grubby, who Bolan noticed was smirking, and better dressed, but the soldier still towered above him. He glared up at Bolan, who returned the stare.

"Cousin say you not pay! If not pay, get off boat now!" The man was in a foul mood, spittle flying from his mouth.

"No. I said that I would talk to the captain. Are you the captain?" Bolan kept his voice calm, quiet.

"So, cousin is liar! You not pay, then say family is all liars! You off boat now! Now!" The man was all but screaming, shrill in his exclamations. Bolan could feel the situation slipping out of control. The other two bridge members were slowly approaching, spoiling for a fight. Grubby, in the background, was rubbing his hands together. Bolan reached into his pocket and removed a fifty-dollar bill. He waved it under the irate man's nose.

"I'll give this to the captain and only the captain. If I have to leave, then fine. But it will have consequences." He leaned in close, invading another man's space for the second time in five minutes. "I know that my employers have already paid the *Cape Faith*'s owners. I know that there was a generous bonus included for the captain."

He saw the crewmen's heads snap around at that revelation. They hadn't been aware of it. "When I disembark, I'll phone my employers, who will then contact the owners to inform them of the breaking of the contract, something that we call theft. Then I'll make another call, this one to the US Embassy. As a reporter, I'll tell them that I learned the *Cape Faith* is smuggling drugs and weapons to terrorists. You can expect to be boarded by American soldiers the minute you leave Yemeni waters. They'll impound your ship and arrest you for everything from piracy to tax evasion."

Bolan straightened. "Or that need not happen. I've already paid. This is a small gift for the captain. Perhaps he can buy a bottle of rum with it. Now, are you the captain?"

The man was quiet for a moment, glowering at Bolan's threat. Slowly his demeanor changed, the anger bleeding away, a farcical smile of delight spreading across his face. He stuck out his hand, keeping an eye on the fifty-dollar bill.

"I am captain. Captain Abu. No need be angry. All friends here!" Abu waved his crew away. Grubby cursed and gave Bolan a vicious look before skulking away through a door in the bulkhead of the bridge.

"Forgive anger. Bad day in office. Cousin lazy. Bad day, bad day. But I buy rum next time, we drink together!" Abu was still smiling as he pocketed the fifty dollars. "Come, come, good friend Mr. Balansky! I show you where you sleep."

Bolan didn't bother to correct Abu on the mispronunciation of his cover name.

The captain continued. "Thank you for travel on good ship *Cape Faith*. Bad business at airport, no? Many people go splat!" Abu led Bolan through the same door Grubby had disappeared through and down a ladder into the heart of the superstructure. The condition of the ship's insides weren't much better than its outsides. "Come, Mr. Balansky. You stay in fine cabin with nice lady. She is from Neverland. I have been to Neverland many, many times. Rotterdam is good, no? Good beer! You go to Rotterdam?"

Bolan smiled. "I have been to the Netherlands. Rotterdam is a good place."

Abu reached a door and banged on it. "Mrs. Clapton," he yelled. "Mrs. Clapton! You have visitor friend! Mrs. Clapton! Open up!"

The metal door did open to reveal a woman. Her sharp eyes blazed contempt and indignation at Captain Abu. In her hand she held a hairbrush. She was either busy with her short curly brown hair, Bolan thought, or she was going to beat Abu with it. Abu beamed at her. Her expression did not alter.

"What do you want now?" she demanded.

"Mrs. Clapton! You have guest. My good friend Balansky. He stay with you in cabin!"

The woman took a deep breath, and Bolan could see she was about to erupt. He was about to ask if there was another cabin, when the volcano exploded.

"It is Clayton. Mrs. Clayton. And no! This is my cabin! Mine! I have paid for it. My organization paid for it. Now go away! Leave me alone, you pirate!" She hadn't even glanced in Bolan's direction, her eyes firmly fixed on Abu, who was still smiling inanely.

"No, Mrs. Clapton! You pay for bed. For bunk. Not cabin. I throw my cousin and sailor out of here for you. Now Mr. Balansky also stay. You like him. He funny, make me laugh, always giving gifts. Now I go. We slip moorings. We sail for Djibouti. Just like cruise ship, yes?" Abu cheerfully sauntered off, leaving Mrs. Clayton staring angrily after him, making a growling noise behind clenched teeth, her knuckles white around the hairbrush.

Slowly she directed her gaze to Bolan, who smiled disarmingly. He put her height at around five foot six and could see bright intelligence behind the burning fire in her eyes. He raised an eyebrow, indicating the cabin behind her with a jerk of his chin.

"Maybe I could just stow my bag here," he said. "Don't worry. I'll stay out of your way as much as possible. And nothing will happen, believe me. I'm Mike Blanski." He held out his right hand. Clayton stared at him, not giving ground. Bolan adjusted his hand, indicating that he wanted to shake hers. Finally she conceded, transferring the hairbrush to her left hand and shaking Bolan's with her right.

"Nancy Clayton," she said.

"Mike Blanski," Bolan repeated. "May I?" He indicated the cabin.

"Go ahead, be my guest, make yourself at home. It's not like I have a lot of choice." She stood aside, allowing Bolan to enter.

The cabin was small, a bunk bed on the left, a metal desk and wardrobe on the right. Facing him was an open porthole, the noise and smells of the harbor pouring through it. The MV *Cape Faith* shuddered and began vibrating harder. He could hear shouting on the decks as the ship cast off, a small tug just visible outside. He placed his sports bag on the top bunk, noting that the lower one had been claimed.

"I'd advise you to turn the mattress over," Clayton said. "They aren't very clean. I shudder to think how old they are. The captain's cousin sleeps up there. I have never met a more repugnant creature."

"Ah, yes, Grubby. He doesn't like me much."

"Ha! Grubby! Yes, that is a good name for him. Grubby. This whole ship is grubby."

"Your accent? Chicago? Abu said you were from the Netherlands."

"Abu is an idiot. I doubt he has his master's license for this boat. But, yes, I was born and raised in Chicago. I live in Holland, working for a Dutch charity organization, Help Without Borders. You?"

"Journalist. Freelance. Covering the famine on the Horn of Africa. How come you're on board a ship? Isn't that dangerous for a woman? I was always under the impression that you guys were flown everywhere."

"Huh! I didn't want to be here, believe me. Our shipment of rice is on board. I was supposed to meet with colleagues in Djibouti after supervising the loading, making sure nothing accidently disappeared, but the airport is shut down, so I had to hitch a ride with the Misfits of the Caribbean. Not something I wanted to do. Yes, it could be dangerous. I'm not happy about it. I fully intended to lock the door and stay in here, no matter how hot it gets. Speaking of hot." She tugged on her T-shirt, a vain attempt to circulate some air around her body. "Do you think they have any cooler rooms on board? The ship must have a freezer. What a sweatbox."

"Our rice?" Bolan inquired.

"Yes, I work for a Dutch charity. Don't ask. It's a long story. Anyway, I'm supervising the delivery. I worked for other big organizations before this one, covered disaster relief in Indonesia, Haiti, Thailand,

Somalia, which is why they thought it was a good idea to send me here to Djibouti. My husband and son are worried sick, what with the bombings there."

"Bombings?"

"Yes, the bombings. There was a big one two days ago, car bomb outside a hotel where a lot of aid workers were staying. Where I was supposed to stay. Loads of people were killed. How can you be a journalist and not have heard of it?"

"I've been busy," Bolan said. He reached into his back pocket and removed his cell phone. He still had a connection with the local networks. They hadn't cleared the harbor yet.

"I'm just going to make a call. I'll be back soon."

Bolan left Clayton in the cabin and proceeded up onto the main deck. He moved away from the busy area and worked his way to the counter deck at the stern of the ship where no crew members were present. He typed in the cutout number for Stony Man Farm and gripped the hot taffrail, hoping that the call would go through on his cheap cell phone. It took a little longer than usual, but he was connected through to the Annex Computer Room. Carmen Delahunt, a former FBI agent and now one of the top cyberwarriors for the Farm, answered.

"Striker," Bolan said as a way of greeting, speaking loudly over the noise of the engine. He put on his sunglasses to cover the intensity of the blue sea and sky. The harbor was trailing away in the wake of the ship, the MV *Cape Faith* marking her passage with a long stream of black funnel smoke.

"Hi, what's burning?" she said cheerily.

"At the moment, I am. You apprised of the situation?"

"Sure am. Got briefed just before the rest all went off to bed. What can I do you for?"

"Two things. First give me a bare-bones rundown on one Nancy Clayton, formerly of Chicago, now resident in the Netherlands, working for Help Without Borders. Second, I just heard there was bomb blast in Djibouti yesterday. Am I walking into something I should know about?"

"Hold on. I'll check." Bolan could hear keys clacking as Delahunt rapidly typed in the multiple queries. She came back on a minute later.

"Okay, the bombing was at the Waverley Hotel. Seems it was a car bomb planted on a guest's car. The guest, a French national, was killed along with his driver and four soldiers at the hotel checkpoint. Six aid workers for various charities were killed, along with a Danish journalist and nine hotel staff. Sixty people were injured, some seriously. The injured foreign nationals were moved to Lemonnier's military hospital. The locals went to various hospitals in the city. Get this. One of the seriously injured was a CIA spook. Another spook was slightly injured."

"Anybody claim responsibility?"

"Not as of yet, but the government is blaming FRUD, the Front for Restoration of Unity and Democracy. They signed a peace treaty with the government more than a decade ago, but it seems that the government is beating its chest and pointing fingers. The leaders of FRUD are denying all responsibility and are blaming the government for the carnage."

"Wonderful. Do I need to look into it?"

"I don't know. I'll ask the boss when she wakes up. In the meantime you may soon have more pressing problems at sea."

"Yeah. And Clayton?"

"Forty-four, a former teacher from a high school in a disadvantaged neighborhood in Chicago. Married and joined a large charity organization. Been to hot spots all around the world. Has one son, aged nine. Resident of the Netherlands for the past four years due to husband's job. Specializes in communication and education. Changed from one charity organization to the current one. They were glad to have her, promoting her experience and success on their website. One of their highfliers. She seems to be aboveboard. Do you want me to dig deeper? Is she part of the mission?"

"No, she's a passenger on board. If the fireworks start, I'll shut her in the cabin. Don't bother digging deeper. My gut tells me she is who she says she is. I think my cell connection is about to go. I'll be in contact soon." Bolan broke off and returned the phone to his jeans pocket.

On his way back to the cabin, he came across the galley. Nobody was in the room. All hands on deck, he supposed. A quick search of the cupboards turned up several plastic bottles of water, which he pilfered. He then navigated his way back to the cabin. The door was locked from the inside. He gave it a rap with his knuckles.

"Who is it?"

"Me. Mike."

There was a rattle, the door opened and there was Clayton, looking more disheveled than when he had left. He handed her one of the bottles of water to which she muttered a quick thanks before downing half of its contents. Bolan put the others in a locker, keeping one out for himself. He perched himself on the desk, taking several gulps of water. Clayton lay back on her bunk, groaning.

"I hate boats," she stated. "This one rattles and shakes like nothing I have ever experienced. If you close the porthole, then you suffocate. If you leave it open, the fumes from the funnel come in and then you suffocate. Well, I don't hate all boats—we went on a cruise once—that was nice—but this one is awful. So, did you contact a friend about the bombings?"

"Yeah. They're keeping an eye on it. Maybe they'll ask me for a photo or to do an interview. Seems the government is blaming an old enemy and the enemy is blaming the government. I've seen that so many times."

"You know," Clayton said, "I probably knew some of those people who were killed. Oh, God, that's awful. I didn't think of it. Oh, God." Her hand was at her mouth. "I'll be showing up not knowing who's dead. And I was just worrying about this rotten boat."

Bolan reached into his back pocket and pulled out the cell phone. He held it out to her. "If you want to make a quick call, you can use this. There's still one stripe, but you'll have to stand on deck to have a chance at reception."

She looked at the offered phone, then nodded. Getting up from the bunk, she rooted around in a bag, removing a battered address book. She found a number, typed it into the phone and then looked at Bolan. "Walk with me?" she asked.

Bolan led her back onto the deck where he had

stood and moved off a little to allow her some privacy. Clayton pressed the tiny green call button and waited for a connection. Bolan could make out mutterings, a disappointed "Oh, no," followed by a "Yes, I remember him." After a minute she broke the connection and handed the cell phone back to Bolan.

"Thank you," she said.

"Any problems?"

"Somebody I once met is among the dead. Several others are in hospital or are being flown home. They think that twenty-five are dead, and many are wounded. Why would anybody want to do this?" She gripped the taffrail with both hands, staring at the horizon, not focusing on any one thing. "I hate bombs. Bombs, guns, anybody who uses them."

Bolan remained silent. He understood the sentiment, wanting nothing more than a world free of death and destruction. Unfortunately he knew that would never come to pass.

"Did I tell you I was a teacher in Chicago?" Clayton continued. "We used to confiscate guns from eight-year-olds. Eight-year-olds! They needed them for 'protection' because they didn't feel safe. What sort of world do we live in where children need to protect themselves, and aid workers are blown up for helping others? Monsters, Mike. Monsters walk among us. I'm going back down. Thanks for the phone."

She left Bolan on the deck, reflecting. Monsters did indeed walk among them. It was the reason the Executioner existed, to fight evil by any means available. He sat down in a shaded patch of the deck, contemplating, remembering fallen friends and family as Aden slowly slipped under the horizon.

TOWARD THE END of the afternoon, they sat opposite each other in the ship's cramped galley, managing to eat a simple meal of chicken and rice, which the cook had prepared for them, as the ship rocked leisurely from side to side. Neither the vibration nor the stink of oil fumes had abated once the ship had left harbor; what slight wind that there was conspired to blow the funnel smoke down onto the deck and into any open porthole. They had been instructed by the cook—a friendly Filipino—to eat up because the first shift of the crew would be down soon and seating space would disappear. Along with all available food.

As they downed their surprisingly good meal, Clayton informed Bolan of the difficulties in moving the rice from Djibouti City to northern Obcock, the region where the shipment was destined, a rugged, mountainous area that bordered Eritrea. There was a tiny airport at Obcock City, but her agency had considered the flight too expensive. There was a tiny harbor, also in the city, but the agency couldn't find a boat willing to transport the shipment across the Gulf of Tadjoura from Djibouti City to Obcock—no reasons had been forthcoming. The Help Without Borders agency had settled on a small convoy of trucks to drive around the bay that divided the country almost in two. And there were so many tales of how dangerous it was. Bolan had inquired if there was an escort, and Clayton replied that she believed the army or the police would be providing something—that was, if there was any rice left to deliver, the black market in Djibouti being so huge.

Bolan was about to ask more when he heard a commotion coming down the corridor. Somebody was yelling, screeching incoherently. The cook fled into a store room as Captain Abu burst in, waving his hands in the air, Grubby close on his heels. Abu spotted Bolan and approached the table. He shouted hysterically at Bolan, who raised his hand and gave the man a look that cut off the torrent of words in an instant.

"Calm down," Bolan instructed. "Take a deep breath and tell me what's wrong."

Abu took a deep breath and then relaunched his tirade, but this time in English.

"You lie! You lie! You tell all lies! Why? Why? Did Abu not give you his ship? Was Abu not nice enough? Did cousin not say sorry?"

"I have no idea what you're talking about, Abu. Tell me again."

It was Grubby who picked up the thread, his look one of contempt.

"You phone American Army. They send two helicopters to us. They radio, say we must stay on course and speed…"

Bolan was already moving. He grabbed Clayton by the hand, hauling her to her feet. "Abu," he said quickly, "I called no one. But if the US Navy is here, then you need to return to the bridge immediately. It means there are pirates in the area. Nancy, come with me."

He pulled the aid worker along, back down to their cabin, leaving Abu and Grubby standing openmouthed. Clayton protested but didn't resist. Once in the cabin, Bolan released her and began rummaging in his sports bag.

"You hurt me," she said, rubbing her wrist.

"Sorry. There's no time to explain."

Her eyes widened as Bolan removed the pistol and the spare magazines.

"Oh, no! No guns! Why are you carrying that with you?"

Bolan turned to her as he tucked the pistol into his waistband, pulling his shirt over it. He pushed the magazines into his rear pockets.

"Again, sorry. Now listen. You have to stay here, no matter what happens. Close and lock the door. Only open it for me. No one else. And keep the porthole closed, as well. No matter what you hear, stay here!"

Bolan left her, pulling the cabin door shut behind him. He hoped that Clayton would be sensible enough to lock it. He charged down the corridor and found an open door that led him onto the deck. He could clearly hear the helicopters, the thunder of their engines and rotors getting closer. Then they were over the ship, flying no more than fifty feet above the funnel. Two gray Sikorsky MH-60R Seahawk helicopters roared overhead. Bolan could clearly see the door gunners gripping their General Electric GAU-17A miniguns, a six-barreled Gatling gun that was capable of firing up to six thousand rounds a minute. Several of the deck crew fell to the ground, clutching their ears, expecting to be shot at any minute. Bolan scanned the horizon. Where was the terrorist strike team? He'd have a better chance at locating them from the bridge.

He ran back, retracing his steps, taking ladders and stairs quickly upward where he found Abu, Grubby and a couple of others looking decidedly nervous. Bolan grabbed a pair of binoculars and proceeded out onto the flying bridge, a tiny piece of superstructure that afforded the captain an outside view of his ship and the sea. The Seahawks were peeling off, heading toward the starboard horizon. Bolan followed them with his binoculars. Then he saw the tiny boats in the water, charging at high speed toward the *Cape Faith*. He nodded to himself.

The attack was on.

CHAPTER EIGHT

The murder took place seven yards from where Peter Douglas stood, staring out of his first-floor bedroom window, watching with horror and feeling powerless to prevent it. The skinny black guy had come out of an opposite building, holding aloft what appeared to be a chicken leg, brandishing it as if it were a sword captured from an enemy on the battlefield. Douglas had no idea what the building opposite housed, but he suspected that it was being used by black marketers selling food and other items at overinflated prices. And this guy, pleased as punch, waved his expensive piece of chicken around for all the world to see.

It caught the attention of three punks, all hungry, who demanded that the chicken be turned over along with anything else the skinny guy had—at least that's what Douglas assumed they were saying. Punks were the same the world over. The skinny guy refused, was about to take a bite when the punks lunged. There was a scuffle, a flash of a knife, and the skinny guy relinquished his chicken, falling into the grime of the gutter.

The punks laughed, one of them clutching the chicken leg, and together they ran down the litter-strewn street, fading into the darkness. Nobody approached the dying man, whose blood was spreading through the filth. Nobody cared. It was just another death in Djibouti. The corpse, when found, would be taken to a mass burial pit outside the city to join the growing pile of dead.

Douglas let the black curtain fall back into place. He sat heavily on the corner of his single bed, its worn springs protesting. He rubbed his eyes with his bandaged hands, thinking of the madness of the world, of the dead body under his window, of Saint-Verran blown to pieces, of Peter Davies lying in intensive care at Camp Lemonnier, unable to be moved due to the severity of his injuries. How was it possible that Davies was knocking on death's door when he had only cuts to his hands and a few bruises to show? Davies had been standing right next to him when the car bomb exploded. It was madness.

After his discharge from the military hospital, he had been debriefed by the station chief, who wanted to know how he could have allowed this to happen. Why hadn't he foreseen an assassination plot against Saint-Verran? Did he know that French Intelligence was up in arms about one of their own, an ex-employee but a very useful ex-employee, being murdered just after he had a chat with the CIA? And just what was the chat about?

Douglas had wearily relayed all that he could remember, but no, he didn't know how many mercenaries there were or even if there were mercenaries; no, he knew nothing about American oil prospectors being in the same area. And what about the factions in the local government, demanding the removal of all foreign troops from their soil? Did he know anything about that? No, Douglas had answered, wasn't that a task of one of the other agents on the ground?

The chief didn't answer him. Instead he went on about how important Djibouti was to the United States, how important it was to the French. Didn't the locals understand that without the French, the country would financially fall apart? The only other source of income they had was the large harbor and its single railroad line to Addis Ababa in Ethiopia.

Douglas was sent on his way, instructed not to return to his own apartment—the French were probably watching it—but instead to a safehouse on rue de Londres. Once there he was to type up his report, submit it, then wait for further instructions. Douglas could read between the lines on that. He was in the doghouse. An agent under his care had been gravely injured, an important source was dead and a hotel was half blown to smithereens, killing and injuring a load of journalists and aid workers, not to mention the locals who had jobs there.

So there he was, stuck. The apartment was tiny. A single bedroom, a tiny bathroom where the shower sometimes allowed a dribble of yellow water to seep out of its head, and a living room cum kitchenette, which did admittedly have bottles of water and enough packaged food to last a week. The living room was dominated by a threadbare orange sofa, a computer desk in one corner where an old laptop and a printer were located, and a locked gray metal cabinet that Douglas knew contained various weapons. He hadn't opened it yet, didn't feel the need. He didn't expect to be there long. The transfer orders to Greenland were probably being drawn up at that very moment. He found his coffee, lukewarm, on the scratched table and took a sip. Even cold coffee was better than what some of those unfortunate bastards outside were drinking.

The printer started to rattle. The laptop was permanently on. It had a live VPN link to Lemonnier, and Douglas had no idea how that had been installed with nobody noticing. Internet was virtually unheard of for individual citizens. The printer heads slid back and forth, slowly spewing out a single sheet before going silent. Douglas observed the paper from across the room. There it was, orders to go to Greenland or Antarctica or back to Langley for "training." He didn't want to pick it up, but he did. And what was on it stopped him in his tracks.

It was indeed orders, but not a transfer. He was instructed to report to the harbor in the morning, to be at Wharf 16 when a ship, the MV *Cape Faith*, docked. He was to meet with a male passenger, an American named Mike Blanski, and escort him to Lemonnier, where he would board a military flight. Journalists— if there were any—were to be kept far away from Mr. Blanski. The whole transfer to Lemonnier was to be hush-hush, no fuss, use a nondescript vehicle as transport. Destroy this document. End of message.

Douglas frowned. There was no signature, no other name apart from this Mike Blanski. The message was in plain language, not in a form of code that was normally used, and in any case, any message would come from the station chief, having been passed down the chain of command. Something was highly unusual about this message. Nobody, apart from the CIA, had access to this computer or its printer.

Douglas sat on the desk chair, logged into the network at Lemonnier and navigated to a secure web portal at the CIA. He typed in his password and jumped through several virtual hoops before entering the database to perform a search. He typed in the name of the ship. Not much information was returned: 4,000 ton displacement, tramp freighter, operated in the Middle East and around the Horn of Africa, suspected of being sometimes involved in the black market but nothing proved.

Next he entered the name Mike Blanski. And he waited. And waited a little more. Something was wrong. Usually when something took a long time, it meant that the computer had crashed. Or other departments were being notified of the search.

Information finally appeared on the screen, a few lines, written in red. Douglas frowned as he began to read. The text stated that the information was locked. No access was permitted. The request had been flagged. Cease the inquiry. The hair on his nape and arms stood up. He had seen something like this before. A long time ago, a lifetime ago. It spelled trouble. It spelled deep black ops.

Whoever was arriving the next day specialized in one thing: death and destruction. What had he gotten himself into now?

MACK BOLAN OBSERVED the helicopters circle the tiny speedboats. He could make out five, possibly six, low in the water. A drone high overhead had to have spotted six wakes heading in the direction of the *Cape Faith*. The boats were getting closer. Abu and Grubby joined Bolan on the flying bridge, pressing a little too close. Bolan wondered if they or other members of the crew were in on the plot. But if they were, then why hijack the ship to start with? No, these men were not in with the terrorists, of that Bolan was certain. Or he'd be getting a knife between his ribs, he thought.

"What is it? What's happening?" Abu asked nervously.

"Watch," Bolan replied. "You're about to see some action."

There were flickers of light from the speedboats. Muzzle-flashes, Bolan knew. The two helicopters responded in kind, but the flashes came not from small arms but Gatling guns. Two boats disintegrated. Brief blazes of flame from the gas tanks, and they were gone. There would be no survivors. Both Abu and Grubby gasped. The remaining four boats split away from one another, all keeping their vectors on the *Cape Faith*. The two helicopters swooped again. Except this time the terrorists retaliated harder.

A contrail shot away from one of the boats, heading toward a Seahawk. The helicopter pilot saw the approaching RPG rocket and jerked the helicopter aside but not quite quickly enough. There was an impact and a bright flash. Bolan heard the boom a second later. The helicopter had been struck on the underside. The rocket-propelled grenade had bounced partially off before exploding. The damage was severe enough for the Sikorsky to break off the attack and limp eastward, trailing a black stream of smoke. Bolan focused on the second helicopter. Another RPG shot upward, this one missing. No second chance was given. The helicopter fired its Gatling gun and another boat disappeared.

"Then there were three," Bolan muttered.

The Seahawk rose higher and turned slightly to

bring its nose to face the closest two speedboats. There were more muzzle-flashes from the terrorists, but they were unable to hit anything due to the wild bouncing across the waves. The gunfire and the buzz of the outboard motors could now clearly be heard. There was a whoosh from the Seahawk and two heat-seeking Hellfire missiles shot away, targeting the outboard motors. Both boats exploded within a second of each other.

The last boat was the farthest away from the remaining helicopter, and it was the closest to the *Cape Faith*. The helicopter pursued, but Bolan realized that they would not fire if the speedboat got too close. The terrorists would almost certainly try to board if they didn't break off their attack. And with the latter option a suicidal one, Bolan knew that he would have to join the action. He drew the Beretta from his waistband and faced Abu, pistol pointed skyward.

"Stay on course, and whatever happens do not slow down or stop. Do you understand?"

Both Abu and Grubby nodded, their eyes fixed on the pistol that Bolan wielded. He pushed past them and ran through the bridge. Seconds later he was on deck, brushing past gaping crewmen who had come out to watch the action. The speedboat was close; he could hear it. The helicopter was also close, the rotors thundering, a loudspeaker blaring words about surrender and slowing down. The words were meaningless to terrorists.

Bolan ran to starboard and looked down the hull. The speedboat was alongside, four terrorists: one operating the outboard, two more pointing grappling hooks up at the side, the fourth firing potshots at the hovering helicopter, which was keeping its distance at one hundred yards. Bolan drew back as the grappling guns fired, the hooks flying up, then landing on the deck. He waved the crew back, not wanting them to interfere. Let the terrorists come to him. What they were attempting was incredibly dangerous. There was a good chance they would fall into the sea before they reached the deck. The grappling hooks were pulled back and became stuck and taut on the railing. Bolan heard the men clambering up the side. He looked over to see they were almost level with the deck. He took two steps back and brought his pistol up as the first terrorist popped his head up over the side.

"Surprise," Bolan said as he fired. The terrorist's head snapped back and disappeared from view. The second terrorist appeared a moment later, unable to comprehend why his companion had fallen. The Executioner offered an explanation by firing a second round. The terrorist also dropped back, eliciting angry cries from the speedboat.

Bolan approached the railing, pistol leading the way, and looked down. One body was lying in the boat, the two remaining terrorists looking upward to see what had gone wrong. Bolan took the one armed with the AK-47 first, firing three shots at him. The terrorist shuddered and toppled backward into the churning water. Bolan brought the remaining terrorist into the pistol's sights, even as the guy was getting to his feet, shouting insults.

"He says you are the son of a whore," Grubby said from behind him.

"Does he, indeed?" Bolan fired the pistol twice more, not at the remaining terrorist but at the outboard motor. The engine coughed, as smoke began to pour out of it, then gave up entirely. The speedboat immediately lost its way and was soon drifting in the wake of the *Cape Faith*, its lone survivor waving frantically.

"Why you not kill him?" Grubby inquired.

"Because the Navy can pick him up and question him. Ask where the mother ship is, how many crew on board. Things like that." Bolan ejected his partially spent magazine as he spoke, slapping in a fresh one. Grubby nodded and moved back, no longer wanting to stand next to the American, in case the earlier misunderstanding over money was suddenly remembered.

The helicopter moved in closer, until it was flying no more than ten yards above the deck. Bolan ducked from the heavy rotor wash, the whirlwind whipping up all manner of dust, dirt and rust. The crew cleared the deck, disappearing down open hatchways. Two polyester lines dropped from the helicopter, followed by two men who fast-roped down to the ship. Once on deck they released their harnesses, one man signaling the helicopter. The aircraft banked away, heading east toward the speedboat. The two men, dressed in black combat fatigues, bristling with weaponry, approached Bolan as the racket of the Seahawk decreased. The Executioner tucked the Beretta away under his shirt and extended his hand. He had them pegged as SEALs. One commando shook it as the other scanned the ship for possible threats.

"Are you Blanski?" the man asked.

Bolan nodded.

"Yeah, we were told that you would be on board. I'm Linck. That's…well, that's someone else," he said, indicating the other man. "Is there somewhere we can go?"

"Follow me." Bolan led the way into the superstructure to the galley. Several crewmen were present, animatedly discussing the attacks. They went silent as soon as Bolan and the two heavily armed SEALs entered. Bolan indicated with his head that they should clear the room.

As they scuttled past, Linck asked, "Is one of them the ship's master?"

"Abu," Bolan called after them. "Send Abu here now. Only Abu!" Bolan wasn't sure if any of them spoke English, but the message should be clear enough.

"Thanks for your help, Blanski. I understand that the intel came from you?" Linck believed Bolan to be a spook, probably CIA. The Executioner didn't say anything to contradict that mistake.

"I was never here, Mr. Linck," Bolan said softly. "What's the status of the other chopper?"

"Understood, sir. Last I heard Buzzard One was limping back to the coast. No fatalities. Just a lot of shaken-up guys." He grinned. "Serves them right for getting too close. Buzzard Two has gone to pick up that lone survivor. Unless he decides to play games and take potshots. Then he'll be vaporized. The mother ship has been located and will be intercepted by a French frigate. Scuttlebutt is that Zaid abu Qutaiba has been killed in Yemen. Was that you?"

Bolan said nothing.

"Just asking. The Yemeni army can't shoot for shit."

Linck fell silent as Abu scurried in, looking anxious. The SEAL turned to face him. "Are you the ship's master?"

Abu nodded, eyes wide.

"Sir, on behalf of the United States of America, I wish to thank you for your assistance in the interception of these notorious pirates. I understand that the Secretary of State will be in contact with the ship's owners, praising you and your crew's bravery. Maybe your boss will inform Al-Jazeera of your actions. You may even get to be on TV." Bolan smiled slightly as Abu's face lit up. Whether or not any of Linck's praise was true or not, it had certainly bought Abu's full co-operation.

"You stay for party? We have party on ship for brave American soldiers!" Abu's smile spread from ear to ear.

"No, sir. We will, however, be staying on board until the ship reaches Djibouti. You do not need to arrange quarters. We'll be on deck. You may also hear other helicopters buzzing around during the night. They will be assisting in your protection. We will leave you now, to your party. Mr. Blanski, what will be your role when we enter Djiboutian waters?"

"I'll be first to leave. No fuss. Somebody should be around to get me through customs."

"We can have the bird come back and give you a lift."

Bolan thought for a moment. Hitching a ride on the helicopter would cut down his extraction time. On the other hand he felt a strange commitment to explain something to his bunk mate. And a night's sleep would not be amiss.

"No, I think I'll stay and sneak off in the morning."

"Very good." Linck turned to his companion, muttered a "Let's go check the rest of the ship" and left Bolan with Abu. The captain grinned up at Bolan, rubbing his hands in glee.

"Television! Abu now be famous. Very good for business. Maybe get bigger ship, you think?"

"Yes," Bolan agreed. "I think. Now I'm going to find our other passenger, see how she's doing."

Bolan entered the superstructure and worked his way to their shared cabin. He banged on the door.

"Who is it?" The woman's voice came across force-fully.

"It's me."

"Go away."

"You can open the door now."

"Go. Away."

"Nancy, it's safe. It's all over. The Navy has fought off the pirates. You can come out now."

"I. Said. Go. Away!"

Bolan was exasperated. "Look, I know you don't like guns. I get that. But sometimes they're neces-sary. I'll find somewhere else to sleep, but I need my clothes."

The door suddenly swung open, no sound of it being unlocked. She stood there, glaring up at Bolan.

"You are not really a journalist, are you?"

Bolan was in the process of replacing the gun in the bag. He looked at her. "Yes, I really am a journal-ist. But I used to be Army. Before I got on the ship, I was asked to keep an eye out in case there was trou-ble. They passed me the weapon in Yemen. That's all there is to it."

"So you knew that we would be attacked?"

"Not really, no. There was a possibility. My editors thought I would make a great firsthand story if there was."

"I was watching, you know. I saw the helicopter being shot down. Are they all dead?"

"No, they're all alive. All flying back to base or to their ship. Only the pirates are dead."

"Did you shoot any of them?"

"That's not important."

"But did you? I think it is important. I want to know if I'm sharing a room with a nutcase."

"I'm not a nutcase. You're perfectly safe. So where is this coming from? Why the dislike?"

Clayton sat down slowly on her bunk and stared at her shoes, her anger and energy bleeding away. It took several attempts before she eventually said, "I told you. I told you, but you didn't listen. God, you smell of gun smoke. Just like they did."

"I'm listening now."

A pause. Then, "I told you that some of the kids, they would sometimes bring guns to school. I was in the school yard, during the morning break, talking to a colleague, when they did it. Two eight-year-olds, their whole future in front of them, decided to play cowboys. Not twenty yards away from me, they stood there, like Clint Eastwood, John Wayne, and they shot each other. Both of them dead. A little boy died in my arms. As he lay there, he said that I couldn't tell his daddy that he took the gun, that he was going to put it back. And he died." She stopped with a deep sob, unable to go on. Bolan lowered himself next to her, made to put a comforting arm around her, but she pushed him away. "Go away," she said, her voice breaking. "Just leave me for a while. I'll be all right."

Bolan stood. "I'm sorry," he said. He left her to fight her memories, heading toward the galley, where he could hear cheering as Abu promised the crew that their next ship would be a cruise liner and how they would all be stars on their own television show.

CHAPTER NINE

Northern Djibouti

The stray camel stumbled on the rocky ground, falling to its front knees before struggling back upright. It was lost, dehydrated, exhausted. It was nearly at the end of its life. The animals were famous for their ability to store water on their long desert treks, but this one had depleted its reserves long ago. It staggered forward on its journey to nowhere, searching for water where none was to be found.

The camel was closer to death than it realized.

The sniper lay concealed one hundred yards away, his rifle aimed at the camel's head. The rifle was old, a World War II French-made MAS 36 that had been issued to the French Foreign Legion shortly before their famous battle against Germany's Afrika Korps at Bir Hakeim. Even before the war, it was out of date, the French military having achieved the distinction of introducing the last bolt-action rifle into the military arena when all other armies of the world were working on self-loading rifles. The bolt to reload the weapon was bent at an awkward angle, supposedly so that the soldier would be able to find it easily during combat. The French designers had completely neglected to include a safety catch.

The sniper wasn't interested in design flaws. His

concentration was completely on the staggering camel and how its head fitted into the rifle's sights, since there was no telescopic sight attached. He adjusted his aim to take into account the shimmering heat waves rising from the rocky ground. He let his breath out slightly, then squeezed the trigger. The rifle bucked against his shoulder, and the bullet flew downrange at 823 meters per second. The camel died instantaneously, the top of its skull disintegrating. The beast toppled sideways and was still, a cloud of dust and sand marking its passage. The sniper worked the bolt, forward, up, backward in one quick maneuver as the boom echoed around the barren, rugged hills.

"Good shot, Major."

Two men rose from behind a pile of rocks that had hidden them from the camel. Both were dressed in a light green military uniform, complete with slanting green berets. If anybody had spotted the men, they would have incorrectly identified the two as French military. They would have been wrong. Both were mercenaries; both were American.

The man who had spoken was several inches taller than his companion and a lot bulkier. He lowered the binoculars that he had used to witness the camel's death and replaced them with dark sunglasses. The sniper didn't bother with sunglasses. He kept his eyes firmly on the kill. Soon the creatures that lived in the desert would move in, drawn to the scent of fresh blood. There would be a feast this night, for many nights, as the scavengers fed off the carcass.

"You know, Krulak, I almost feel sorry for that camel. What do you reckon, a stray? Ran away from the camel train? Wild? I wonder what its story was."

Krulak laughed. "Now, now, Major. Don't get all soft on me. Feel sorry for a camel? The thing was already dead on its feet. I can see the headlines now. Heat causes Major Victor Streib to go la-la, starts feeling sorry for camels. Brave, handsome Sergeant Henry 'Hank' Krulak assumes command. So, what did you think of the general's gift?"

Streib examined the old rifle. "Nice sights. Trigger is a little sloppy, but I put that down to age. Nice and thin and basic. Recoil is a little up and to the left. I was aiming for the camel's eye."

The sergeant laughed again. "Are you kidding, sir? You missed its eye by an inch. You blew the camel's freaking head off, sir!"

"Yes, I suppose I did. Speaking of the general, we'd better be getting back to camp. We wouldn't want to keep the man waiting, now, would we?"

"No, sir, we would not. We might hurt his inflated sense of pride again, and that would never do."

Streib chuckled at the reference to the Djiboutian general's vanity and size. He worked the bolt of the rifle several times, ejecting the rounds of ammunition from the rifle's staggered box magazine. It wouldn't do to stumble when carrying the rifle, seeing as there was no safety catch.

The two mercenaries had known each other for years, serving in the US military together in Afghanistan and Iraq. It was Iraq that had brought their joint downfall. While manning a checkpoint outside Baghdad, they had come under fire by militants in a battered old car. The militants hadn't stood a chance. The soldiers had returned fire, destroying the car, killing the occupants.

It was all caught on camera by an embedded CNN reporter—including the cross fire and ricochets, which killed several Iraqi children in a nearby bus.

There was an uproar over the shooting of children; the fact that some of the fatal shots came from the militants' wild firing was completely ignored.

Streib, as checkpoint commander, took the fall for the deaths and resigned his commission after a court of inquiry found him indirectly guilty. Krulak also resigned, believing the commission and the Army bureaucracy to be out of touch. Months after the shooting they were back in America, unemployed, drinking beer and wondering what to do with themselves. Civilian life didn't have anything to offer, and neither did working for one of the big private-security contractors. So they'd gone into business for themselves, starting a small private-security firm that trained bodyguards for celebrities and rich private citizens.

They'd been moderately successful in a very competitive arena known as The Circuit. Soon they had recruited another twenty ex-military men, all disenchanted at the thought of life on Main Street, USA. Countries in Africa had called, wanting their troops to be brought up to scratch. The money and clientele had rolled in. It was then that Trenchard Oil Industries had contacted them.

They always met Robert Trenchard's chauffeur, never Trenchard himself. The great man probably deemed himself too high to fraternize with such pond scum, they theorized. But neither man cared. The chauffeur was himself a former soldier, thus military terminology never presented a problem. The assignment was simple. Go to Djibouti, make contact with one General Dileila Bouh of the Djiboutian army and train a small group of a hundred men in tactics and weapons. The tactics required were that of street fighting, moving door-to-door, clearing rooms, fighting from rooftops. The weapons would be supplied by Bouh, all of French origin. Trenchard Oil Industries would meet all costs through a variety of shell companies. The objectives were never explained, but Streib had learned enough to know that the general and the oil baron were planning a coup.

Streib did not have a problem with that. What happened in some backwater African country was of little consequence. Coups happened all the time. As long as his men were not called on to go into combat, then it didn't matter what happened. As far as he could see, very little would change if there was an uprising. One lifetime dictator would be replaced by another, the United States would still have its base at Lemonnier—the Djiboutian army was nowhere near good enough to take that on—and the French would still be in country. As long as they were paid, there would not be a problem.

Getting into the country unnoticed had been easy. Trenchard Oil Industries had hired an old freighter and the twenty men in Streib's team had simply slipped over the side on a dark night, quietly rowing away in black dinghies as the ship entered Djibouti's harbor. The ship's master and crew had been paid enough to keep their mouths shut about their mysterious passengers. The former soldiers had then made contact with General Bouh, who had them transported to the Obcock region to train his men. That had been three weeks ago.

They approached their vehicle. It, like everything they had been supplied with, was French made. And at least twenty years old. The rifles, the armored personnel carriers and the all-terrain truck. All of it was pristine but out of date. Streib wondered if Bouh had been hiding equipment for years. The 4x4 ACMAT two-and-a-half-ton vehicle looked more like a stretched Land Rover than a truck. Built especially for long-range patrols over difficult terrain, the ACMAT had a range of a thousand miles, carried two hundred-liter water tanks for personnel and could be fitted with either a .50-caliber machine gun or a Milan antitank missile launcher.

Streib stowed the French rifle in a side compartment and climbed into the passenger seat as Krulak clambered behind the steering wheel and started the engine. Within moments they were bouncing across the desert, heading for the training camp and mock village that they had constructed.

"Do you think Bouh will be able to keep his promise, you know, to keep the Foreign Legion at bay?" Krulak had to shout over the roar of the diesel engine while fighting to keep the truck in a straight line over the rough terrain.

"What concerns me more is how he'll do it. I can't see Legionnaires being confined to barracks, even if the US Marine Corps is. And how do you bribe a Legionnaire? The only way to stop a patrol would be to take them out. And once the patrol is missed, the rest of their friends will begin searching for them. And there is no way that Bouh's troops are good enough to take on the 13th Regiment." Streib braced himself as the ACMAT leaped over a sand dune. He pushed himself back from the dashboard. "A little slower, if you don't mind."

"Sorry, Major. And those men who Bouh wants trained? They're not regular Djiboutian soldiers."

"Nope, they're cannon fodder, nothing more. I suspect that they are Eritrean or Ethiopian, promised a better life by Bouh. It's quite a simple plot when you think about it. Trenchard discovers oil and wants to drill it, or mine it, or suck it out with a straw, whatever they do. But they don't want to share with other oil companies. Trenchard learns that Bouh is susceptible to a bribe. They work out a plan of action whereby Bouh gets into power and Trenchard gets exclusive drilling rights in the country, with Trenchard picking up the tab. Our job is to train the cattle so it looks as if there's civil unrest and the country titters on the brink of civil war. Then Bouh's real troops move in, restore order, but not before the cannon fodder have assassinated the main political leaders. A nice bit of treachery for one and all."

"Yep, that's what I figured. Those mooks that Bouh has us training have no idea how to fire those FAMAS rifles. Why he just didn't give us AKs is beyond me."

Krulak downshifted the gears, driving the truck up a steep slope. After several seconds of engine strain they reached the crest and looked down into the valley below. Krulak put the truck into Neutral.

It was more of a large crater, running north to south, two miles long and three miles wide. A massive hole in the desert. Completely hidden from outside view, it made a perfect base of operations. At the top end was a large cluster of sand-colored tents, housing the men. Parked nearby were several more ACMAT trucks, all fitted out as troop carriers. Next to them were a couple of armored personnel carriers. The middle of the valley had an obstacle course and a shooting range. Toward the end was a series of mock buildings and alleys, where the trainees had to practice their street-fighting skills. Trainers made the trainees jog from one end to the other, with threats to shoot dead anyone who fell behind. The empty threat carried weight. So far, none of the trainees had been shot.

"Not exactly state-of-the-art, is it?" Krulak stated.

"No, and with any luck we won't be here much longer. I have just about had enough of Bouh's hospitality, I've had enough of this heat and I definitely have had enough of these flies! Where the fuck do they come from?" He waved the irritating insects away from his face. "Two or three days more, then we'll extract. Trenchard has paid the money, and Bouh's 'soldiers' are almost ready to leave. I see no reason to hang around. Once the coup starts there's no reason for us to be caught up in it."

"The ship will pick us up again? You heard from them?"

"They dock in the morning. They'll pick us up when they depart, same place."

Krulak nodded. He put the ACMAT into gear and drove slowly down the side of the crater and into the camp. He parked next to the two Renault VAB armored personnel carriers. The APCs were the four-wheeled version, capable of carrying ten fully equipped men as well as a driver and commander. The vehicles were fitted with a one-man, roof-mounted turret that contained a single 7.62 mm machine gun. When it came time to leave, Streib intended to borrow them in a dash to the coast where the dinghies were hidden.

Krulak turned off the engine and the two men clambered out of the uncomfortable truck. Another man, dressed in a khaki combat uniform, promptly joined them beside the vehicle. He saluted Major Streib. Old habits die hard, Streib thought as he returned the salute.

"At ease. Report."

"Sir, we have received notification that General Bouh will be joining us within the next few minutes."

Streib closed his eyes. He heard Krulak mutter "shit." The last thing he wanted was to see Bouh again. The man was infuriating with his casual disregard for the men under his command. Bouh was a menace, a vainglorious menace, and was not to be trusted as far as he could be thrown.

"Very well. Have a couple of snipers posted around, just in case the general goes nuts on us."

"Yes, sir!" The former gunnery sergeant saluted again and turned, hurrying off to a nearby tent. Within moments several ex-soldiers were scrambling up the slopes to find hiding positions behind outcrops. Streib retrieved his rifle from the ACMAT. He reloaded the magazine, making sure that it was ready to fire.

"Expecting trouble, Major?" Krulak asked as he checked that his own pistol was clear of blockage and ready to fire. It was another French weapon, a 9 mm MAS 50 based on the trusted Browning design. Krulak didn't particularly like the weapon, but again there was no choice. At least it worked and carried a nine-round magazine.

"Not really, but you never know with that fat asshole. If he does try to pull a fast one, then he'll send in his men and stand well clear. Coming here personally means that he has something to tell us. And, if I am not mistaken, here's the gluttonous bastard now."

Both men turned to watch the approaching APC. Whereas the Renault VAB had a practical look, this combat vehicle was pure intimidation. The South African–built Ratel command vehicle approached the tents, following the same path that the ACMAT had taken. The Ratel was far more heavily armed than its Renault counterpart. A fully armored top turret contained a 12.7 mm machine gun, and two more 7.62 mm machine guns were mounted externally. It was an awesome APC, and Streib did not want to go up against it in combat.

The heavy carrier roared to a stop several yards away. The rear doors opened, ejecting four Djiboutian soldiers, who took up defensive positions. Streib wasn't impressed by the general's show. The soldiers could be easily mowed down, defensive position or not. His snipers would take them out in seconds if the situation warranted it. Both Streib and Krulak tried not to laugh as the driver ran around to the side door of the APC, opening it, then assisting the overweight general in exiting the vehicle.

Streib could just make out the large heavily padded red leather chair that was built inside the APC so that the general could ride in relative comfort. Streib thought it was a designer piece but had no idea who would make such a thing for an armored vehicle. A massive vanity piece for a massive man. Some of Streib's men had taken to calling him General Jabba, something Streib had quickly ended in case one of the trainees caught wind of it and reported it. Not that he really thought they would catch the *Star Wars* reference. Krulak had commented in private that if the general were to die, then the entire population could feed on his carcass for a month.

Streib eyed General Bouh with disgust. There was no way that any man would let himself go in such a manner in any army of the Western world. Or give himself so many medals. The general's chest was covered with ribbons, most of them self-awarded, of that he was sure. He was careful to keep his face neutral as the general approached, accompanied by the driver, a man who worried both Streib and Krulak. Driver, bodyguard and killer rolled into one, the guy was the general's attack dog. He was no taller than Krulak, but thinner, wiry. Light brown in skin color and bald, the man was covered in scars, including a particularly vicious one across his throat. Somebody had gotten close but not close enough. He sensed Krulak's hand hovering near his French pistol.

"At ease, Krulak," he whispered.

Both Streib and Krulak saluted the general, who returned it. A wolfish grin spread across Bouh's face and he slapped Streib on the shoulder.

"So, you have been playing with my little gift." Bouh indicated the rifle that Streib held in his left hand. "How did you like it?"

"Not bad for World War II vintage. Throws a little to the left, but it is still a good rifle. What brings you back to us so soon, General?"

Bouh's smile fell. He took half a step back and Streib tensed, ready to bring the rifle up and shoot the scarred bodyguard before shooting Bouh. But the smile returned.

"The schedule has been moved up. My men must be ready for action in two days."

"Two days?" Streib didn't allow the concern to show on his face. The rendezvous with the freighter wasn't for another four. If Bouh were to betray them, then they would be trapped in the country with nowhere to go. "Why so soon? Your men are not yet ready for extended street operations."

Bouh waved his gold-ringed fingers, dismissing the observation. "It matters not. The attack on the Frenchman did not go as planned. Many were injured, including two American spies. I do not want American spies walking around. Spying."

A few days before, Streib had been informed by the general of the Frenchman's inquiries. Did the general know the Frenchman? No. So he would not object if the Frenchman were to have an accident. But wasn't that drastic? The general had laughed, then boasted about a car bomb being placed and detonated after the Frenchman left his home. Streib had argued against the plan, saying that others could be killed. The general didn't care. It would be blamed on the radicals, on the ineffective government. The Frenchman's death would serve its purpose. But Streib wasn't happy. Car bombs were the work of insurgents like those who had attacked his checkpoint.

"I did warn you against it, General. So, what is the condition of the two CIA agents?"

The Djiboutian general gave Streib a hard, cold look, a warning not to push too hard or criticize too much. "The man who made the bomb explode too late is no longer with us, Major Streib. Xiblinti," Bouh said, pointing at the scarred bodyguard, "opened him up, displaying his insides to the sun. The one spy is in the hospital in Lemonnier. He may yet die. The other is, how do you say, walking wounded? It concerns me that he may begin to spy again. He will have to meet with an accident, as well. I am moving up my schedule so that no other spies can interfere with my plans."

Streib openly grimaced at the way Bouh casually spoke about assassinating a CIA agent. It could create a hornet's nest, with the CIA and other agencies investigating, something that could very easily expose his team. He took a deep breath.

"General, sir, I think that would be a mistake. The CIA will not have enough time to investigate. Killing one of their men will, however, attract a lot of attention. It's something that you may regret in the future."

Bouh stared at Streib in silence. A silence that lasted much too long, during which a cruel smile grew on Xiblinti's face. Streib wondered if the man was thinking about gutting him, as well. After a full ten seconds Bouh spoke, low and menacing, fire burning in his eyes.

"I do not make mistakes, Major Streib. Other men do. Be sure to remember it." Bouh's smile returned to his pendulous face. "Do not concern yourself about the CIA man. We know how to find him. He will meet his fate in the morning. The other man is not a concern. Just be sure to have my men ready to leave in two days. That's all, Major."

Streib and Bouh saluted each other and the general was escorted back to his APC and pulled inside by two of his soldiers. The side door slammed shut as Bouh squeezed himself into the red chair. Xiblinti stood for a moment, staring at Streib and Krulak, before mounting the cab. The engine bellowed to life, its exhaust fumes pouring from the pipes. The APC turned and departed the way it had come. Streib waited until it was out of sight before speaking.

"Sergeant, make the preparations to leave, not for the Africans but for us. We'll be using the Renaults. I have the nasty feeling that Bouh is planning a little accident for us, as well. I don't want to wait around to see if I'm correct or not."

"Yes, sir." Krulak turned and left Streib staring at the dust trail the APC had left in its wake.

CHAPTER TEN

Djibouti City, Djibouti

Bolan didn't get his good night's rest as he had hoped. The bunk was too small, the mattress was tired, thin and mean, and his bunk mate gave him the cold shoulder for the rest of the evening. Eventually he got up, gathered his belongings and joined the two SEALs on deck. Little was said between the men. Bolan couldn't tell them much without revealing his knowledge of Special Forces, and the SEALs did not trust a CIA man enough to tell him anything interesting, other than that the surviving terrorist had surrendered and been picked up and that Buzzard One had made it safely back to shore. Bolan intended to make contact with Stony Man in the morning, learn what had happened to the remaining terrorist and hear if there was anything that he could follow up on. He lay on the hard, rusty deck, using the sports bag as a pillow, the ship's irregular vibrations eventually lulling him to sleep.

The MV *Cape Faith* entered the harbor as dawn was breaking, passing several larger vessels that were anchored in the bay awaiting their turn at the docks. The *Cape Faith* would have no problem berthing at a smaller wharf, and in all likelihood, arrangements would have been made to get her docked as swiftly as possible. The freighter passed within three hundred yards of the frigate USS *Ford*. Bolan could see several of the crew standing on deck, waving. Obviously the good news had been passed on. Now Bolan had to get off before television and news crews showed up wanting a scoop on the previous day's activities.

The harbor was bustling even at that early hour. Several large cargo ships were in the process of being unloaded, bright containers being lifted off by large blue cranes or the ship's own derricks. The *Cape Faith* made a lazy turn to port, slowly moving toward an empty section of the dock. A harbor pilot had come on board an hour before. If he had been surprised at the presence of the two black-clad SEALs, he gave no sign of it. Bolan decided to go below, find something for breakfast. He had seen Djibouti harbor before and wouldn't be in country long enough to see it again.

Within the hour the ship was moored. Bolan had grabbed a quick bite and was wearing his black sunglasses and baseball cap. He said a quick goodbye to Abu, nodded at Grubby, realizing that he didn't even know the man's real name, and went to the gangway, which was being lowered. Of the SEALs, there was no sign. Bolan wondered if they had already slipped off the ship or were sequestered below out of sight. He saw nothing of Nancy Clayton and decided there was no need to bother her anymore. With his sports bag slung over his shoulder, he disembarked the freighter, passing several uniformed Djiboutian men at the bottom of the gangway. They glowered at Bolan but did not demand to see a passport. Bolan assumed they had been given instructions not to interfere with any Americans on board. As soon as he was off, they jogged up the gangway.

Looking for his contact, Bolan dodged around a few forklifts, around a couple of battered trucks that had seen better days. Men were shouting instructions at one another, diesel engines of vehicles throbbed and the containers boomed as a massive crane piled them alongside a towering ship moored behind the *Cape Faith*. Bolan would be unable to hear his name being called above the cacophony of the docks. Two stevedores jogged past Bolan on their way to who knew where. Where was the contact? The soldier jumped to one side as a forklift almost ran him down, its driver's attention taken up by looking in the wrong direction.

It was then that he saw the man staring straight at him from under the shelter of an overhanging warehouse roof.

The guy was Caucasian, his skin now reddish brown from exposure to the African sun. There were several cuts on his face, and his hands were lightly bandaged. The guy was wearing a whitish sweat-stained T-shirt that appeared to be a size too large for him, along with tatty light green trousers. The man's eyes were behind sunglasses, but he raised a hand when he saw Bolan looking at him. Bolan was naturally wary. The stranger appeared nervous, apprehensive as if expecting something to happen at any moment. The way he licked his lips and looked around at his surroundings... Something didn't add up.

Bolan surveyed the docks, watching for suspicious activity. Nothing. Nobody was paying him the slightest bit of attention. There could be a sniper hidden on a roof or up on a derrick, but Bolan didn't sense an ambush. He turned back to the man, who hadn't moved. Bolan approached cautiously until he stood directly in front of the stranger, towering over him by several inches. He said nothing. The man seemed to recognize him, which could mean that Stony Man had passed on a description.

The stranger licked his lips again before asking "Are you, um, are you Blanski?"

Bolan nodded.

"Okay. I'm Peter Douglas. I've been sent to pick you up. Take you to the base. Get you on a flight out of here." Douglas offered a bandaged hand, then withdrew it. "Um, better not. My hands are not in the best of shape. Hurt like hell just driving over here."

"What happened?" Bolan scanned the dock again, looking for anything that resembled trouble.

"Got caught in a bomb blast. I was in a hotel when somebody decided to blow it up. Can't tell you more than that. Shall we go? I expect that you want to leave as soon as possible."

Another lick of the lips. The man seemed in a hurry to get Bolan out of Djibouti as fast as possible. Was he up to something, or was it trauma from the bomb blast? He meant to keep an eye on Douglas until he was out of the country.

"I heard about that. A car bomb. You were one of the two caught in the blast?"

"Uh, yeah. My vehicle is around the other side of the warehouse. They wouldn't let me park any closer. Too afraid I might steal something. Like it matters. A third of what you see around here will go to the black market, if not more. Shall we?" Douglas indicated the direction, and Bolan followed him.

"Yeah, I was there. I got off lightly. Even my eardrums survived. Just cuts and bruises. Go figure. But a friend was killed and my colleague is still in medical in Lemonnier. They may fly him out at the end of the day. Depends. He might make it. He might not. They don't know."

Bolan merely nodded. Words from a stranger would never ease the pain of those who'd survived a terrorist strike. They walked around the massive warehouse, dodging workers and forklifts until they arrived at a rusting, dented red Nissan pickup. Douglas unlocked the passenger door for Bolan, then unlocked his own. Both men climbed in, Douglas gasping at the imprisoned heat inside the vehicle. Bolan sat on the sagging passenger seat, which had rips in various places, the foam pushing its way out. He shoved his sports bag into the foot well and attempted to wind the window down, but the glass became stuck halfway. Douglas wound his down as well, wincing every time he squeezed his hand too hard. The engine, however, started on the first try. Douglas put the pickup into gear and drove away, heading toward the dock exit.

"No air-conditioning. Sorry. And it isn't fancy, either. The engine is okay, though. I get it tuned up over at Lemonnier, let the Marine mechanics have a go with it. Thing is, if you drive anything half-decent around here, then you won't be driving it for very long." Douglas went silent for a few minutes as he navigated his way out of the port facilities. Bolan still wanted to know why Douglas was so edgy. He looked over his shoulder, peering through the grimy rear window, but he couldn't make out anybody following. Several tractor-trailer trucks were pulling in behind them, all of which had the light blue–colored Maersk containers on their loads. Bolan turned his attention back to the road ahead.

"It's busy here," Bolan commented. "Busier than I expected it to be. I was under the impression that everybody was starving."

"Huh! Everybody is starving. Unless you happen to be in government, be in the army, have a good job here at the docks or be a gangster. You can easily tell who is who by their cars. The government guys like to roll around in black Beemers. Guys here at the docks have Korean or Japanese cars like this or Hyundai. The gangsters drive around in shiny silver Mercedes-Benz. They wash the things every day, using enough water to keep a refugee family going for two weeks. Then they drive around, letting the poor know where the power is. If you touch a silver Mercedes-Benz, then you're dead. They lean out of the windows and gun you down. If you're in a fender bender with one, then you're dead, along with anybody else in the car at the time. Everybody on the roads avoids them, pulling over to the sides. Unless it's the military. Their guns are bigger and their trucks better armored. Welcome to life in Djibouti, where life is worth nothing at all. Yeah, it's busy here. Business still goes on. That railroad over there—" he indicated a poorly maintained locomotive and its train "—goes all the way into Ethiopia. Chinese money rebuilt it after EU money vanished into thin air. Nobody bothered to find out where it went."

They stopped at the docks checkpoint. Douglas showed a card to an official along with a ten-dollar bill, which promptly disappeared into a pocket. They were waved through without any further delay.

"Yeah, corruption is everywhere. US dollars are the favorite, the only currency the black marketers accept."

They merged into the early-morning traffic. Green-and-white-colored taxis were joined by pickups similar to their own, one of which had a scraggy-looking camel standing in the back of it. Motorbikes and scooters of unknown makes zipped by, overloaded with passengers. Up ahead somebody tooted, a signal for everybody else to start using their horns, as well. Douglas turned down a litter-filled side street.

"Hunger and poverty are everywhere," he continued. "There are refugee camps outside the city, while here there is very little to buy, except by the black marketers, who overcharge for everything. There's also a lot of unrest. People are fed up with going hungry while the top tier of government and the military need to go on a diet. Something is going to give soon. I can feel it." He braked suddenly as an African woman stepped into the road, looking neither left nor right as she ambled across. Several other cars honked, but she paid no attention. Douglas beeped as well, wincing as he used his hand. She was past, and they continued on their journey. The roads were getting busier. It reminded Bolan a little of New York, except here it was a lot dirtier—piles of trash lay in the gutters, being poked through by urchins looking for something useful—and the cars and minibuses a lot rustier and more faded.

"Morning rush hour," Douglas said apologetically. "We should be out of it soon."

Bolan could feel the man's agitation, almost as if he were on the verge of saying something but choking it back. The soldier looked around again for people too interested in them, but saw nothing. He removed his sunglasses and stared at Douglas, hard, his blue eyes boring into the CIA agent. Something wasn't adding up, and Bolan wanted to know what it was.

"Spit it out."

"What! What? Spit what out?" Douglas gave Bolan a glance, then looked quickly away.

"You've been antsy since you picked me up, no, before you picked me up. So what is it? I don't like surprises." Bolan's ice-cold gaze remained fixed on Douglas, who was sweating, and it wasn't just from the heat. "Well?"

"Well, what?"

"I'm waiting."

Douglas became quiet, weighing his words. He turned past a green-and-white taxi parked on the corner of a road and found a street that was less congested.

"Still waiting."

"Well, I, well, I...I was wondering..."

"Yes?"

"I was wondering on whether you were staying here for a while. If going to the airport was a ruse or something." A motorbike burped past, overtaking them, four passengers on the seat.

"And why would it be a ruse?"

"Well, I thought maybe you had been sent over to look into the bombing, the one that killed the Frenchman and injured Davies. That's all." Douglas kept his eyes firmly on the road ahead, avoiding Bolan's penetrating gaze. The soldier sat back a little in his seat.

"I haven't been sent to do anything. I'm leaving. Next flight out. Unless you've heard something to the contrary. Have there been new instructions?"

"What? No. No new instructions."

Something still wasn't right. Bolan could feel Douglas holding back.

"I'm still waiting."

A pause, then it came out.

"I know who you are."

The assertive voice came out of nowhere, replacing the nervous, subservient one that Douglas had been using. It was as if a wall had been broken down, and Bolan froze for an instant. The uncertain Douglas had been replaced by one an inch taller and more in command, as if a sudden weight had been removed from his chest. Douglas took a deep breath of the warm, unmoving air.

"I know who you are," he said again.

"And who am I?" Bolan growled.

"You have to be some deep-cover CIA shadow man who specializes in wet work, an assassin. Black ops. You really shouldn't have used that Blanski alias. It's what tipped me off. I probably crashed one of the Langley databases last night when researching you. At one point I was kicked out altogether. Told to cease the inquiry. You must have had something to do with the sudden death of Zaid abu Qutaiba."

"People die all the time. Qutaiba's dead. So what? I'm not staying. I'm out of here today."

"That commotion I heard about on the ship. Was that you?"

"Intelligence only. I was a spectator. And does that put your mind put at ease?"

"I don't know. The professional in me wants you gone, but—" The back window suddenly shattered. A bullet hole appeared in the front windshield.

"Jesus!" Douglas yelled.

Bolan ducked and twisted to peer through the broken rear window. Two black Toyota pickups were behind them, rapidly closing the distance. The front vehicle contained two men in the cab, with two more in the bed, each holding on to a roll bar with one hand while trying to level machine pistols with the other. He couldn't see the second pickup clear enough for an analysis but assumed it was similarly crewed. The passenger of the truck was trying to lean out of the side window, gun in hand. One of them had opened fire too early. The element of surprise was gone, and Bolan intended to make them pay for the error.

"Floor it!" he yelled at Douglas.

"Here?" Douglas had his hand on the horn, keeping it there, the warbling making people jump out of the way. He maneuvered into the middle of the road, squeezing past a taxi and an oncoming minibus, which claimed his wing mirror. More horns sounded; people were yelling, screaming. More shots were fired. Bolan could make out the boom of the revolver over the excited zip of the machine pistols. Bullets impacted on the tailgate of the pickup, another hole appeared in the windscreen, and a bullet audibly scraped the roof between Bolan and Douglas.

"Jesus!" Douglas yelled again.

Bolan was rummaging around in the sports bag for his Beretta pistol. He found it and pulled it out. Still hunched over, he checked the pistol and released the safety catch.

"I can't go faster here! I'll kill someone!" Douglas was trying to get past a motorbike, its pillion passenger clutching six-foot lengths of wood and pipes lengthways down the street, its rider refusing to get out of the way, oblivious to the danger behind him.

Douglas heaved the steering wheel to the left, mounting a crumbling sidewalk. People screamed as they ducked into doorways or jumped out of the way. Once past the bike, he drove back onto the road, the biker mouthing obscenities. But only for a moment. The next second he was dead, along with his passenger, as one of the attackers opened fire on them, bullet holes appearing in their chests. The bike fell to the road, the two dead men and their cargo promptly driven over by the Toyota pickups.

"They don't seem to care about bystanders," Bolan shouted. "Go faster!"

"I can't!" Douglas shouted back.

"Then find somewhere with no civilians."

"Where? There are people everywhere!"

"Just do it!"

Douglas took a right-hand turn onto a one-way street. The Nissan's tires protested, as the back end swung out. Douglas fought the wheel, apparently beyond registering the pain in his hands and the blood running down his fingers. The smoking wheels regained their traction, and their car shot up the street, heading against the traffic. Bolan hung on to the side of his seat with his left hand, the Beretta pistol in his right. He watched as the black Toyota pickup tried the same maneuver, the revolver guy hanging out trying to line up a shot. The driver was traveling too fast and didn't have the skill to make the turn. The pickup barreled sideways into the faded yellow wall of a colonial-looking building. There was an awful, inhuman scream and the screech of metal as the driver accelerated, completely oblivious to the fate of his passenger, who was being smeared down the side of the building. A second later the whole body was ripped out of the cab and was gone, the driver noticing nothing, fixated on the target. Bolan could see his grin, even from a couple of dozen meters away. The machine gunners were banging on the cab roof, and the black pickup accelerated.

"They have more power under the hood than we do!" Bolan shouted at Douglas.

"No kidding!" Douglas looked manic, eyes wide, dodging around bicycles, motorbikes, taxis and minibuses. Everybody seemed to be on the road that morning.

"They're coming in! Brace yourself!" Bolan yelled.

There was a lurching thump as the attacking vehicle rammed their less powerful red pickup. One of the gunners let out a war whoop and began clambering over the cab. He paused on the hood, getting his balance, then with a yell, leaped into the bed of the red Nissan pickup, wild eyes bulging out of the head of a man who was sure of a kill. Bolan showed him the error of his ways by pumping three shots into the assailant's chest at point-blank range. The man shuddered, then fell back, the machine pistol falling from his fingers. His corpse landed on the hood of the Toyota pickup, just in front of the driver, who seemed as unconcerned about the second passenger as he had the first. The second machine gunner didn't seem as crazed. He was lining up a shot, hoping to riddle the cab with bullets. Bolan fired several more shots, trying to hold his aim true despite the bouncing and lurching pickup. One round connected, and the gunner spun and disappeared from view.

"Road's clear!" Douglas roared. "We can go faster now!"

"Do it!"

Bolan brushed the broken safety glass of the rear window aside and crawled into the pickup's bed. He rose to his knees and brought the pistol to bear, pointing it at the feverish face of the driver. Only now did the driver seem to realize his predicament, but self-preservation came too slow. Bolan squeezed the trigger three times and the cab of the black pickup filled with blood splatters.

The black pickup instantly lost speed and spun to one side, momentum tipping it onto the driver's side. There was a loud smash of impacting metal and glass as the second Toyota pickup careened into the wreck. The sudden loss of velocity catapulted both men in the pickup bed high into the air. Screaming, they plunged down, their lives ending on contact with the black asphalt. Bolan couldn't see the fate of the two inside the cab of the second black pickup, but he guessed that if they were not wearing seat belts, then they would have exited the vehicle the hard way.

He crawled back into the cab. His face blanched, Douglas was breathing heavily, peering out of the one corner of the windshield that wasn't starred or bearing holes in it. Bolan looked back at the wreckage. People were already coming out of hiding places to crawl over it, looking for something to salvage.

"You know what I said earlier?" he said to Douglas.

"What? What! What about?"

"About leaving. I've changed my mind. I'm suddenly interested in seeing the local culture. Take in some of the sights. Find somewhere to dump the pickup. Then we'll catch one of those green-and-white taxis back to your place. It seems I'm going to pay Djibouti a visit."

CHAPTER ELEVEN

They abandoned the red Nissan pickup on the edge of a rough neighborhood, a no-go area unless you had a death wish or an armored car. Three young toughs spotted them and began to swagger over, apparently thinking that they had scored an easy mark with some lost white men. Bolan slowly exited the pickup and stood at his full height, coldly gazing down on the punks. The death stare brought the three up short, unsure whether to back off and lose face, or to proceed with their mugging and kidnapping. Bolan saved them the trouble. He held out his hand to Douglas, who had also climbed out of the vehicle, brushing fragments of shattered windshield off his clothes. Douglas tossed the car keys to Bolan, who promptly tossed them at the feet of the lead punk. Without a word both men turned and walked away, heading into a slightly safer part of town where a taxi could be found.

They changed taxis twice, hoping to lose any followers, although it wouldn't be too hard to locate two white men in Djibouti, one tall, the other with bandaged hands. They proceeded on foot to the safehouse, having the taxi drop them off two blocks away.

"Does anybody else know about this place?" Bolan asked, as they stood at the end of the litter-filled avenue, surveying the street.

"As a safehouse, no. I was told that my own apartment was under surveillance, so I came here. Who the watchers are, I don't know. Those attached to the bombing would be my guess, wanting to know what Saint-Verran told me before he died. Or it could be the French. I heard that they're quite pissed off."

"Who are those guys?" Bolan indicated several men guarding the building opposite the hopefully still-secure apartment.

"Black marketers. Dangerous if you bother them. Well, probably not for you. I think they're selling food. I watched one guy get murdered here yesterday for a chicken leg."

"Then let's not bother them. We've drawn enough attention to ourselves already."

Bolan thought Douglas muttered a "no kidding" as he led the way down the avenue to the safehouse apartment. The city was divided into blocks, similar to a North American city, making it easier to navigate. Bolan could feel the eyes of the two black-marketer guards on him as he followed Douglas. He watched them surreptitiously out of the corner of his eye, but the guards made no suspicious moves, even looking away when they lost interest.

Douglas unlocked the rotting brown door, which opened onto a flight of stairs, a threadbare, stained tan carpet leading the way up. Bolan put a hand on Douglas, holding him back.

"Hold this. Stay here," he whispered, handing over his sports bag. The Beretta pistol was already out and ready. Douglas nodded. Bolan crept up the stairs, back against the wall, the pistol leading the way. The stairs creaked and groaned under his weight. The soldier entered the tiny apartment, wary for trip wires, and quickly covered the rooms. The place was empty, and there were no booby traps. He called back down to Douglas, who came upstairs and dumped Bolan's bag on the sagging orange sofa.

"You want a drink?" Douglas asked. "Something to eat?"

"What have you got?"

"Ethiopian coffee and plenty of MREs."

Bolan didn't feel like eating Meals Ready to Eat, but knew from long experience that it was always best to eat and drink when the opportunity arose.

"Coffee is good, and an MRE with something resembling beef in it."

"*Resembling* is the right word. Meals Refusing to Exit is a better name for them. I had one of these years ago, couldn't shit for four days after." Douglas set an ancient coffeemaker to work, then dug around the MRE box for something that said *beef* on its label. He prepared it for Bolan, who was sitting on the sofa dismantling the Beretta pistol and spreading its parts across the table.

"So, what now?" Douglas asked.

"For starters, open that for me." Bolan indicated the locked cabinet. Douglas dug a key out of a drawer and unlocked it, revealing two M-16-A-2s and two Beretta 92s. Boxes of ammunition were stacked at the bottom along with some gun-cleaning kits. Bolan reached over for one, and Douglas noted the expression of disappointment etched onto the man's face.

"What, five guns isn't enough for you?"

"It's enough for half an hour. I was hoping for something compact, an Uzi or Ingram, something easy to conceal."

"Sorry to disappoint. This safehouse wasn't meant to be a fortress, so it only comes equipped with standard Marine fare. You'll have to make do. You have enough bullets here to shoot up the neighborhood."

"Like I said, enough for half an hour. What about that laptop, is it secure?"

"Runs straight through Lemonnier," Douglas said, returning to the kitchenette, where the coffeemaker was gurgling.

"In other words everybody from the National Security Agency to the IRS is listening in. I'll need to use it later. After you finish your coffee, I have a task for you."

"Yeah, about that..." Douglas placed a plate and a fork on the coffee table, the MRE spread out so that it resembled an edible meal.

Bolan finished cleaning the Berretta pistol, reloaded it and placed it within arm's reach. He picked up the plate and started on, what was for him, breakfast.

"You said something about staying. I take it that means you intend to kill people," Douglas said.

"I have an aversion to people shooting at me. Makes me want to know why. How many people knew that I was arriving today?"

"A few." Douglas began pouring coffee into two chipped mugs. "How do you like it?"

"Black. I don't think they were after me. They were after you."

"Why me and not you? You were in Yemen yesterday. Don't deny it. Lots of people will be pissed about Qutaiba. Then you had some adventures on that freighter, which will not have gone unnoticed. I'd say that you were the target."

"If an enemy knew I was here, then they would not have sent amateurs. Those guys in the black pick-ups were high on something and too trigger-happy for pros. No, they were after you. So what happened in the hotel? Were you the target?"

Douglas handed Bolan a coffee cup, then sat on the desk chair opposite the sofa. He gazed into his brew for a moment before turning his eyes to Bolan.

"So I only warrant druggies, do I? I don't know whether I should be insulted or not. No, I wasn't the target. A Frenchman by the name of Pierre Saint-Verran was. His car exploded as he was climbing into it."

"Who was he, and what was your relationship with him?"

"I met him in Djibouti years ago, then became reac-quainted with him when I was reposted here. He used to be DGSE but retired over here. He ran his own little agency, offering intelligence analyses for businesses and aid agencies, guides and translators, that sort of thing. He still dabbled in intel, knew a lot of people, fingers in a lot of intelligence pies. What he passed on to me was always reliable. I suspected that he was being used by the Deuxième Bureau to pass on infor-mation unofficially. Anyway, I have been back a little over a year now and met with him on four different occasions. Most of the intel was about undesirables entering the country."

"And this time?"

"The same. People who had entered without us or the government knowing about it."

Bolan finished his MRE and washed the feel of it away with a mouthful of coffee as Douglas narrated what Saint-Verran had told him during those last few minutes.

"So you learned about the mercs and oil prospectors minutes before the blast. Do you feel that they're connected to Saint-Verran's assassination?"

"I don't know. There's no evidence to prove it. As I said, he had his fingers in a lot of pies. But I have to assume it was. I also think that the bomb was meant to go off before he reached us. Why detonate it after he passed the information on? That doesn't make sense. But so far I have no other leads. And my station chief wants answers yesterday."

"You know a lot," Bolan said. "Trenchard Oil, for a start. What do you know about them?"

"Small-time production business based in Dallas. Started by Robert Trenchard over a hundred years ago, is now run by his grandson, Robert Trenchard III. Seems a pretty clean company, always paying taxes on time and has happy employees. Langley looked into them while I was hospitalized. It seems Trenchard did have some people over here. However they failed to turn anything up and are now back stateside. Officially Trenchard has nobody in country at the moment, and I can't say that I blame them. There's no oil here, despite the close proximity to the Gulf States.

"Then there's Saint-Verran himself. As I said, he has an agency here, some small offices. Sometimes worked with a guy called Gullon. I wanted to go over there today, with or without permission from the chief, but instead I had to babysit your ass."

"I heard rumors of a civil war that is supposed to

be coming," Bolan said, changing the subject. "What is that about?"

"Now, that one is strange." Douglas thought for a moment. "I wouldn't even call it a civil war, more of a civil unrest. Nobody seems to be behind it, and I do mean nobody. The last civil war ended after nine years of bloodshed between the government and the FRUD Afars. The Afars are the main tribal group to the north, with the Issars in the south. The Afars are made up of Eritrean and Ethiopian stock. The Issars originate from Somalia. The government was Issar, the Afars felt neglected, so the two sides were at each other's throats. When it was all over, the president of the country was Issar and the prime minister Afar. Together they run a corrupt, secular Muslim state. Both sides seem happy but for the drought and the fact that the politicians are eating when the rest of the people starve. But nobody wants a new war. There was once an attempted coup by the police, but that was crushed by the army as soon as it started."

Bolan drained his cup. "And what about the rioters. Have any of them been picked up?"

"Yeah, and there's not much info there, either. The ones in prison claim they want Djibouti free of America and France, that they only joined the protest when it passed outside their front doors. They saw another Arab Spring, an uprising for television. But who was organizing," Douglas said, shrugging, "nobody knows. It's claimed that an extremist Muslim group may be behind it."

"Political, maybe, but I doubt extremist. Not enough violence. Has anybody claimed responsibility for the bomb?"

"Several groups and nut jobs have claimed responsibility, but not one has been able to give accurate information about it. I don't see how the rioters would be connected to the hotel bombing or the attack on us today.

"So what do we do now?"

"We? You're going to work with me?"

Douglas sighed. "I don't know. I think so. Is it always like this morning with you?"

"No. This morning was easy. Normally the bad guys put in a lot more effort. I've been in Djibouti before, but I don't know my way around. I would appreciate a guide. And I think that you would like some sort of closure on this."

"Okay, I'm in. It's not like my career was going anywhere anyway."

"Good. Now, do you have a slush-fund stash?"

Douglas nodded.

"Then get us some new transport, nothing flashy. We're going to pay Gullon a visit. I'm going to call home, let the folks know that I'm camping out."

"Anything else?"

"Yeah. Got a spare toothbrush?"

ONCE DOUGLAS HAD LEFT, taking with him one of the Beretta pistols, Bolan sat behind the laptop. In the internet browser he typed in a web address that navigated him to a website that sent anonymous emails. He typed a short message—Lovely weather, staying for a few more days. Mike—then sent it to another anonymous email address. The email would be around the world in seconds and arrive in a secure email box that was monitored by Stony Man Farm.

After that he quickly changed his clothes, exchanging the white shirt and blue jeans for the black T-shirt and trousers that he had purchased the day before in Aden. The black boots he also put on. The T-shirt he left hanging out so that he could keep his pistol tucked into his waistband at his back. Uncomfortable and not practical, but he could live with it.

He turned his attention to the weapons in the cabinet. The M-16s were too big to lug around, but were possibly useful. He stripped down both weapons and placed the component parts in his sports bag, using his clothes to wrap the pieces in to prevent rattling. The remaining Beretta joined the rifle parts. He placed several magazines in his rear pockets. His cell phone beeped several times. He retrieved it and found the device was almost out of juice. There had been no adapter sold with the phone. The soldier turned it off and chucked the now-useless device onto the bed. And then he waited, using the old laptop to do a little research on Trenchard Oil Industries on various public websites.

He didn't have to wait long. Douglas returned, thundering up the stairs.

"Okay," he said, "I have a vehicle, nothing fancy."

"Let's go."

After Douglas locked the door, Bolan followed him down the stairs, shouldering the heavy sports bag. Parked outside was a small dark blue four-door Hyundai Excel sedan. Bolan raised an eyebrow at Douglas.

"Hey, it was the best thing I could get at such short notice. Only…it has a 1.3 liter engine."

Bolan's other eyebrow rose.

"It drives okay, although the steering wheel is very thin. Come on, I'll drive. You might need to shoot."

"What's the spoiler on the back for?"

"How should I know? Gives you something to hold on to when you need to push?"

Bolan chucked the sports bag onto the backseat and climbed into the passenger side, finding the springs shot in the seat. Douglas clunked the manual gearshift and drove away. Bolan noted that the two black marketers paid them no more attention than they had earlier in the day. The car's air-conditioning blasted warm air around. Bolan cranked down a window. At least that worked.

The offices of Saint-Verran were on rue Clochet, not far from the Ethiopian Embassy, only five blocks north of their own address. Bolan noted that all the streets were named either after cities or countries. The trees that lined the streets seemed either dead or dying; the whitewash on the colonial-style buildings was faded and peeling. They passed a long line of people at one point, standing and waiting for food to be handed out. Douglas maneuvered the car around slow-moving minibuses, scooters and the ever-present green-and-white taxis, until he pulled over to the side of the road.

"The offices are over there, second floor," Douglas said.

Bolan saw that the police and army had a heavier presence here. A couple of Dacia squad cars were driving down the street, and Bolan spotted two old AMX-10RC 6x6 armored cars. Their 105 mm guns pointed to the sky, but he knew that they could be brought into play quickly.

"There are a lot of embassies around here, and the shiny parliament building is just down the road," Douglas stated. "It would be slightly embarrassing to the government if something were to happen."

Nobody seemed particularly interested in the office building. Bolan wound up his window and climbed out. He carried the sports bag with him and placed it in the trunk, not wanting opportunists to make a quick smash and grab. Douglas joined him at the rear of the car.

"What's the plan?" he asked.

"Go in and ask questions. Be nice to normal people. Shoot any bad guys."

They crossed the road, dodging traffic, ignoring the beeps and hoots. A nameplate was fastened next to the surprisingly clean brown double doors, proclaiming a shipping company could be found on the ground floor. Nothing for upstairs. Bolan pushed open the door and entered the cool foyer. It was tastefully decorated in white, the furniture and various vases all French and seemingly costly. Bolan proceeded to a large staircase that wrapped itself along one wall and led up to a landing that was covered in a rich, patterned carpet.

The first door on the landing was open and Bolan could hear a lot of movement inside. He entered into a large lobby, decorated in the same manner as the rest of the building. It seemed no expense had been spared. In the middle of the room was a large receptionist desk, behind which were two doors, presumably, Bolan thought, one for Saint-Verran, the other for a partner. Sitting at the desk was a beautiful Somali woman who was supervising two other women packing files and folders into boxes. The receptionist looked up as Bolan and Douglas approached, offering the two men a smile that did not reach her sad eyes.

"Bonjour," the woman said. The two women behind her stopped their packing and looked up at the strangers.

"Er, yeah, *bonjour*," Douglas replied. He then started to speak in halting French, mispronouncing several words. Bolan knew enough of the language to know that Douglas was asking to speak to Monsieur Gullon.

"I am sorry," the woman said in perfect English, "but we are no longer in business. I am afraid that it is quite impossible to speak with Mr. Gullon. He is very busy tidying up."

"Yeah, I'm sure he is. We don't want to disturb him, we just want to ask him something," Douglas stated.

"I am sorry, but Mr. Gullon does not want to be disturbed." The smile had fallen from her face. "As I said, we are no longer in business. I can provide you with other addresses of companies that offer similar services. They are very good and come highly recommended."

Bolan stepped forward and spoke in a low voice before Douglas could reply. "Tell Gullon that the last people who saw Saint-Verran alive are standing outside his door. We really would like to discuss what cost Saint-Verran his life and inform Gullon that his might also be in danger."

The receptionist looked blankly at the Executioner for a moment, weighing whether to grant the request or not. Finally she climbed reluctantly out of her chair and went to the closed door on the right. She knocked, opened it and poked her head inside. There were inaudible mutterings, audible cursing. The two packers got back to work, keeping their heads down. The receptionist turned and indicated with a jerk of her head that the two men could enter the office.

Gullon turned out to be a small and extremely thin Frenchman in his late fifties. Boxes were piled on the chairs and desks. All the bookshelves in the room were empty. Gullon had his back to them, displaying what appeared to be a tailor-made Versace suit. He waved irritably behind him, not looking up from the box he was peering into.

"There are no chairs. You will have to stand," Gullon said, speaking in heavily accented English.

"Fine. Then we'll stand. But we won't wait. We aren't patient men, Mr. Gullon. If you don't feel like talking to us, then somebody from the French or American authorities will come to escort you to Lemonnier. Or you can talk to us, here and now," Bolan said.

Gullon turned slowly, glaring at Bolan through his thin spectacles.

"Do not expect me to be intimidated, Mr. CIA spy. I am not to be intimidated." His glare focused on Douglas, softening slightly. "I know you. How are your hands? How is your friend?"

"My hands are fine. They'll recover. My friend is still in intensive care. I don't know how he is at the moment. The doctors believe that he will recover."

"Pah! Doctors! Quacks! What do they know? They lied about my wife's condition, and they will lie to you, as well."

He turned back to Bolan. "I do not know you. What do you want?"

"My name is not important. What we want is information on Saint-Verran's activities."

"Pah! You spies are all the same. Wanting to know secrets, keeping secrets from each other. Always playing little games. Well, Pierre's little games, little secrets, cost him his life. And now we are all paying the price. Without his contacts we have nothing. I have to throw the ladies who work for me onto the streets where they can starve. I will have to return to Lyons to live, where my daughter will not speak to me. All because Pierre could not leave the game alone. And because of his obsession, he got a lot of people killed at the hotel."

"We think that was a miscalculation on the killer's behalf. We think that the bomb should have gone off earlier," Bolan said.

"Think? Think? What difference does it make? People are still dead, I am ruined. It makes no difference when the bomb goes off! It did go off!"

Douglas held up his bandaged hands. "Please, we just want to find who did it, stop them from doing it again. That's all."

"*Oui!* You stop them with more bombs!" Gullon stopped ranting, took a deep breath and looked down at his feet. "This helps no one. Very well. What is it you want?"

"We want to know what Saint-Verran knew about the mercenary camps in the north and about Trenchard Oil."

Gullon shook his head. "I know nothing about the mercenaries. I do know that Trenchard paid their bills on time, for the hire of two guides and other costs. They have not returned to the country."

"What about Saint-Verran's papers, documents, computers?" Douglas asked.

Again Gullon shook his head. "Not long after the bomb, hours maybe, friends of Pierre's, spies from DGSE, came in and took everything. The room is now empty."

"And the guides? What about them? Do you have an address for them? You must have paid them somehow."

"They are two brothers. I do not know their names. All payments were made in cash. They do not have bank accounts. They would not know what to do with them. You cannot buy food with a bank account. Marie!"

The attractive receptionist hurried in. "Give these two men the address of the brothers," Gullon barked. She nodded, returning to her desk.

"I am sorry," Gullon continued, "there is nothing more I know. I handled the financial side. When companies want to open offices, start trading, I handle that. I guide the way. Pierre, he would do the rest, play the spy, learn what the politicians, what the army, were doing."

Marie returned, clutching a small yellow sticky note. She looked at Bolan and Douglas, then decided to hand it to Bolan before returning to pack her things.

"Thank you," Bolan said to Gullon.

"Yes, yes. Now, please, leave. I do not wish to play spy. I have to return to France, penniless. Now, please leave! *Au revoir! Au revoir!*"

CHAPTER TWELVE

"Penniless!" Douglas imitated Gullon's accent as the two men exited the building. "I am penniless! *Sacre bleu!* Who is he trying to kid? Did you see the suit he was wearing? That would cost me six months' salary! I bet you that he has been cooking the books. Running off with the company money. And that chick! I bet that she is in on it, as well."

"Not our problem. I don't look into financial theft. If it makes you feel better, you can always fire an email off to someone you know in the government. This address, where is it?" Bolan handed Douglas the yellow slip of paper. Douglas studied it, thinking before pulling a face.

"South of here. It was once a reasonably good neighborhood, now gone to seed. Nothing but the starving and the gangbangers."

"Then let's go. Maybe the two brothers can tell us something about Trenchard Oil. We can hire these guides ourselves. They no doubt need the money now that Saint-Verran is dead."

The two men crossed the road, dodging the traffic that obeyed no rules. Their Hyundai sedan was still intact; nobody had paid it any interest. They headed south, threading their way between the other cars and trucks that occupied the roads. Mangy, skinny donkeys pulled carts piled high with junk that nobody wanted. The farther south they traveled, the less affable the neighborhoods became. The stares of people changed from disinterested to mildly curious to outrightly hostile at the intrusion of the white men. Houses and buildings that were once painted white were streaked with black-and-brown grime. Whole sections of paintwork and mortar had fallen away, and nobody seemed to care. Bolan stayed on alert throughout the entire journey, which was only a couple of miles but felt like a voyage to another planet. Trash lay everywhere, garbage overflowing into the streets. People waded through the mess, and malnourished children played in it. It was a sorry sight to witness.

They were forced to slow at one junction, as children were sitting in the middle of the street, listless in the scorching heat. Bolan looked around, noting the enmity from nearby adults. Everybody was staring at them. They began to move forward, lurching as if they were zombies. Douglas tooted on the horn, but the children didn't move.

"Ambush!" Bolan said. "Lock your door quickly. Go around the kids." The soldier reached over the back of the seat, making sure the two rear doors were still secure. Douglas cursed and banged on the horn again. Several adults, mainly men, were standing in the way, hands pressed on the hood, teeth bared, glaring at them. More people ran up and began hammering on the windows, screaming, demanding money from the two rich white men. Women pressed their emancipated children against the glass as a sign of poverty; others offered items for sale, even their sisters. Men were yelling, pulling on the door handles, trying to open them. The car was shaking from side to side. It would be only moments before either the windows caved in from the pressure or the Hyundai sedan was turned on its side and the mob pulled them both out of the car.

"Go!" Bolan yelled. "Push your way through them!"

"I can't see shit!" Douglas screamed back. "I'll run over someone!"

"They'll get out of the way! Just go!"

As Douglas accelerated the vehicle, the banging on the roof and sides grew even more frantic. Several men had clambered on top and were jumping up and down. The roof began to crumple.

"Go!" Bolan shouted again.

Douglas made the effort. The car shot forward, both wing mirrors snapping off. The men on the roof tumbled from sight; people jumped out of the way. There was a lurch as the Hyundai sedan drove over something, then they were free of the mob, back onto the main road. Insults and jeers were hurled after them, along with bricks and other rubbish. Bolan looked back to see somebody sitting on the road, clutching at their legs, screaming.

"God! Did I kill someone?" Douglas demanded.

"Someone hurt their legs," Bolan told him.

"Jesus, I thought that was it. That we'd be pulled out and beaten to death. Jesus!" He continued to mutter, his lips moving but making very little sound.

Bolan said nothing. It had been close. Even if he had fired several rounds into the air, nobody would have noticed. They were making far too much noise. And Douglas was right: they would have been beaten to death by starving, anxious people. People who were so desperate that they used their own children as a barricade.

"Much farther?" he asked.

"No. Jesus! No. We are almost there. This is the street. Shit!" The temperature in the Hyundai sedan was unbearable, the air conditioner blowing nothing but warmth, but there was no way Douglas was going to open a window after what had just happened.

"Calm down," Bolan said. "We're still alive."

Douglas gave Bolan a look as if to say how could he take that incident so calmly? Then he focused on the road, making a right turn and slowing.

"I think this is it," he said. There were no street names and no house numbers, so Bolan hoped that he was right.

"Pull over here. Quickly." Bolan pointed to where he wanted the car parked. As soon as they'd stopped, Bolan unlocked his door and was out, surveying the street. Something was wrong.

Douglas switched off the engine and climbed out. He mouthed a "What?" at Bolan. The soldier indicated the end of the street with his head. He then moved around the front of the car to join Douglas. The feel of the street had alerted him to the danger. It looked no different from any other that they had just driven through, except there were no people. Everybody had vanished. Bolan suspected they were in hiding, peering out through holes in the walls and gaps in the curtains, waiting for the danger to go away.

"What?" Douglas whispered.

Bolan reached behind his back and withdrew his Beretta pistol. Douglas saw the pistol and groaned.

"Oh, no. You're not going to start shooting again, are you?"

"Probably. Look down there."

Douglas, still shaking from their encounter with the starving mob, finally realized what had caught Bolan's attention.

Two black Toyota pickups were parked end to end, identical to the ones that had been used in the attack earlier that day.

"Shit, we're too late."

"Get my bag out of the trunk. We may need it."

Douglas automatically crouched but not before noticing the massive dents in the roof of the Hyundai sedan. He cursed. He had bought the car only hours ago, yet already it was a near write-off. He retrieved the heavy bag, not bothering to close the trunk in case it made some noise. Seeing that the fake spoiler had been ripped off, he cursed again. He rejoined Bolan at the side of the car.

"What now?"

"Follow me. Try to act normal."

"What, in a hood that doesn't know what a white man is? Act normal, he says."

Bolan was already walking nonchalantly toward the first of the two pickups, holding his Beretta pistol by his side, releasing the safety with a flick of his thumb. Douglas saw that and decided that he should do the same, falling in behind his comrade.

There was one man in each pickup cab, both behind the wheel, both keeping watch. A very loose watch. They were too relaxed, felt too safe in their own territory. Kings of the heap.

The Executioner moved slowly toward the first

pickup, knowing the driver only had to look in his rearview mirror to spot Death approaching. The gunmen were too lazy to even notice that the street had cleared of people. Or maybe they were just used to that reaction when they showed up. Bolan was glad there were no civilians present. A gunfight in a busy street was something that he always tried to avoid. Now he could eliminate the two drivers without anybody else getting injured.

It never got that far.

A small alley separated the target building and the house next to it. There were muffled shouts, fired shots, a scream and the tinny roar of an engine.

A white Vespa moped shot out of the alley, a terrified African astride it. The Djiboutian twisted the handlebars over to the left, almost losing control. He skidded several feet before regaining his balance. Eyes wide, the man pulled the throttle back and sped down the street, burning rubber, moving as fast as the moped allowed him to.

The Toyota drivers came alive, twisting the ignition keys and starting the heavy engines. Bolan closed the distance to the first driver, poked the pistol in through the open window and shot the man through the head, the bullet exiting through the passenger's open window, taking a good portion of the man's skull with it. The guy died without even knowing he was in trouble. The engine of the pickup stalled. A group of shouting gunmen poured out of the house, four killers who jumped into the open bed of the first Toyota. The driver gunned the engine and pulled a U-turn, giving chase to the fleeing moped before the last man was safely in.

All of them were too excited to even notice Bolan, Douglas or their dead companion.

A second group of gunmen ran out of the alley and did notice Bolan, but it was too late for them. They plunged straight into Bolan's gun sights. The Executioner had swung his right arm around, extending it, the Beretta pistol pointing at a gunman's forehead. The killer opened his mouth to shout, but a Parabellum round beat him to it, coring through his head and splattering his friends with blood and brain matter. The remaining three men staggered to a halt, trying to bring their diverse collection of sidearms to bear. Shocked by the appearance of an adversary and the sudden death of their cohort, their reactions were fatally delayed.

Bolan already had target acquisition on the second man and fired the Beretta pistol repeatedly. Two more gunners collapsed to the dusty sidewalk, all life already gone. The fourth man tried his best, managed to fire a single shot from a scratched revolver before succumbing to Bolan's superior marksmanship. He fell on top of his buddies, twitching. He was dead before the sound of the shot had finished echoing around the street.

Bolan swung his head around, looking for Douglas. The CIA agent was standing where the soldier had last seen him, frozen, a look of stunned disbelief on his face. His own Beretta pistol was still pointing at the ground; he hadn't even had the time to raise it to defend himself. Bolan cursed, worrying that Douglas would become a liability in a serious gunfight. He yanked the door of the Toyota pickup open, pulling the corpse of the driver out. Douglas just stood there.

"Hey!" Bolan used his best drill instructor's voice. "Snap out of it. Get over here, now! Bag in the back! Move it!"

Douglas looked blank for a second, then joined Bolan, a dumbfounded expression on his face. He heaved the sports bag into the pickup bed. "You shot them all. Just like that. It was so fast."

"I'll give you an autograph later. Right now you need to drive. We need to get to that scooter guy before the other team does. Get in and drive."

"Shouldn't we check the house first?"

"The chances are the guy on the scooter is one of the guides. He'll be dead if we don't move it. Drive." Bolan climbed into the back of the pickup.

"What about our car?" Douglas asked as he scrambled into the cab.

"This one has more horses. And has side mirrors. And the seat is more comfortable. Why are we still here?"

"I'm sitting in blood! Some of that guy's head is stuck to the windshield! That's so gross!" Douglas twisted the key, started the powerful engine and spun the power steering over. The pickup turned smoothly and shot off down the street in pursuit, with the soldier tightly holding on to the roll bar in the back.

It wasn't hard to follow the first Toyota pickup. It was already several blocks ahead, having left a trail of destruction behind it as the gunmen tried to shoot the moped rider. The road conditions made accurate shooting impossible. Bullets flew in all directions, striking other vehicles, buildings and fleeing civilians. The moped zipped in and out of the traffic; the pickup plunged through it. Bolan could just make out the scooter as it dodged around a taxi. The pickup approached the vehicle, the killers firing into it. The taxi, its driver either dead or dying, spun right and crashed nose first into a building. Cars skidded to a stop, and others smashed into them. The killers poured murderous fire into those as well, not caring who died. Bolan hammered on the roof of the cab.

"Go faster! We need to catch them!" he yelled.

"I'm trying!" Douglas yelled back. He jerked the vehicle over to one side, throwing the soldier off-balance. A pedestrian lay in the road, broken and twisted, where he had been flung over the roof of the gunmen's pickup. Bolan growled in anger as he hung on tightly. Douglas spun the wheel back just as a donkey and cart began to cross the road, its owner oblivious to the sounds of chaos around him. There was no avoiding them. Their pickup clipped the rear of the cart, smashing it, knocking the wreckage over onto its side, nearly taking the braying donkey with it. The owner screamed obscenities at them as Douglas regained control of the pickup.

Bolan was aware of pedestrians on the side of the road, wailing, crying and shaking fists. There was nothing he could do for them other than halt the killers in their tracks. Douglas kept his hand on the horn, wanting people to get off the road. They shrieked past the shot-up taxi, its driver unmoving. Bolan wanted the killers more than ever.

They were gaining, no more than half a block behind. The moped turned hard right, its rider almost pulled off from the forces exerted on him, the side of the bike scraping the ground in a shower of sparks. He regained control a second before disaster struck, the edge of a building only inches away, the moped's rear tire gaining traction and burning rubber. The enemy's vehicle followed, skidding around the corner too fast. The squeal was audible to Bolan, as was the terrified scream of one of the gunmen as the ruffian lost his grip on the roll bar, momentum taking over and flinging him at sixty miles per hour against the building that the moped had narrowly missed. The scream was abruptly cut off on impact, the broken corpse bouncing into the street.

And then there were four, Bolan thought. He braced himself against the pickup's side, hunkering down as Douglas imitated the maneuver of spinning the vehicle. Their pickup slid around the bend sideways in a cloud of burning rubber, crushing the corpse lying in the road, slamming into the side of the building. Metal crumpled, the wing mirror disintegrated and there was a terrible, sharp scraping noise as Douglas changed gear and pulled away, scouring the black paint from the left side of the pickup, driving half on, half off the sidewalk.

"Didn't Langley teach you how to drive?" Bolan asked.

"Shut up! I'm trying to drive," Douglas yelled.

Bolan regained his feet, clutching the roll bar tightly. They were gaining on the hunters and their human prey. He made out the moped making a left turn at the end of the road. The gunmen continued to take potshots, but it seemed they were beginning to conserve their ammunition. Either that or they were shaken by the death of their comrade in arms and were too busy holding on to do much shooting. They still were not aware that they in turn were being pursued.

But somebody else was. The wail of a police siren sounded behind them. Bolan glanced back to see a Dacia police sedan join the pursuit, its lights flashing.

Douglas must have seen the lights in his rearview mirror. "Shit! Can you do something about them?" he shouted as he drove back into the middle of the road, dodging a stalled minibus.

"I don't shoot cops," Bolan shouted back. "Try to lose them, but don't lose the Vespa."

"Try to lose them, he says!" Douglas spun the wheel to the right to avoid a foolish man stepping into the street to see what all the commotion was. The man jumped out of the way as the Toyota pickup banged into a parked taxi. The right wing mirror was now ripped away, and the steering wheel spun through Douglas's hands. He quickly regained control of the slaloming vehicle, apparently realizing the police car was gaining, that he was losing ground to the moped. Bolan felt him floor the accelerator. The pickup's tires spun, and the vehicle shot forward, the pursuing police car close behind.

"Left! Left here!" Bolan thumped hard on the roof. Douglas complied, pulling the steering wheel hard over. They fishtailed, Bolan fighting to hold on. The enemy's pickup was up ahead, accelerating away. They hadn't caught the moped rider yet. It was the police car's turn to crash into the side of a building as the underpowered Romanian-French car failed to take the corner at high speed. Bolan saw the right side of the car crumple, its headlight exploding in a shower of glass. Their engine stalled, delaying them, but he knew that they were not out of the game. He could see the officer in the passenger seat speaking into a radio. More police would be on the way, maybe even the army. They had to catch the moped driver and quickly disappear.

They came upon another right turn, then they shot out onto a main road. Horns blared as angry drivers braked to a sudden halt. The moped rider was on the left side of the road, driving into the traffic, causing minibuses and a large truck to swerve out of the way. The scooter mounted the sidewalk, where two screaming children were yanked back by a protective mother. The gunmen's vehicle stayed to the right, swerving around traffic. They drew level with the buzzing moped, deciding to resume shooting at it. Bullets flew in all directions, striking cars, walls and shattering grimy windows. Douglas narrowly avoided the swerving truck, its protesting horn drowning out almost all noise.

Above the din Bolan could just make out the siren of the police car as the damaged Dacia barreled out of the side street looking to take up the pursuit again. The police failed spectacularly as they crashed head-on into the truck. The Dacia lost the argument, spinning like a top as the fender and hood crumpled, one front wheel flying off. Bolan could only hope that the police officers were not too badly injured. His attention returned to the pursuit as he heard Douglas yell, "Shit!"

Up ahead a large passenger train was crossing over the road junction on its long journey down to Addis Ababa, Ethiopia, the blue diesel locomotive belching fumes. It was directly in front of them, blocking the road. Cars came to a stop, waiting for the train to move away. The gunmen had seen the obstacle, as well, the driver making the decision to follow behind the moped. The gunmen's vehicle shot across the road unmindful of oncoming traffic, mounting the curb just behind the terrified moped rider. The gunmen were laughing at him, wanting to see him run over instead of shot, banging on the roof, encouraging the driver to speed up. Maybe the moped would crash into the side of the train.

"Follow them!" Bolan ordered. The sidewalk would be clear; people would be avoiding the first two vehicles. Douglas kept his hand on the horn, drove across the road and up onto the sidewalk. They drove over the remains of somebody's wooden chair, gaining on the first Toyota pickup, which had now slowed, its crew wanting to torment the moped rider before they killed him.

The scooter turned left, onto another main road, which paralleled the railway. The two Toyota pickups followed, white smoke from their tires creating a screen that blocked the view from other drivers. There were several crashes as cars came to a sudden halt, the sound of crunching metal and exploding glass adding to the cacophony. The noise dramatically increased as, a mile down the road, a Boeing 747 took off, flying barely a hundred feet above the highway. Bolan could easily read the Air France Cargo slogan on the aircraft's side.

"We're approaching Ambouli Airport! And Camp Lemonnier!" Douglas yelled.

Would that help or hinder them? Bolan wondered. There would be US soldiers stationed at the gates to Lemonnier, but they wouldn't interfere in anything off base. However, at the airport, there would be more police, who would. He had no time to think about it.

The moped shot across the road, getting closer to the train until it was parallel to the last carriage. The rider kept glancing at the carriage, as if trying to make a decision. Between the train tracks and the road was a brown strip of earth and sand about ten feet wide. The gunmen's pickup joined the scooter on the strip, creating a dust storm that all but obscured Bolan's view.

Narrowing his eyes and raising a hand to protect them as Douglas joined chase over the dirt, the soldier could just make out the moped driver reaching toward the passenger car. A brown arm shot out from inside, someone stretching out to grip the rider's hand. In one quick movement, the rider placed both feet on the saddle of the Vespa moped, then leaped onto the train. The moped fell to the ground, spinning, and the lead Toyota pickup crashed into it, knocking it away, back onto the road.

The killers in the pickup bed were agitated, banging on the roof, urging the driver to increase speed. Bolan realized what they were intending to do and banged on the roof himself.

"Catch up with them! They're trying to board the train!"

"I'm trying!" Douglas yelled back.

The buildings of the city were now behind them, the massive complex of buildings that belonged to the airport and the military to the left.

"I've got to get on board that train before the gunmen kill everybody! We need to catch up quickly!"

"Tell me something I don't know!"

"The police won't be far behind!"

Their pickup left the ground for a second as they hit a rut. Bolan gripped the bar hard, eyes squinting against the dust cloud. Small stones peppered the 4x4, some cutting the Executioner's face. He ignored the stinging wounds. Up ahead he could make out the lead pickup coming level with the passenger car. One man was poised to jump, the driver holding the pickup as steady as possible. After several seconds, the gunman leaped and disappeared inside.

The rear door had to be open, Bolan realized. The second man, encouraged by the success of his comrade, also made the jump. The final man was more hesitant, and Bolan knew this was his opportunity to act. A plan of action formulated in his mind. He banged on the roof of the Toyota pickup again.

"Hit their rear fender!"

"What!"

"Hit their rear fender! Hold it for a couple of seconds!"

"Why?"

"Just do it!"

They were not far behind the enemy's vehicle. A few more beats and Bolan could implement his idea. He could clearly see the side of the train carriage now. It had originally been painted dark green and cream, but the colors had been bleached away by the hard African sun. The paint was peeling from the old wooden sides, revealing the SNCF letters, which told Bolan the carriage had originated in France and been imported. He could also see that not only was the door gaping but also the windows were either fully open or completely removed. There would be no air-conditioning on the passenger cars, so the Djiboutians had created their own.

Frightened faces peered out of the windows, ner-

vously watching the pursuing vehicles. Douglas
brought their pickup right up behind the enemy's transport. He was finding it difficult to keep the bouncing
pickup under control; the strip was getting rockier and
bumpier. There was another huge roar as a massive,
unidentifiable aircraft took off from the airport, flying
right above them. As he was preparing to ram the lead
Toyota, Douglas saw the remaining gunman look up,
then look directly at him. A nervous grin covered the
man's face; he seemed to be looking for encouragement from his fellow anarchists. What he found was
encouragement from Death.

Even as he struck the leading Toyota pickup, the
CIA agent heard Bolan on the move. There was a
thump on the roof the cab. The next moment he saw
Bolan catapult himself onto the bed of the vehicle.
The gunman opened his mouth to scream or to shout
a warning, but he never made it that far. Bolan's right
fist lashed out in a powerful undercut. The gunman's
head snapped back and his body lifted over the roof
of the vehicle. He landed on the hood of the pickup,
and Douglas lost sight of him. The driver was looking
into his mirror in disbelief at the apparition that had
appeared from nowhere.

Bolan whipped out his Beretta pistol, giving the
driver a double tap of Parabellum rounds. The soldier
thrust the handgun into the waistband at the small of
his back, twisted and leaped away from the now out-
of-control vehicle, reaching for the doorway of the
passenger car. Douglas briefly saw his partner hanging on by one hand but had no time to observe more.
He slammed on the brakes as the driverless Toyota
pickup spun onto its side, then flipped over onto its

roof. A body flew from the tumbling pickup, presumably that of the gunman Bolan had punched. Douglas's own car fishtailed and spun 180 degrees before finally coming to a stop.

He sat there for several seconds, his hands tightly squeezing the steering wheel. After closing his eyes and taking a couple of deep breaths, he looked into the rearview mirror. The train had drawn well ahead; he could no longer see Blanski on its side. He lowered his gaze to the city. The cherry lights of several police cruisers were visible in the distance, but they would not catch up for a least a minute. He had to leave.

The CIA agent took a final deep breath to steady his nerves, then put the pickup into gear. With any luck he would be able to keep pace with the train, even though the railroad tracks would lead into the desert. And hopefully he would be able to help Mike Blanski get off the train.

That was if the man was still alive.

CHAPTER THIRTEEN

The Executioner was very much alive.

Bolan twisted after shooting the driver, quickly flicking on the safety and pushing the pistol into his waistband. The speeding train was a mere five feet away.

Terrified faces stared back at him from the carriages, but Bolan ignored them. He focused for a split second on the handrail next to the open door. Bolan placed his foot on the rim of the Toyota's bed and hurled himself forward. As he pushed away, the Toyota spun out of control, causing him to lose his balance. He grabbed desperately at the warm, corroded metal, feeling his hands slip. His body slammed into the wooden paneling, knocking the breath from his lungs. He kept his feet up, not wanting his boots to be ripped away as they dragged along the ground. He managed to get them onto the foot plate, levering himself up and into the swaying, rattling passenger car. He crouched, drawing the Beretta pistol. No gunshots greeted his arrival, no cries of anger or aggression. The soldier took a few deep breaths, then examined his surroundings.

He stood slowly, rocking side to side with the train's motion. The interior was wood—wooden floor, wooden seats, wooden paneling—every surface was scuffed, scratched and riddled with tiny woodworm holes. Names and other graffiti had been scratched or scribbled onto the interior walls.

The car was also overcrowded.

The passengers, terrified and pitiful, cowered from Bolan, pressing themselves against the seats and walls. Their eyes were wide with terror as they huddled against one another, tightly clutching howling children. Many of the adults were moaning with dread, having witnessed the execution of the pickup driver and the death-defying jump onto the train. They truly believed the white man was there to kill them all. The atmosphere was thick with dust, heat and fear. Bolan raised his left hand hoping to placate them. He kept the Beretta pistol hidden behind his right leg.

He spoke in French, hoping that the people would understand him. "I am not going to harm you. I want to help the man who is being chased."

The only reaction was more moaning and wailing, making Bolan wonder if they spoke a dialect and didn't understand what he'd said. He didn't have time to explain again. He firmly but gently pushed his way to the front of the car, only then bringing the pistol to shoulder height, an action that produced more bawling from the passengers. Bolan ignored them and turned the handle of the connecting door.

The dividing corridor separated two cars, its rubber walls bending and shuddering with the movement of the train. In many places the rubber had perished, sunlight shining straight through. Bolan stepped into the passageway, closing one door and slowly opening the next. He glanced through the gap, hoping to spot one of the killers.

The passengers were all pressed against the right

side of the car, which meant that something was happening on the left, just out of view. Throwing the door open, Bolan stepped into the car, Beretta pistol at the ready. He was greeted by the sight of a pair of legs standing on the frame of an open window. As he watched, both legs lifted away as the unknown person transferred his weight to his arms.

The fight was going to be on the roof.

The Executioner didn't waste time wondering whose legs were disappearing from view. He stepped over to the window, grabbed hold of one of the man's ankles with his left hand and pulled downward as hard as he could.

There was a horrified yelp and a man appeared, hanging by his outstretched arms. His eyes were wide with shock as he looked at his assailant. Bolan recognized him as one of the thugs who had jumped from the pickup. The Beretta pistol barked once from point-blank range, a bright red hole instantly appearing in the thug's T-shirt directly over his heart. The thug dropped away without making another sound. Bolan doubted that the killer was alive when he hit the ground. Only one opponent remained. At the sound of the gunshot, the passengers began howling in earnest. Bolan ignored them. He climbed onto the nearest seat, reaching out of the window frame, searching for a handhold. There wasn't one to be found. With the knowledge that the gunman had been holding on to something, he stretched farther and found a fingertip-wide ledge where the body of the car met the roof.

With the Beretta pistol once again stuffed into his waistband, the soldier leaned out even farther, turning his head away from the direction of the locomotive to protect his eyes from the blast of warm air and sand that had been stirred up. He grabbed the ledge with his other hand, placed both feet on the window frame and, with a powerful kick, heaved himself upward. Bolan was a lot taller than the gunman and easily found another purchase. He pulled, dragging his body until he was lying flat on his back, feet facing the rear of the train. The car shook and rolled, diesel fumes from the locomotive washed over him and the sun burned down, broiling him on the torn black felt-clad roof.

Bolan rolled carefully onto his stomach. He estimated the train was now traveling at about fifty miles per hour. Djibouti City was far behind. He looked down the length of the train. The moped rider was standing on the locomotive itself, taking steps backward, his arms outstretched to balance himself. His assailant was slowly approaching, a machete in his hand.

There was nowhere for the moped rider to go.

Bolan pushed himself to his feet. There was no point in drawing his pistol. The rocking of the train made accuracy impossible, and there was a good chance that he would kill the man he had come to rescue. He had to get closer.

The soldier began to run down the length of the car as fast as he dared. He jumped onto the next car, then the next, all the while fighting to keep his balance, all too aware that the machete-wielding killer was drawing closer to his prey. He needed to distract the enemy and quickly. He leaped onto the blue roof of the locomotive. It was still thirty feet to the thug, who was raising his machete, ready for a downward chop.

"Get down!" Bolan yelled. "Lie on the roof! Get down now!"

The moped rider's eyes widened as he took in the impossible sight of the black-clad white man on the roof of the train. It took a second for the meaning of the words to register, then he threw himself flat, literally at the feet of his would be killer. Machete man spun, equally amazed to see somebody other than his fellow killer. The amazement passed quickly as he saw that the white man was empty-handed. A large grin split his pockmarked face. An easy kill. He made his move toward the stupid white man.

Bolan let the thug come close, giving the illusion that he wanted some sort of fistfight. As his adversary got to within ten feet, Bolan drew the Beretta pistol, pointed it at the machete man's chest and fired two shots. The thug's look changed from aggression to shock in a split second. He staggered backward, swaying before gravity took over, the machete falling from nerveless fingers. It dropped over the side of the locomotive, quickly followed by the corpse.

"'Never bring a knife to a gunfight,'" Bolan muttered, quoting a line from a movie he'd once seen. He turned his attention to the moped rider. The man had raised his head and observed the death of the assassin. He stared at Bolan, terror etched into his face. The soldier stuck the Beretta into his waistband, then held out his hand.

"I'm not going to hurt you," he called out above the roar of the engine. "I just want to know about the Americans you took to the north. That's all."

The rider didn't react. He continued to stare unblinkingly at the Executioner. Bolan shook his head in frustration.

"Look, if I wanted to hurt you, I would have done

it already. All I want is to talk to you. Nothing more."
Bolan slowly approached. They had to get off the train,
otherwise they would end up somewhere in Ethiopia.

"Why they kill Abdullah?" the man called out for
the first time. "Why they kill my brother?"

"I don't know, but the only way to find out is to get
off this train. Will you help me?"

The man nodded and slowly rose. He was a foot
shorter than Bolan, dressed in a tattered white soccer
shirt and tan trousers. Close up, Bolan could see that
he was in his midthirties.

"We need to get off this train," Bolan shouted.

"Who are you?" the man shouted back.

"Later. Come on." Bolan lurched to the front of the
locomotive. Once there he lay down on its roof, wincing from the heat of the metal.

The soldier eased himself forward over the lip,
holding on to the metal molding. Below, the tracks
rushed under the locomotive at a terrifying speed.
Bolan did his best to ignore the velocity. He spotted
the engine driver, sitting at the controls behind the
dusty, bug-splattered windshield. He rapped on the
glass. The engineer's head shot up, his mouth falling
open. Bolan briefly eased one hand from its purchase.
He waved at the controls, trying to indicate that the
engine should slow. The Executioner then powered his
way back up, helped onto the roof by the moped man.

"Hold on to something! The train is about to stop!"

The moped rider threw himself to the roof, clutching at a protruding metal pipe. There was a shudder
as the train began to decelerate, a squeal as the brakes
were applied. The loss of forward velocity wasn't as
bad as Bolan had imagined. Neither he nor the other

man was in danger of being flung off the roof. Within a minute the train came to a shuddering halt.

"Come on. This is our station," Bolan said, climbing to his feet. He noticed the look of distrust in the other man's eyes. "I told you, if I wanted to hurt you, I already would have. I just need information. Nothing more."

They climbed down a service ladder that was attached to the side of the locomotive. The driver was leaning out of his cab, saying something that Bolan couldn't make out. The soldier smiled and waved. The passengers were equally unfriendly, now that the immediate danger had passed, shouting and gesturing from the safety of the passenger cars. With a roar and a cloud of black smoke, the train slowly accelerated away, resuming its long journey to Addis Ababa. Soon it was lost to sight, leaving Bolan and the moped rider standing in the broiling desert.

"It is a long walk to city," the man said. "Can you make it?"

"Probably," Bolan replied, "but I'm hoping a friend will pick us up before long. If he hasn't gotten himself into too much trouble. Tell me something. Are you the guide who worked for a Frenchman named Saint-Verran?"

"Yes, I sometime work for him. He dead, too. Bad men kill him. They kill my brother. They kill everyone." The guide sounded bitter and angry. Bolan didn't blame him.

"What is your name?"

"Abdourahman. I cannot go back to house now. Police there. Don't trust police. Maybe uncle's house. Don't know. What I call you?"

"Blanski." They walked past the corpse of the man Bolan had shot. Abdourahman spit on the body.

"He not even from Djibouti. Maybe from Eritrea or Somalia," Abdourahman said vehemently. They quickly searched the body for some form of identification but found nothing. The machete was nowhere to be seen. Abandoning the body to the vultures flying overhead, they resumed their trek toward the city. Bolan pondered what Abdourahman had just said.

"You said that man was from a different country. I thought the rebels were local militia."

"Militia? What that? Don't talk now. Too hot. Save strength. Talk later."

They had been walking for ten minutes alongside the railroad tracks when they spotted a distant dust plume that seemed to be heading toward them. Bolan shielded his eyes against the shimmering heat, hoping to make out some details. Abdourahman had seen it, as well.

"I hope this is friend. If police, then is big problem," he said.

Bolan silently agreed. There was nowhere to hide in the desert, so the pair could only wait to see who it was.

A few minutes later a dust-covered and battered black Toyota pickup rolled into view.

"It's a friend," Bolan said.

Peter Douglas leaned out the window as he brought the pickup to a halt. He grinned through the dirt and sweat that covered his face.

"What kept you?" Bolan asked.

"Had to lose some friendly cops that I picked up," Douglas replied. "I suddenly remembered that Langley taught us evasive-driving techniques. I took their underpowered Dacias on a trip across the desert and left them there. Is this him?"

"Yeah."

"Shit. Let's hope that he was worth it."

THEY TOOK THE long route back to the city, following a track that Abdourahman knew of, one he assured the Americans that the police knew nothing of. It was used only by herders and smugglers. They would leave the track at the suburb of Balbala, a former shantytown to the west of Djibouti City that had been integrated into the city proper sometime in the late seventies. Abdourahman had an uncle there who could help them. The Toyota pickup would be on everybody's look-out list following the trail of devastation and carnage that had been left behind. Douglas had mildly protested. The pickup had working air-conditioning.

They passed Balbala's large livestock market, once a thriving place full of goats and camels, now run-down and neglected, the camels and goats having become food long ago. The shantytown loomed before them.

"Oh, boy," Douglas muttered, "this place does not look promising. I have never been in this area. White folks are generally unwelcome. The town is a complete maze inside. Supposed to be schools and a good hospital in there, but I have no idea where."

"Do not worry," said Abdourahman, who was sitting in between the two Americans. "My uncle has that building over there, right on edge of N1 Road."

The N1 was a major artery that cut across southern Djibouti, linking all the major towns and villages with the city. Large trucks and buses traversed the highway heading into or out of the city. Douglas stopped at the edge of the road, waiting to drive straight across. The moment there was a break in the traffic, he accelerated; a bus thirty yards away tooted in protest. Abdourahman pointed to a yard behind the dirty yellow building that was proudly displaying two signs, one the famous Coca-Cola logo, the other a local boutique.

"Oh, Coca-Cola." Douglas sighed. "How I'd love one of those. A cold one."

"I ask my uncle," Abdourahman said as the Toyota pickup came to a halt, "I see what he has. But I first tell him about my brother."

"We need a car," Bolan said, "and a place to hide this one."

"Yes, yes," Abdourahman agreed. Bolan climbed out, allowing Abdourahman to run past him into the building.

"You trust him to return?" Douglas asked as Bolan got back in.

"I don't know. He owes us, so let's hope he honors that. Keep the engine running. I don't like sitting here in this yard."

"What's going on, Blanski? I mean, you have more experience with this sort of thing—car chases, jumping onto trains from moving vehicles. I've been with the Agency for years, but this is the first time I have ever done any of that."

"I have no idea what the threat is or where it's coming from. I only know that so far, it has been too easy."

"Easy?"

"Yeah. All the hitters that we've encountered have just been hoodlums. Useful for beating up old ladies but very little else. Now that we've taken out two groups

of them, the enemy may up the ante, send some pro-
fessionals in to do the job. It could get a little tougher
from here on."

"Tougher. Great. How did they find us this morning, when I picked you up at the docks?"

"They must have had spotters along the route, people from the organization who phoned our location in.
Or they were using several cars to follow us, because
I didn't spot a tail. All of which indicates that there is
a professional organization behind this. But what the
goal is? No idea."

"Great. A professional organization."

"Don't worry about it. You have something that
they don't."

"Yeah? What?"

"Me."

They waited five minutes before Abdourahman returned, waving them into the building. The two men
got out of the pickup, Bolan retrieving his sports bag,
which had been sliding around in the bed during the
journey. He brushed off some of the dust and sand
before following Douglas, alert and ready to fight or
flee, depending on the situation.

Abdourahman led them into a large but empty
room, which was considerably cooler than the tem-
peratures outside. He pointed at a scuffed Formica
table where two open bottles of Coca-Cola stood.

"A gift from uncle," he explained. "He see what he
can do about a car. The black one will go to the slums
where it disappear."

Douglas accepted the cold bottle, remembering that
the last time he had seen cola was when Davies had
ordered one in the Waverley hotel. He wondered how

his partner was doing. But business came first. Abdourahman was sitting on a wooden chair, eyeing them nervously. Bolan sat on the opposite side of the table.

"All we want is some information," Bolan stated, "and then we'll leave you. We won't harm you. If you decide to tell us nothing, then we'll still leave. I would prefer it, however, if you tell us about the men who hired you, the men you and your brother led into the mountains."

Abdourahman lowered his eyes at the mention of his brother. He gazed at the floor for a few seconds.

"My aunt very upset about Abdullah. My brother was favorite," he said softly.

"Look," Douglas interjected, "if it makes you feel any better, I was with Saint-Verran just before he died. He was telling me about the Trenchard people you led into Obcock."

Bolan narrowed his gaze at the mention of Obcock. The name rang a bell, but he couldn't put a finger on what it was.

Abdourahman stared at Douglas with new respect.

"That was you?"

Douglas held up his hands, displaying the dirty bandages.

"That is how this happened. Hurts like hell, especially when driving over sand dunes."

"Abdourahman," Bolan broke in, "what happened in Obcock?"

"Nothing."

"Nothing?"

"Nothing happen. Monsieur Saint-Verran, he call, he say have job. We take two Americans into Obcock mountains. Very dangerous. Many bandits there. Many rebels. We take boat, over Tadjoura Bay to Obcock. Then truck into mountains. Americans take many small machines. Many computers. Also—" Abdourahman paused, searching for the right word "—small round dish, like for television."

"A satellite dish," Bolan prompted, "for communications?"

"Yes. Yes. To talk to America. They talk many times. We are in mountains maybe ten days. No bandits. No problems. One American, he find it too hot. His friend say it is like Arizona."

"What did the Americans do?" Douglas asked.

"Work with computers and machines. Always with computers. They bring sun panel for electric. Lots of sun. Adbullah and I, we walk around, look for bandits and snakes and scorpion. We come back. The Americans talk to computer. They not seem happy. They talk to man called General. They say lots of 'Yes, General.' They stop with computer and talk to each other. Then we stay for three days, then leave for city. Men go home. That all I know."

Bolan turned to Douglas. "You researched Trenchard Oil Industries. Is there anybody who works there with the title of general? A retired military man perhaps?"

"Not that I know of. Everybody in the upper management seemed to come from stuffy business schools."

Bolan turned back to Abdourahman. "Can you lead us into the mountains, to the place where you took the Americans?"

Abdourahman shook his head. "No. I not go back. I stay here. Bandits want me dead. I not know why. I know nothing."

"Maybe not, but the bandits think you know something. Did you see any soldiers around there?"

Douglas chimed in. "Saint-Verran said there were mercenaries in the same area. Did you see them?"

Abdourahman continued to shake his head. "*Non.* I see no one. I not understand what men say to computer. It was difficult English. I only know they find no oil."

"What!" Douglas exclaimed. "Then why did they return? Saint-Verran was certain the Trenchard guys came back."

Bolan looked steadily at Abdourahman. "Are you certain they found no oil?"

"*Oui!* They say 'there is no oil, General.'"

"But they spent another three days there. What were they doing?"

"I not know. They work with computers and machines. We look for snakes and bandits. I know nothing. Nothing. They kill brother for nothing. They want to kill me for nothing." Abdourahman slumped into his chair.

Bolan glanced at Douglas, then turned his gaze back to Abdourahman.

"Can you read a map?" he asked. Abdourahman nodded. "Then I would like you to find a map and show us where you were for ten days. Then we will leave."

Abdourahman nodded again, got up and left the room.

"And exactly how are we going to get there without a guide?" Douglas wanted to know.

"I have an idea," Bolan said.

Abdourahman returned a few minutes later, holding a brand-new road map of Djibouti. He spread it out on the table.

"My uncle say you have this. Also car is ready outside. You keep it."

"Tell your uncle that we are very grateful," said Bolan.

They waited while Abdourahman studied it. Then he pointed to a spot well north of the town of Obcock.

"Here," he said.

Bolan studied the map, then marked the spot with a pencil. "Thank you. We'll leave you in peace now. To mourn for your brother."

Abdourahman led them through the boutique. The two Americans saw neither the uncle nor the aunt in the shop full of junk. Several scruffy men were hanging around, but they barely gave the two strangers a second glance. Bolan turned to thank Adbourahman again, but the guide was gone. Outside, a rusting white Peugeot 205 was waiting for them.

The keys were in the ignition. Bolan placed the sports bag in the car's tiny cargo area as Douglas squeezed into the passenger seat, complaining about Europeans and their small cars. Bolan climbed behind the wheel, adjusting the seat to fit his large frame.

"Great," Douglas muttered. "We have to go into Obcock without a guide. You know it will be suspicious if we don't have a cover story."

"I have a cover story. I'm a journalist, remember. And I suggest you get a cover as a photographer."

"And how do we get there? Drive this rust bucket? This will just get us to the city and no more. I guess the uncle wasn't too grateful."

"I know someone. The name Obcock rang a bell. An aid worker and a convoy of rice will be traveling there in the morning."

"I sense a big *but*."

"Yeah," Bolan said as he twisted the ignition key. "She doesn't like me. You'll have to do the talking."

THE PEUGEOT 205 gave up a half mile from the safehouse. Its engine coughed once, then it coasted to a stop in the middle of a junction, forcing Bolan and Douglas to push the tiny car to the side of the road while angry, impatient drivers honked their horns in frustration. They abandoned the car, keys in the ignition, and walked the rest of the way, checking all the time for surveillance from the authorities or even would-be muggers. Nobody showed much interest in them, not even a police car that cruised by.

They reached their destination in the early evening. Bolan noted that the black-market guards had changed shifts, their replacements sporting soccer shirts of European nations. The safehouse was still secure. Bolan dropped the heavy sports bag on the floor while Douglas busied himself with the old coffeemaker.

"I have to report in," Douglas announced. "Let them know what has been happening. I'll probably get my ass handed to me for shooting up the city and destroying police cars. Even though I did no shooting."

"I only fired five shots, if that helps."

"Yeah, sure, great. I'll just let Langley know that I am running around with you."

"Listen, how much money have you got left in that slush fund?"

"A couple thousand. Why?"

"The M-16 is a great rifle, but I couldn't assemble it today for it to be useful. The Beretta pistol was underpowered. I need something small and compact, like an Uzi. You make your report. I'm going shopping."

"And where the hell will you find an Uzi?"

"Your neighbors, opposite. The black-market boys. They sell everything, right?"

"They are more likely to shoot you."

"Not if I shoot them first. But I don't think they'll shoot. They're more interested in business. White man, black man, it doesn't matter as long as cash is involved. You want anything?"

Douglas shook his head. He dug out the money and handed it to Bolan, who left him to his coffeemaker.

"Hey," Douglas called after him, "I might know somebody up in Obcock. I'll see if I can arrange a meeting. Transport or something."

But Bolan was already gone.

CHAPTER FOURTEEN

An hour later Douglas was finished making his report. As expected he had been chewed out. The job was unauthorized. There had been no instructions from Langley. He was supposed to be lying low, working some angles on the bombing investigation, not tearing around Djibouti City in stolen vehicles, shooting anything that moved, causing untold damage to police cars, not to mention civilian deaths. And then he was hanging out with an unknown agent. The chief was furious at the thought that somebody in America had commandeered one of his men without informing him. And why hadn't he reported in earlier, before he decided to have fistfights on train roofs and destroy half of a city in two car chases?

Douglas had protested, saying that the agent he'd met at the dock had happened to be with him when the hotel bombers had attempted to kill him; the rest had just followed. The station chief had fallen silent, then asked what Douglas needed to continue on this quest of his. Cover documents for a reporter called Mike Blanski and for a photographer called Peter Douglas. The CIA section chief said they would be delivered at first light, that Douglas was to make regular reports and that he was not to trust Blanski. And he was to put everything in writing. Immediately.

Douglas started to shake shortly after completing his written report and sending it in. Doctors would refer to it as something fancy, like post-traumatic stress disorder, but Douglas knew that he was just plain scared. Car bombs, car chases, people shooting at him... There had to be a contract out on him; the police probably had their version of an APB out on him. What would Cindy, his ex, say when they informed her that his bullet-riddled body had been found in the desert? Would she even care?

Then there was Blanski. Where was he? Only popped out to the local store to buy a couple of guns. He could be dead by now; one of the black-market villains could have knifed him in the back. Another thought occurred to Douglas. Did the faceless enemy know about this safehouse? There were people watching his own apartment, but had anybody managed to follow them here? Douglas brushed the back of his hand against his face and was surprised to find it wet. Tears were streaming down his face.

He wiped his face with a tissue. Then pinched himself, hoping to snap out of his morbid pensiveness. There was no going back. The following day they would travel to Obcock, to the heart of the problem, to look for two mysterious oilmen and a camp of armed mercenaries. Men who were not hoodlums, men who were dangerous and knew how to shoot straight.

"Are you okay?"

The voice was soft, but Douglas yelped and all but jumped out of his skin. He spun to find Bolan standing a mere foot behind him.

"Jesus! You almost killed me! How long have you been standing there?"

"Just as you were submitting your report to the Agency."

"Shit. Look—"

Bolan cut him off with a wave of his hand. "Don't worry about it. But I need to know something about you. Are you up for this? If not, then say so now. I can go on alone."

"It's not that, it's… Aw, shit. It's just that nobody has ever shot at me before. I've never been involved in a high-speed pursuit, and I've never seen anybody jump from an out-of-control pickup onto a speeding train. I guess it just caught up with me, that's all. But I have been ordered to find out about these Americans in Obcock, so I have to go, like it or not."

"But can I rely on you?"

Douglas returned Bolan's gaze. "Yes. Yes, you can. I owe it to Davies and to Saint-Verran to see this thing through."

"Good. Now look up a Dutch charity called Help Without Borders and a woman called Nancy Clayton. Find out where she is in Djibouti."

"Okay. Did you have any luck with the neighbors?"

"Yeah. Quite friendly guys once they were encouraged to talk. They sold me some gear at discount prices, and even had some clothes that should fit. I also managed to persuade them to donate some of their food to the poor in the neighborhood." Bolan indicated a large plastic bag that he had managed to bring up the stairs without Douglas hearing a thing. He pulled out two matching sets of desert-camouflage battle fatigues in the six-color pattern favored throughout Africa. Wrapped up in the clothes to prevent rattling were two new-looking Skorpion machine pistols, along with ten fully loaded magazines and two M26 fragmentation grenades. At the bottom of the bag Bolan produced shoulder holsters and slings for the Skorpions and their Berettas.

"I plan to change clothes once we leave the aid convoy and go on recon," Bolan said.

"How much did this all cost?" Douglas asked, wondering how he would explain it to his boss.

"I knew from previous experience that the going price for an AK-47 in Ethiopia is around $250. I got the Skorpions for $200, including the ammunition. The grenades and uniforms for $75. The food they threw in."

"Are we going to have any problems with them?"

"Not as long as we're here. They may move in tomorrow after we leave and vent their frustrations. It will pay for you to inform the Agency and have them send some guys around to clean the place out."

"Great. A safehouse blown. Why couldn't you just get some stuff from the Marines at Lemonnier?"

"I don't want to involve them. I'm here unofficially. I just can't walk in and ask for the keys to the armory. Have you found anything on Clayton yet?"

"Yeah. It's on their main website. A wonderful blog telling the world what they are doing, where they are going and when they are leaving. Idiots. They should be departing at nine in the morning from Warehouse 4 at the main docks. What dumbasses. Don't they know what security is?"

"Probably somebody back at main office typed all that in to show off to sponsors. That sort of stupidity happens all the time. I'm going to clean the weapons and then get some shut-eye. What about that person you were going to contact?"

"A guy called Samar. He's a bit of a rogue. He does things for the French and sometimes for us. He'll meet us on the city outskirts."

"Good. Now, where is that coffee you were making?"

THEY CAUGHT A taxi to the docks the next morning, departing just as two men showed up with a van, ready to remove the safehouse furniture and equipment. Across the road Douglas saw two hoods guarding the entrance to the black-market building, both sporting black eyes and bruises. Douglas wondered how persuasive Blanski had been. The two thugs glared back, then looked away once they spotted the tall American, pretending to take no interest in the activities opposite.

Bolan gave them a little wave as he placed the heavy sports bag in the taxi's trunk, noting that the seams were beginning to split. The quality in replica goods was definitely falling, he mused.

The taxi took them to the harbor without any problems. Bolan spotted the MV *Cape Faith* still moored but dwarfed by two new container ships that had to have docked the night before. They paid the driver and gave him a generous tip, then walked into the warehouse, removing their sunglasses in the sudden change of light. The building wasn't that large, and the offloaded rice took up only half the floor space. Several Africans sat around looking bored. Bolan nodded to a small office unit at the end and walked toward it, Douglas trailing him and lugging the sports bag.

Bolan found Nancy Clayton sitting with her back

toward him, elbows resting on an old metal desk that had seen better days, a black telephone handset pressed against her ear. She was speaking loudly to whoever was on the other end of the line. A bad connection, Bolan thought.

"No, forty…forty percent, not fourteen. It disappeared during the night…No, the guards saw nothing…most likely they helped carry the stuff out…No, the trucks haven't shown up. Two water tankers have, but the rest…I think that we will only need three now, not five…No, nothing has shown up…I don't know where to find more trucks. You were supposed to handle that…Well, find me some trucks then, with drivers…Yes, the translator is here, as is the guide. They wanted money before they even said hello…Yes, okay, I'll talk to you later."

She hung up the phone and groaned, muttering something inaudible.

"Hello, Nancy," Bolan said.

She spun, saw Bolan, then closed her eyes, placing her hands against her forehead.

"And just when I thought things couldn't get any worse, you show up. And I see you've found a friend. And he carries your bag for you. How nice. Does he know there's a gun in it?"

"Yeah. And the gun has been joined by several more. We need a favor. One that may be beneficial to you."

"How can anything you do be beneficial? Unless of course you're here to recover my stolen rice. They took it during the night, the bastards. Go shoot them or something. Stealing from their own people. Bastards. And there are no trucks to carry it. The company we hired claims that somebody else offered them more money to carry another shipment, so they went with them instead. Probably carrying my stolen rice. Bastards, the lot of them. And my so-called colleagues, who were supposed to be here waiting, decided to get sick. Both of them. Can you believe that? And how did you find me?"

"It's on your website. Times and everything. It's probably how your thieves knew when to visit and what you were shipping."

"Brilliant. Just brilliant. Stick it on the website, why don't you? I tell you, when I get back to Holland I'm going to kick some ass, then quit. Stupid fools. They couldn't organize sex with a hooker. So, who's your friend? Does he shoot people, as well?"

"His name is Peter, and he doesn't like shooting people."

"I like him already. More than I like you."

To Douglas she said, "Do you know that Mike here shoots people?"

"Yeah, I gathered that yesterday when we were driving around the city."

"Driving around the city? Oh, marvelous. That was you? I might have guessed. It was on the radio, you know that? They were scraping bodies off the streets."

"We aren't here to discuss yesterday. We're interested in today," Bolan said.

"And what happens today?"

"You're going to Obcock. We want to go to Obcock. So I figured we could hitch a ride and maybe protect your rice shipment from any bandits who show up."

"We aren't going anywhere. I told you, no trucks. And only a little more than half of the rice is left."

"We'll arrange some trucks," Bolan said. "Peter here can make some phone calls—"

"I can?" Douglas queried.

"—and arrange something pretty quick. If we do that, can we ride with you?"

Nancy Clayton thought for a moment. "Fine. Arrange some trucks. Only don't think you're riding in the same one as me. How long will it all take to arrange?"

"Let's say an hour," Bolan replied, oblivious to the look Douglas gave him.

"An hour? That fast? Who on earth do you know?"

"Lots of people in extremely low places."

"Then I better get some organizing done. Shift some of those lazy butts outside. An hour? I can hold you to that?"

"We'll do our best," Bolan said, now looking at Douglas, who just shrugged.

"Then I'll leave you to it."

"Wow, she's a handful," Douglas stated the moment Nancy Clayton had left the office.

"You weren't cooped up on a small ship with her. Now, phone's there. Make good on my promise."

Douglas picked up the receiver and got to work.

PETER DOUGLAS WISHED that he were somewhere else. Anywhere else. Anywhere but sitting in the stifling cab of an ancient Mercedes-Benz truck during the middle of the day, with the sun burning down and no air-conditioning for a hundred miles. The foam that had been in the passenger seat when the truck had left the factory had worn away years ago, leaving Douglas sitting on springs and a metal frame. He had placed a towel on the seat for extra comfort, but it didn't help. The truck bounced, rattled and shook over every pothole in the road, and there were many. He felt every single one of them. Painfully. He groaned as the truck hit another rut. The African driver seemed as impervious to the discomfort as he was to the heat.

Douglas took another sip of his rapidly dwindling bottled water. The vents were blowing a gale of heated air and bits of grit around the cab. He had fiddled with the dial, vainly hoping that the truck would be able to dispense cool air, as well. He quickly came to the miserable conclusion that the thing had only one setting—hot. All others were broken. And the window wouldn't wind down, either. Sweat poured off him. He wondered how Blanski was faring in the rear truck. Or that Clayton woman, sitting in the fourth truck, one of the two water tankers. The driver whistled tunelessly, adding to Douglas's discomfort.

Earlier that day he had phoned an acquaintance, who had put him through to somebody else, who had put him through to another person, who had diverted the call to another department in the Djiboutian Ministry for Transportation, which had passed him on to yet another person. This time a woman had tried to help without being helpful. Douglas had lost patience by then and threatened to phone the US Embassy and CNN to tell them that not only were the Djiboutian people stealing rice but they didn't want to help deliver what was left. He was quickly passed to a minor official who promised to do what he could. Half an hour later the man phoned back, apologizing profusely,

promising that three trucks were on the way, that he
would come and supervise the loading personally to
make sure nothing else was stolen, that a police escort
would stay with them all the way to Obcock.

The official showed up as vowed, along with three
trucks that looked as if they had just been rescued from
the scrap yard, and a solitary police car. The man assured Nancy Clayton that the rice would be safe now,
nobody would attack a police car, that the government
was grateful for all she was doing and the owner of the
original truck-hire company would receive firm words
from the government. And with that, the convoy left
the docks, the police car leading the way. The three
Americans decided to ride with the trucks that had
the most tread on the tires; one water tanker and one
rice carrier looked decidedly dangerous. Bolan took
the last truck in the convoy, wanting to keep an eye
on the rear in case anybody was following.

Douglas peered out of the grimy side window. They
were heading up a steep hill, the edge of the road a
mere two yards away. The drop to the ravine floor
below looked terrifying. On the opposite side was a
rock face, the road barely wide enough to accept two
vehicles. The engine labored heavily, the driver shifting and grinding gears to try to keep the momentum
going. The vehicles in front were not faring much
better, the water-carrying tanker suffering the worst.
Douglas moaned softly and hoped that the ride would
be over soon.

Bam!

"What the…?"

Douglas shot forward in his seat as the driver
slammed on the brakes, the truck lurching to a halt,

the tanker in front doing likewise. From somewhere up ahead, a heavy-caliber machine gun opened up, followed by the excited chatter of other, smaller weapons. He watched as a man jumped out of the cab of the tanker and took two steps before disintegrating as the bullets tore him apart.

"Shit!"

Douglas had his Beretta pistol in his hand but didn't yet know what to do. Beside him his driver was squealing in terror at the sight of the bloody remains as what was left of the man collapsed to the ground. Douglas cursed his folly at not assembling his M-16. It was still in his sports bag. He reached for the door handle, only to have it yanked away. Douglas started, then stared into the business end of a rusty AK-47. The African holding it was screaming at him, but Douglas had no idea what the words were. Another man joined the rifle man. He reached up and grabbed the pistol out of Douglas's hand, throwing it to the floor.

The CIA agent snapped out of his trance, realizing too late that he could have shot the rifle-wielding thug and his friend instead of sitting there staring down the barrel of the Kalashnikov. The man reached for Douglas again, hauling him out of the cab. The American started to comply, stepping out and down, but he missed the foot plate and fell to his hands and knees, gravel cutting through his bandages. Cursing he started to rise, only to be kicked back down again, a heavy workman's boot crashing painfully into his side.

Douglas groaned. He could hear one of the two men shouting and the truck driver shrieking. Both men started yelling as the noise continued. The Kalashnikov opened up and the shrieking cut off abruptly, replaced by the sound of broken glass and the sensation of hot cartridges dropping on Douglas's head.

Another kick and Douglas rolled over onto his back, eyes shut tight against the men. Now the Africans were screaming at him. There was more rifle fire somewhere close by. Douglas was seized by the scruff of his neck and dragged farther up the road to be dumped next to several other men. The African with the rifle suddenly cut off his tirade, and all at once it was quiet. Douglas opened his eyes, seeing that the men next to him were the remaining drivers and various workers who had been squeezed into the cabs and the leading trucks. They were all kneeling with their hands on their heads. The man closest hissed something at him, indicating that he should get into the same position.

Douglas struggled to his knees, wincing from the pain in his side and hand. Only when he was in position did he manage to take stock of what was happening. The hostages all had their backs to the empty space behind them, the toes of their shoes right on the edge of the near-vertical drop. The remains of the police car were at the front of the convoy, burning, acrid flames rising into the air. Douglas knew there wouldn't be anything left of the two officers. In front of the wreck was a technical, a pickup truck with a large machine gun fixed in its bed. The gun was pointing in his general direction, the gunner just waiting for an excuse to let rip.

Douglas shifted his gaze to what was happening in front of him. The soldiers or bandits or whatever they were had formed a rough semicircle, all of them pointing weapons at their prisoners. He wondered if he would have a chance to escape. There appeared to be only two possibilities, and neither was acceptable. One was to run past the eleven or so bandits, but that would be suicidal. The other option would be to jump off the cliff. The drop was not sheer, but chances of surviving it without injury would be impossible.

Where was Blanski? Douglas risked a quick look around. His was the only white face in the lineup; Nancy Clayton was also missing. Douglas felt a glimmer of hope. Blanski had to be somewhere close by. Unless he was already dead. The glimmer faded. There had been a lot of shooting when the ambushers stuck. Perhaps Blanski had been killed in the skirmish; it would take only one bullet. If Blanski was gone, then there would be no way out. Unless the bandits wanted hostages. Douglas eyed them. Their demeanor discouraged him. The men had formed a loose firing squad. They were just waiting for the command to open up, and the corpses would fall backward into the ravine, never to be seen again.

The man beside him, the translator if Douglas remembered correctly, began whimpering in terror. Douglas resisted the temptation to join him.

A young African stepped out of the semicircle and approached Douglas, who recognized him as the one who had pulled him from the cab. In the man's hand was the Beretta pistol that Douglas had lost. The man crouched in front of the American, grinning. His eyes shone wildly as he held the pistol in front of his face. He admired it for a moment before giving Douglas his undivided attention. Reaching out, he plucked Douglas's sunglasses from his face and placed them on his own, smiling all the while. Douglas blinked furiously in the bright sunshine. The man spoke with a deep voice that belied his youth.

"It is a mighty fine pistol. Mighty fine. Thank you for such a wonderful gift. And your sunglasses. Perfect fit. I like it. And now, my friend, who are you? Hmm? To be out here with such a mighty fine pistol as this. You are American? CIA? Hmm? Sent out here to spy on us? To spy on me? Hmm? Where is your friend? Well? No answer? Well, Mr. Spy, I shall tell you this. We are the Front for Restoration of Unity and Democracy, and it pleases me to tell you that you will die by your own pistol. Your own pistol that you were sent here to kill me with. Still nothing to say? Hmm? Then thank you for your pistol and for all the food and water that you have brought us. My men are mighty pleased. Mighty pleased. They will feast in your honor tonight. And now you will take a message of death back to your President, to all your American people."

The man rose to his feet and pointed the Beretta pistol directly at Douglas's skull. The American squeezed his eyes shut, waiting for existence to end. Beside him the hostages began to whimper louder.

Bang!

Something warm and wet splattered across the top of his head.

Something heavy hit the ground hard, right in front of him.

Pandemonium broke out.

Douglas opened his eyes to find his would-be killer lying in the dust in front of him, the top of his skull missing, the sunglasses gone. The firing squad broke apart, looking around wildly, yelling, firing in random directions. They had no idea where the shot had come from. The rest of the hostages were in the dirt, hands over their heads, hoping that the FRUD soldiers would ignore them.

The Beretta pistol was only inches away. Douglas grabbed it and was getting to his feet when one of the FRUD revolutionaries saw him and ran over, his AK-47 pointing at Douglas. The CIA agent didn't hesitate. In an instant he drew target acquisition and fired, putting two hot rounds into the screaming man's face. The insurgent collapsed as if his strings had been cut, falling onto his back. Douglas kept the pistol raised, ready to fire at another target. He didn't have time to dwell on the fact that he had just shot a man for the first time. He crouched again as several wild bullets passed too close for comfort.

He looked around for cover. The ground was littered with corpses. It could only be Blanski! He darted to one of the trucks, hunkering down behind the front wheel. All of the so-called FRUD gunners were now firing up the cliff. Obviously they had located Blanski. How many were left, and how could he assist his comrade in arms with only a pistol?

He was reaching for a discarded AK-47 when his eyes fell upon the technical. The gunner had already been neutralized, his body draped over the vehicle's cab. Blanski had to have killed him an instant after shooting the leader.

How hard would it be to fire a heavy machine gun?

His heart was pounding in his ears as he made the charge toward the vehicle. Gunfire surrounded him as the rebels engaged Blanski. Another rebel had the smart idea of using the technical, as well, and he was making a break for it when he and Douglas locked eyes. The CIA agent skidded to a stop and adopted the Weaver stance that he had learned during firearms training ages ago. His two shots were lost in the cacophony as the rebel tumbled and fell. Douglas continued his charge, reaching the vehicle unharmed.

Shoving the pistol into his rear pocket, he clambered onto the technical, trying his best to ignore the corpse, the blood and smears of what he presumed was brain matter. Douglas quickly examined the heavy-caliber machine gun. He didn't know the make, but it looked old and appeared to be of Russian origin. It seemed simple enough. Point, squeeze, shoot.

He swung the machine gun around so that it was pointing at the back of the closest FRUD rebel. He quickly counted six others, who were all crouched along the side of the cliff, firing upward at where they presumed their enemy to be. Several of their friends lay dead beside them, testament to Blanski's killing skills. Douglas squeezed the trigger. The old Soviet weapon roared to life, sending a stream of 7.62 mm death toward the first rebel. The man came apart like a rotten tomato. The others quickly realized their predicament but were unable to do anything about it. Screaming incoherently, Douglas walked the barrel along the line of figures. Some of the bandits managed to get to their feet in time to be ripped in two; others never felt their heads exploding off their shoulders. Within seconds it was over.

Douglas ceased firing and ceased screaming as the remains of the last rebel fell. He was shaking, his bandaged hand hurt like hell, but he had done it. He had saved Blanski and taken out eight bad guys in less than a minute.

He began to laugh hysterically as the shock of what he had done set it.

Could Blanski rely on him?

Hell, yeah!

CHAPTER FIFTEEN

Mack Bolan had already assembled his M-16, ignoring the nervous glances of the driver. Both his Beretta pistol and Skorpion had been cleaned and readied for use. The pistol was tucked into the waistband of his trousers, poking him whenever the truck hit a rut. The Skorpion hung on a sling, under his right arm. Like Douglas, he found the journey uncomfortable. Unlike Douglas, he was experienced enough to ignore the jolts of the truck and the heat of the day.

He was in motion the moment he heard the initial gunfire and explosion. He threw the passenger door open before the truck had come to a halt and jumped out. The truck was a mere two feet from the edge of the precipice. Glancing down, he noted a wedge of rock sticking out of the ridge face, maybe six feet down. It would be perfect for what he had in mind. He ran to the next truck in line, reached up and threw open the passenger door. Nancy Clayton looked down at him, her face white with horror.

"What is happening?"

"Out. Now. Right now."

He reached up and grabbed her arm, pulling her out of the cab. She almost fell, but he kept her stable until her feet touched the ground.

"With me. Now."

He pulled her along by the arm, his M-16 in one hand, up and ready for action.

"Where are we… What's happening?" she gasped.

"Down there. Quickly." Bolan pointed to the ledge of rock.

"I…I can't. I'll fall."

"If you don't, then you'll be killed. Move."

Bolan manhandled her down the cliff's side until she stood firmly on the exposed rock.

"Whatever happens, stay here. Don't make a sound. If they find you, you'll die."

With that Bolan was gone, the doomsday clock ticking in his head. He could hear another vehicle approaching from the rear. Moving as fast as he could, the soldier climbed up the side of the cab until he was on the roof and lying prone on the searing canvas top. He could hear the vehicle to the rear disgorging men. Up front, thick black smoke and flames were rising into the air, probably from the police car after it had taken hits from the heavy-caliber machine gun that he had heard.

He turned his head slightly so that he could observe the aggressors. He saw instantly that the attackers were not army. They were dressed in ragtag clothes and carried an assortment of weaponry. Bolan had encountered their type too many times before. Rebels, deserters, looters. Vermin that always preyed on those in need. The bandits proceeded along the convoy, dragging out terrified drivers and passengers. He could hear a similar maneuver taking place at the front of the convoy.

As soon as the last bandit had passed, Bolan looked around for a vantage point. The only thing he could find was a ledge of rock that jutted ten feet above the cab of the second truck. It wasn't ideal, there would be no retreat from the position and it would be risky. He couldn't afford to be seen. Shots were fired from somewhere in front of the convoy. Bolan moved; the numbers had ticked down to zero.

He leaped off the roof of the truck, hitting the ground hard, falling automatically into a parachute roll. Then he was on his feet again, running for the cover of the second truck. Slinging his rifle, he began to climb until he reached the ledge. Nobody was paying him any attention.

Once on the ledge he lay on the hot stone and took in the situation as he pulled the rifle off his shoulder. The police car was burning, a technical was covering the crowd and the truck drivers were gathered at the cliff's edge with the bandits. The machine gunner would have to die first. Bolan switched the selector to single shot, released the safety and took aim. He was about to fire when he saw a man step out of the rebel group and approach something. As the man squatted, Bolan spied Douglas. After a few seconds the man rose and pointed a pistol at the CIA agent's head. Bolan didn't hesitate. He shifted his aim, found target acquisition and fired. The top of man's head flew off in a bloody cloud.

The Executioner shifted his aim, bringing the machine gunner back into focus. Another single shot, and another head disintegrated. Bolan didn't bother to see how the man fell. He switched the selector back to three-round burst and opened fire the moment the scrambling rebels came into view. Two fell, but the others had overcome their shock and returned fire, having quickly located Bolan's position.

The Executioner ducked back as the rebels poured a wall of lead at the ledge. He could feel the rounds hammering into the rock under him, hear the bullets and bits of stone flying past. The rebels were taking positions underneath him, and the M-16 was too long to be brought into play. He laid it aside and drew the Skorpion. Shielding his face, he saw one man break away from the group, running toward the technical.

Easy target.

The rest continued to pour fire at Bolan's position. It wouldn't be too long before one of them figured that they would have a better angle if they climbed up onto the trucks. Bolan was about to fire on the running man when the target collapsed to the ground and Douglas was running past, making for the technical.

The gunfire lessened as several rebels stopped to reload. To remind them that he was still alive, Bolan stuck the Skorpion over the side and gave them a quick burst of retaliatory fire without seeing where the rounds went. The rebels opened up again, filling the air with metal hornets. Douglas was on the technical, swinging the barrel around. It looked to Bolan like an old, Soviet Cold War–era, heavy-caliber machine gun. Then Douglas opened fire.

The thunder lasted several seconds. There were screams that abruptly ended and the sound of bullets bouncing off the rock face and hitting the trucks. Then silence, which was suddenly filled by Douglas's hysterical laughter. Bolan slung his weapons and climbed down. Several limbs had been ripped away from their owners by the metal storm. Grimacing, Bolan stepped over the body parts. He gave a wave to Douglas, who was still laughing. Bolan knew that this was a form of adrenaline release, relief at being alive and out of a life-threatening situation. Douglas would come to his senses in a moment.

But first he had to find Nancy Clayton. He jogged over to where he had left her. She was still there, clinging to the side of the rock face, looking up, glaring in a mix of anger and terror. She started as Bolan suddenly appeared, her expression of surprise instantly giving way to a look of relief. Bolan crouched and offered her his hand, helping her to climb up to the road.

Once there she looked around, likely expecting to see something. From her vantage point she could not view any of the dead bodies.

"Are you all right?" Bolan asked.

"Yes, yes. What happened?" she answered, rubbing her hands on her sides.

"Bandits. But they've gone now."

She looked at him sharply, then looked away. "Did you shoot them?"

"Some of them. I had help. If we hadn't, then they would have shot everybody here."

She looked at him again, the anger replaced by concern. "Is anybody hurt?"

"A few of the workers have been killed or injured. I'm not sure how many."

"Oh, God. Because I brought them up here."

"It's not your fault. It would have happened anyway, if not to them, then to somebody else. Now come with me." Bolan led her over to her truck and all but lifted her inside. "Stay here. We have to clean the place up and assess the damage. When we leave, I want you to look out of the passenger window. Don't look out of the driver's window."

"I have seen dead bodies before, you know."

"Not like this you haven't."

Bolan left Clayton and returned to the technical. Douglas had climbed down and was on his hands and knees, vomiting into the dust. Bolan helped him to his feet and handed him a warm bottle of water, which he gratefully drank. The bandages on the CIA agent's hands were filthy. Blood appeared to be leaking through.

Bolan glanced around while Douglas downed the water. The convoy drivers and other workers appeared to be recovering their nerve. Some of them had begun to scavenge the corpses, pulling boots off dead feet and going through pockets. Bolan turned his attention back to the CIA agent.

"Shit, Blanski," Douglas gasped, "I thought I was a goner. Then you took out that guy—thanks for that— and I opened up with the machine gun and, well, those guys just came apart. I mean they just came apart. I have never done anything like that before. Shit."

"Killing doesn't get any easier," Bolan said.

"And those cops in the car. Some escort. They didn't stand a chance. Hey, and there's something else. The guy you popped. He questioned me about being in the CIA, wanted to know where my buddy was hiding. And he didn't seem too concerned about questioning me for too long."

That brought Bolan to a halt for a moment. If the FRUD rebels knew about him and Douglas, then it meant the enemy knew they were coming. Somebody in the police or the government had passed on the information, possibly the official who had shown up to see them off. Then, the target of rice and water had to have been secondary to the actual contract of killing him and Douglas. It meant they had to separate themselves from the convoy.

"Get your things out of your truck and put them in the technical. We're taking their wheels and pushing on. I'm going to get my stuff. Have somebody call the cops or the army, and say our goodbyes to Nancy."

Douglas nodded. "Won't the technical be too obvious? Big machine gun on it and all?"

"We'll do our best to stay off road and get a new ride as soon as possible."

Bolan left Douglas and went to grab his own stuff while quickly checking for victims of the aid convoy. It seemed miraculous, but nobody had been killed, not even Douglas's own truck driver, who had passed out from fright when he had been shot at, the bullets going through his truck door and the rebel likely too excited to confirm his kill. Bolan found Clayton still in the cab, sitting still, staring blankly into nothingness.

"We're leaving," Bolan said. "Douglas and I are, anyway. You need to stay here and have somebody call the police or the army for help."

"I can't do this anymore," she said. "First those pirates wanted to kill us, now these bandits. I just can't go on, not anymore."

"I understand. When the police get here, have them escort you back to the city. Go to the embassy and have them take you to Lemonnier. You can get out that way."

"I think that the translator was calling somebody. I'm not going anywhere. What are you going to do?"

"Track down and find out who is responsible for this and see what's going on."

Clayton gave him a faint smile. "It's what you do, isn't it? What should I say to the police about you? I can't exactly say you and your friend were not here."

"Tell them the truth as far as you know it. That we claimed that we were journalists and hitched a ride with your convoy. Then all hell broke loose and we hightailed it out of here. They'll look for us, but so are the bad guys, so it makes no difference.

"So, Nancy, goodbye. I doubt we'll meet again." Clayton nodded sadly, and Bolan turned and walked away.

He placed his bag in the back of the technical and climbed in behind the steering wheel. Douglas rode shotgun. He had already assembled his M-16 and looked at Bolan expectantly.

"Use the Skorpion machine pistol," the soldier advised. "It's more maneuverable if you have to hang out the window and fire." He pulled out the map that Abdourahman had given them, as Douglas turned slightly red and replaced the rifle with the machine pistol.

"We are roughly here," Bolan said, pointing to a spot on the map, "and we have to go here, where the Trenchard men were. Where was your contact meeting us?"

Douglas pointed to a spot on the map, just north of Obcock.

"Then, that is where we are going." Bolan started the engine, checked the fuel gauge and drove away, leaving the aid convoy surrounded by shattered, broken bodies.

NOT LONG AFTER going cross-country, they heard the sound of sirens in the distance as police cars raced toward the ambushed convoy.

"Too fast," Bolan had called out over the din of the struggling engine. "Their response time is too fast. Somebody must have called them the moment the ambush started."

They pushed on, making thirty to forty miles per hour over the rough terrain. Bolan worried about Douglas. The man was an investigator, an analyst, not somebody who was cut out to be in such a situation. Sure the guy had been in three firefights so far, but he was showing signs of cracking under the stress. Bolan considered leaving him in Obcock and striking out on his own. Douglas wouldn't be any use in the desert. He would become a liability. On the other hand, the moment his white face showed in Obcock, he would be picked up, either by the police or the army or some other faction that was after them. Either option didn't bode well for the CIA man, and Bolan didn't want another friendly ghost to join the others who sometimes frequented his dreams.

The pickup hit a ridge of rock. There was a loud snap and the vehicle fell forward, burying its nose into the sand. Both Bolan and Douglas were thrown forward, Douglas striking his head on the windshield. The engine died. Bolan eased himself out and inspected the damage. Both front wheels pointed in different directions.

"What happened?" Douglas groaned.

"Snapped axel. From here on, we walk."

Douglas groaned again. "How far?"

"About an hour or so to your rendezvous. That's

an hour at my pace or three hours at yours. So we'll do it at my pace. Drink some water and change into the army suit that I gave you. Move it, or stay here."

Douglas heaved himself out of the technical and located his bag in the bed of the pickup. He copied his partner in his actions: first water, then change into the military camouflage suit, then put on the weapons. He put his arms through the straps of his sports bag so that the bag sat uncomfortably on his back, all the spare food and ammunition piled together at the bottom. He noted that Blanski didn't sling the M-16 across his shoulder but carried it strapless in his hands. Douglas had heard that the British army's SAS—Special Air Service—carried it that way and wondered if Blanski had picked it up from them. Douglas elected not to carry his similarly; his hands wouldn't take it and his arms would probably fall off long before they reached the rendezvous.

Bolan headed out, setting the pace. He could hear Douglas behind him, struggling to keep up, muttering to himself. Several times the CIA man slipped and stumbled, but Bolan didn't let up, knowing that they had to put as much distance between themselves and the wrecked technical as possible. As it was, the way Douglas was scuffing his feet, even an inexperienced tracker would be able to follow their trail.

Bolan made the decision to leave Douglas somewhere soon, give him something else to do. He had a feeling that the situation would soon escalate. The attacks so far had been rushed and amateurish. Whatever was taking place was so far unclear. There was no confirmation that there were American oilmen in the country, no confirmation of mercenaries. Only the word of a retired French spy who had been assassinated and the numerous attempts on his and Douglas's life by third-party hit men. Something was going on, but Bolan didn't know what.

The hour drew on, the hot sun burning down. Douglas dropped farther and farther behind. Bolan was aware of the situation but didn't let up. So long as the man was still standing, then he could catch up. He stopped for several minutes, taking sips of warm water from a plastic bottle, watching as Douglas struggled over, listening for sounds of pursuit. His ear caught the faint sound of metal banging off metal, somewhere over the next dune. He instantly dropped to a crouch, waving to Douglas that he should do the same. It took the CIA man several seconds to realize what Bolan wanted, but he caught the meaning of the soldier's gestures. Bolan put his water away, slipped the safety off his M-16 and crawled up the dune to the top of the ridge. It took a minute of scrabbling on the loose sand and gravel, but at the top he lay prone, observing the situation.

Below was a thin strip of tarmac road that stretched northward. Parked on the side of the road were two Renault panel vans, facing each other. One van had its hood open. It had either broken down or the two men sitting in the van's shadow were feigning a breakdown. One man was significantly older than the other, the latter being in his early twenties, Bolan thought. The older man's age was impossible to guess. Both Africans wore taqiyah caps and neither, as far as Bolan could see, was armed.

He scanned the area, looking for an indication that this was a trap. He saw nothing. The only movement was a small lizard that was approaching his arm. He ignored it. Men could be hiding in the two vans, but nothing else stirred. Bolan heard and felt Douglas puffing up beside him, making as much noise as a herd of elephants.

"What...whatcha got?" huffed the out-of-shape CIA agent.

Bolan indicated the scene with a nod. "And be quiet. You're making as much noise as a pregnant whale."

"Yeah, thanks." Douglas took in the situation. "Okay, the old guy is Samar. No idea who his friend is. Could be a son. I hear he has dozens."

"What do you know about Samar?"

"Black-market smuggler. Somali. I was introduced to him once by Saint-Verran. Samar is a smuggler but not a bad guy. He speaks excellent English, French and several other languages. According to all my sources, he sticks to alcohol, tobacco, car parts and things that the government would like you to pay tax on. He doesn't do drugs or arms. That's all I know. When I contacted him...when was that? Yesterday? Sheesh, only yesterday! When I contacted him, I asked him to lay on transport and any information he might have. He was one of Saint-Verran's main sources here in the north."

"What's in it for him?"

"Money. Have to give him an IOU. The goodwill of the CIA."

Bolan kept his gun sights focused on the two men. Still he saw nothing suspicious, and that made him suspicious in itself. "Did you give Samar an ETA?"

"Not really, no. I said late afternoon."

"So a smuggler, a bit of a rogue and a rascal, has

nothing better to do than sit around in the middle of nowhere, waiting for a man he only met once?"

"Yeah, I see your point. You think he's up to something?"

"I'd be surprised if he wasn't. Let's see if there is a trap to spring. I want you to go down there."

"Me?"

"Talk to Samar. I'll cover you. If there is anything suspicious, fall to the ground. If I see anything suspicious, then the shooting will start. Again, fall to the ground. Preferably without bullet holes in you. Leave your pack and weapons—no, take the Beretta with you, to have nothing would be unusual—and go and say hi."

"What am I, a tethered goat?"

"Yeah. Big career change. One for the better. Walk slowly down there. Let them see you coming."

"All the more time to shoot me," Douglas muttered as he laid his rifle and sports bag aside. He tucked the Beretta pistol into the front of his waistband, knowing that it went against all good gun-safety rules and not giving a rat's ass.

Bolan watched him stand, take a quick drink of water, then begin his slow trek down to the vans.

CHAPTER SIXTEEN

The Executioner moved.

Quickly and silently he ran halfway down the dune, then turned left, moving as rapidly as possible. He wanted to circle the two vans, coming up in Samar's blind spot while the two Djiboutian men were being distracted by Douglas. He turned again to the left, fifty yards from his last position. Reaching the top of the rise, he observed Douglas with his hands held out at his sides, slowly approaching the two Africans. Both men were on their feet, displaying their empty hands. Samar appeared to be smiling, but Bolan couldn't be sure. What was certain was that both parties were distracted by each other.

He hurried down the side of the dune toward the road, keeping an eye on the vans. Still nothing suspicious. Maybe they were who Douglas said they were. Still the three men hadn't seen him. Then he was on the tarmac. He moved to a position where he couldn't be observed and ran toward the back of the closer van, the one with its hood up. Once by the rear bumper he crouch-walked forward, listening all the time for activity inside the van or close by. He reached the front wheel, still out of sight, listening to the conversation Douglas was having with Samar, ready for anything.

DOUGLAS FELT THE SWEAT run down his face, his back—
in fact he was sweating everywhere. He cursed Blanski for making him do this, felt sure that a dozen rifles
were pointing at him from unseen gunmen. He pre-
tended to stagger sideways, well away from Blanski's
line of fire. Below he observed Samar and the other
man getting to their feet. Could Blanski shoot them
before they shot him? Probably, but the man could also
miss. Douglas slipped on loose stones, almost falling.
His arms windmilling, he cursed Blanski again. The
two Africans watched, a faint smile on the younger
man's face. Douglas reached the bottom of the dune.
He self-consciously brushed the sand from his clothes
as he approached the men. He put a big grin on his
face and held out his hand to Samar.

"Mr. Samar, how wonderful to see you again."

Samar ignored the proffered, sweaty, dirty hand
and merely bowed. Douglas, realizing his faux pas,
lowered his arm and bowed likewise.

"Mr. Douglas, it is indeed an honor to be in your
presence again." Samar's voice was high-pitched,
something Douglas had forgotten. He did note that
the youth was slowly moving his hand toward his robe.
His Beretta pistol felt a million miles away. Was Blanski seeing this? He hoped so. He wished that he had
brought his water bottle, not only for himself but to
pass around, keep the other guys' hands busy.

"This is my son, Omar," Samar continued. "As you
can see, we have brought you transport, something you
can use on your journey. It will not cost you much. I
do it as a favor to poor Mr. Saint-Verran, who, as you
know, died very recently. He was a very nice man, al-

ways kind, always with interesting information for my business."

"I am grateful for your kindness, Samar," Douglas said.

The African nodded. "Then, Mr. Douglas, tell me, are you alone?"

Douglas didn't want to give away Blanski's position nor did he want to lie to Samar before the game had been played out.

"Maybe."

The two Africans scanned the ridge from where they had seen Douglas appear. There was nothing to see, and clearly unsatisfied, they turned back to Douglas, the young man's hand now inside his robes. Douglas began to inch his hand toward the Beretta pistol.

"We have listened to stories, Mr. Douglas. Stories that say two American white men were with an aid convoy when it was hijacked by the FRUD." Samar spit into the dust, the young man doing likewise. "The police and the army are very interested in these two Americans. They left after killing all of the rebels. They say that the Americans need protection from retaliation. They need help. There is talk of a reward. Now you stand before me, all alone. I ask you again, where is your friend?"

"I'm sure he's somewhere close by. Let's talk instead about what information you have for me."

"No. I do not like standing so close to you when the army and police want to talk to you. I think that we should turn you in. I have already called my friend, the army chief of Obcock. He is waiting for me to call back. I am sure that the reward will be most favorable."

The young man sniggered and began to draw what looked like a revolver from the folds of his robes. Douglas felt a shiver run down his spine.

"Where is your friend, Mr. Douglas?"

"Right here."

All three men jumped and spun. Bolan was down on one knee behind the broken-down Renault, his M-16 pointing straight at the younger man's head. Douglas had no idea how Blanski had managed to get into position so silently, without being seen. The young man seemed equally stunned but not stunned enough to do something stupid. He allowed the vintage Webley revolver to fall from his fingers and slowly raised his hands. Bolan indicated with his rifle barrel that Samar should do likewise.

Samar glowered first at Bolan, then at Douglas. He spit again. "American treachery. We came here in good faith and now you threaten to kill us and steal our vans. You Americans think that you can do as you please."

"Hey," Douglas said. "You're the one who wanted to turn us over to the army."

"Ha! You are as big an idiot as Saint-Verran said. Could be led around like a blind dog. You think that I talk to the army? That I would communicate with someone like General Bouh? He would have me shot. You think I come out here alone, with only one son to greet you, if I was to turn you over to army? You are big fool. Saint-Verran was right about you. Big foolish American."

Douglas visibly reddened at the insults and innuendos from Samar. But Bolan wasn't interested in what the Frenchman had said in the past. He lowered the rifle muzzle.

"Put your hands down. All we need to know is what's going on. The trail leads us here. We need to know what you know, and we need your vehicle. I assure you that you will be compensated."

Samar eyed Bolan. "I am not interested in your money, American. That's right, not interested. What I know is that General Bouh has shut down the border between here and Eritrea. Nothing gets in or out. One of my sons was shot at last week for straying too close to the border. Now everything has to go by sea or through Somalia. More dangerous, more bribes to pay."

"And reports of mercenaries? Or other Americans?"

Samar shrugged. "I know very little more. Saint-Verran sent some people up north before Bouh stepped in. I know nothing more."

"So what do you want?" Douglas asked.

"Open the border, foolish one."

"We can't do that," Bolan replied. "We aren't here to fight the army. We're here to find out what happened to the two Americans. Nothing more."

Samar spit yet again. "Then you are truly useless. I will expect a generous payment for the van. Otherwise do not contact me again." Samar made a move to walk away. His son started to bend over to retrieve the revolver.

"We can't let you go, either," Bolan said.

Samar stopped moving; his son froze. "You would kill us, American? Shoot us in cold blood? I hear stories from Iraq about your brutality, are they all true? Then shoot us, cowardly American."

"I'm not going to shoot you, just detain you for a

short while. I don't want you running to the authorities just yet."

Samar laughed. "Foolish American. There are only two directions out here, north or south. South leads to Obcock, and the army and police are already looking for you there. The only direction you can go is north, and they will look for you there, as well. You need to go now if you do not want to be caught too soon. As for me, I never talk to the army unless they want to buy something, and I never sell them information."

"So why were you waiting for us?"

"To see what your friend looked like. Why else? I have heard the stories, stories of big shoot-outs in the city, of two white men causing death, killing people on trains. Taking weapons from my friends in the city. Yes, Mr. Douglas, your stories reach far and wide. I knew where your safehouse was. My friends were watching it for a long time. Then your friend goes and 'buys' things from them." Samar eyed Bolan. "So this is why we wait. To see who has been so busy in the city, in my country. Now I know. So, are you going to detain us? We showed up in good faith. We brought transport. We came alone. We could have brought army or others. We did not. And you dishonor us by making us prisoners?"

"Sorry," Bolan said, "but it is for your own good."

"Ha!"

"If the army learns that you supplied us with a vehicle, something we call aiding and abetting, then they will come after you. If it looks like we stole from you, then they should leave you alone."

Samar stopped to consider that. His eyes narrowed. "You lock us in van with water? So that we not die?"

Bolan nodded.

"Very well, then lock us in. I tell whoever finds us that we were robbed."

The Executioner escorted the two Afars into the back of the broken van, removing a cell phone and two sets of vehicle keys from Samar and a knife from his son. Once the two men were secure in the back of the van, he made a quick inspection of the second Renault, checking it for tracking devices or explosives. Douglas, meanwhile, trudged up the side of the dune to recover their equipment. When he returned with the bags, he found his partner already sitting in the passenger seat, waiting for him.

"Leave me to do all the legwork," Douglas complained.

"The exercise was good for you," Bolan murmured. "Quit bellyaching and climb in."

Douglas, muttering under his breath, got into the van and started the engine. He was about to drive away when Blanski spoke up.

"I'm concerned," the Executioner stated.

"About?"

"You."

"Why?"

"You make more noise than a bull in a china shop. You find it difficult to keep up. You can't shoot straight. One of these things may cost you your life. That's why I want to part ways. You take the other van with Samar and his son back to Obcock town and wait for me there. I'll go on alone, check back with you once I find something."

Douglas was silent, gripping the steering wheel tightly. Bolan could see the CIA man grinding his teeth. Douglas turned to face Bolan, a scowl deeply etched across his face.

"Fuck you, Blanski. Why is it everybody, no matter what I do, thinks I'm a screwup? The Agency thinks I'm a screwup, so they stick me here. My ex-wife thinks I'm a screwup, so she leaves me. And now I learn even Saint-Verran was laughing at me, telling stories to his smuggler friends. The French think I'm a screwup. And now you? Fuck you and everyone else!"

"Finished?"

"Yes. No. I'm in this till the end. No matter what. Even if it means I'm full of bullet holes. At least there'll be no alimony anymore. You are not kicking me out of this. I want to find out what's going on around here."

Bolan considered him and changed his mind.

"All right, you can stay. Just follow my lead, and keep your head down. There's also something you should know."

"And that is?"

"I haven't been to this region before, but I have been to nearby Somalia and Eritrea many times. It is one of the most dangerous places in the world. I go into every situation knowing that I may not survive. I have gone up against the best. I have almost died more times than I can count. You have to be willing to risk your life, even in a situation like now, where we don't understand what's going on. You have to be ready to die for something you believe in, and that is doing the right thing. Somebody wrote something along the lines of 'the greatest sin is to stand by and do nothing.' Are you prepared for that?"

"I'm still sitting here, aren't I? I'm not doing this for the Agency or to find out who killed Saint-Verran. I'm doing this to find out who tried to kill me. I'm doing this because, for once in my career, in my life, I want to do the right thing. To achieve something. So, should I drive this thing or not?"

Bolan smiled. "Yeah, we'd better start putting some distance between us and them. There's one other thing you should consider."

Douglas fired the ignition and drove the van away, heading north. "What?"

"Samar was probably lying about Saint-Verran. Or Saint-Verran lied to him about you. If the Frenchman really thought you were an idiot, then he would never have imparted the information to you back in the hotel. He wouldn't have ever passed anything on."

"Yeah. Yeah. Maybe. And I'll try to be quieter than a pregnant whale next time, okay?"

Bolan nodded, then sat back, watching the horizon, the road, the rocks, looking for any sign of danger.

THE HELICOPTER BUZZED them half an hour later. It was an old sand-colored French Aérospatiale 350 Ecureuil, capable of carrying two pilots and four passengers. Although designed originally as a Navy utility helicopter, it was more than capable of being used as a gunship. Bolan observed that it was armed with a 7.62 mm gun pod. He also saw the bright blue, green and white concentric circles with a red star at the center, which meant that the chopper belonged to the military.

"Shit!" Douglas yelled over the roar of the rotors as the chopper flew directly overhead, whipping up a sandstorm. "Shit! Aren't you going to shoot them?"

Bolan wound down the passenger window and leaned out, getting a better look at the markings on the helicopter. "No. Our argument is with FRUD and maybe the mercenaries. Not the military. Besides, their guns are bigger than ours." Bolan wondered if the military had found Samar first or they had just been spotted from high above. They hadn't made much progress in the past hour. The road had turned into a stone track, making it difficult to drive very fast. Either way it didn't matter. Discovered was discovered.

"I didn't think they had any more of those choppers," Douglas shouted. "They switched over to Russian equipment years ago."

It didn't matter to Bolan what make the helicopter was. He watched it as it spun a hundred yards ahead of them. The way the helicopter lowered its nose gave Bolan an advance warning of what was about to happen.

"Get down!" he roared and ducked in his own seat, even as Douglas was struggling to do the same. The van slid on the stones, the engine stalling as Douglas squeezed behind the steering wheel.

The helicopter opened fire.

Heavy-caliber bullets churned up the ground twenty yards in front of the van, throwing rocks and dirt high into the air. Stones and gravel peppered and shook the Renault like buckshot, the sound of the machine gun reverberating like a thunder roll. Bolan had his hand on the door ready to open and jump out, yet he held back. Not one bullet came close to the van. It was all for show, a demonstration of power. If the people in the helicopter wanted them dead, then they would have opened fire in a strafing run and not bothered with a flyby.

The military performance lasted all of three seconds. Bolan raised his head to witness the helicopter land on its skis, disgorging four men in army uniform, all equipped with what appeared to be FAMAS F1 assault rifles. Once the soldiers were clear, the helicopter lifted off, keeping its minigun trained on the van. The soldiers fanned out, all rifles up and ready to fire, cautiously moving toward their target.

"What now?" Douglas raised his head above the dashboard. He sounded nervous to Bolan.

"Play it by ear. Other than leaving the scene of a gunfight, we've done nothing wrong."

"We left a pile of bodies back in the city, as well."

"Yeah, there's that. Maybe they won't take it into consideration."

"You think?"

The two men exited the van, their hands held high. The soldiers gestured to the Americans, indicating that they should move to the side of the track. The helicopter continued circling, its gun trained on the van. One of the soldiers barked an order at Bolan and Douglas, but neither man understood it. The soldier looked angrily at them, resenting the fact that he would have to speak English.

"On knee. Hand on head."

The Americans moved slowly over to the side of the track, getting down onto their knees and placing their hands on top of their heads.

"Shit, they're going to shoot us in the back," Douglas muttered.

"No talk!" the soldier snapped as he began patting

them down, removing the Beretta pistols and magazines. Bolan didn't believe that they were going to be executed. The helicopter could have done that easily enough. No, they were wanted for interrogation. He listened as two soldiers split off and began searching the van. In no time the bags were found and hauled out for inspection, the contents tipped onto the ground. The soldiers spoke among themselves. Another thought popped into Bolan's head: it would be getting dark soon. The other two soldiers, including the one who had snapped orders at them, kept their French bullpup rifles trained on Bolan and Douglas the whole time. Not a word was spoken to the prisoners. Eventually Douglas could stand it no longer.

"What do you want with us?"

"No talk!"

Douglas shut his mouth, and they waited. And waited. They knelt for more than half an hour before they detected the thunder of a heavy engine in the distance. As it drew closer, Bolan believed it to be that of a tank or an armored personnel carrier. At the same time the helicopter landed and began powering down its rotors. The roar of the engine peaked, then decreased as the vehicle came to a halt, the driver putting the unseen machine into Neutral. The soldiers snapped to attention as a door was opened and somebody jumped out onto the track. The gravel crunched as that person approached the soldiers.

Bolan listened intently, trying to decipher what was happening. Obviously somebody in authority had shown up in an APC. It wasn't a tank because he had not heard the sound of tank tracks. The soldiers were reporting; Bolan didn't understand a word. He made out the soldiers picking up the weapons out of the bags, holding them out for inspection. There was the familiar sound of bolts being drawn back on the M-16 and Skorpion machine pistols. Beside him Douglas tensed, expecting the worst. Then the newcomer approached.

"Get up," the newcomer whispered. "Turn around. Slowly. Keep your hands on your heads."

They got shakily to their knees and turned. Standing in front of them was the most scarred man the Executioner had ever seen. The guy's face was a crisscross of knife wounds, the most prominent one across the throat. Somebody had taken a real dislike to the guy sometime in the past and had to have left him for dead. The man was also completely bald, the crown of his head equally scarred. Bolan briefly wondered what had happened to him, then decided he didn't care. He focused on what the man was holding: in one hand a Skorpion, in the other a large machete. Behind the man idled a six-wheeled Ratel APC, its turret gun trained on Douglas and Bolan. But Bolan knew that it couldn't fire so long as Scarface was standing in the way.

Scarface leaned in close to Bolan, staring him right in the eye. Bolan returned the gaze, his eyes chips of ice that gave nothing away. Scarface sneered, the remains of his top lip twisted upward. He then turned his attention to Douglas, who was far easier to intimidate and began to wilt under the intense hate that emanated from the man. Scarface sneered again.

"So, little CIA spy man, what brings you so far from home?" the man rasped. Bolan suspected that Scarface was unable to speak any louder.

"I, er, we were out for a drive in the country..."

Douglas got no further with his halfhearted quip. Scarface's right hand shot out, slamming the barrel of the machine pistol hard into Douglas's stomach. Douglas made a whooshing sound, taken completely by surprise, and dropped to his knees, his hands automatically clutching his abdomen. Bolan tensed but didn't move. The four soldiers all had their rifles trained on him, their fingers on the triggers.

Scarface looked over to Bolan, his eyebrow raised as if in invitation to act. Bolan refused to be baited, so Scarface turned his attention back to the groaning Douglas. Scarface bent his knees slightly and placed the razor-sharp edge of the machete under the American's chin. Douglas stopped groaning, knowing that he was in mortal danger. Moving only his eyes, he looked up into the leering face of his captor.

"Tell one more lie, and I will open you up. Again, what are you doing so far from home? And you will address me as Captain Xiblinti, since you are dressed like soldiers."

Douglas spoke through clenched teeth. "I...we... were looking for the FRUD insurgents. We'd learned that they were behind the attacks on aid convoys. We...I needed to spy on them. That's all. Captain."

"That's all? Really, Mr. Spy, is that all? And what about your friend here? No, you be quiet," he snapped at Bolan. "Mr. Spy here is going to tell me everything."

"He's, he's a journalist. We teamed up. I thought I could use him, use his contacts to help me find the FRUD."

"A journalist? A journalist who can shoot as well as he can? A journalist who, according to witnesses, can leap from a truck onto a fast train, then fight on the roof? I do not believe you. I told you what would happen if you lied."

Bolan felt the situation slipping out of control. This Xiblinti was clearly unstable. It would take only a moment for him to slice off Douglas's head.

"I used to be in the Army before I became a journalist," Bolan said quickly.

Xiblinti's eyes narrowed as his attention turned to Bolan. "I ordered you not to speak. But it doesn't matter." Xiblinti moved fast, the machete flickering away from Douglas to become lodged under Bolan's chin. Several of the soldiers sniggered, expecting to see an execution. Bolan braced himself, ready to grab the machete and turn it against its wielder, make a play for the Skorpion, then use it against the soldiers. Extremely risky but better than dying without doing anything.

"I am sure that you were in the Army," Xiblinti said, sneering. "I think you still are. The general is most interested in meeting with you before you die. And you will die. You will join the pig Samar in having his stomach exposed to the air." Xiblinti removed the machete from Bolan's throat and slapped the flat of the blade against his cheek. Xiblinti turned away and motioned to one of the soldiers, who shouldered his rifle and stepped forward, removing two pairs of metal handcuffs from his pockets. Bolan's and Douglas's hands were secured behind their backs.

Xiblinti grinned or sneered at them, Bolan was unable to tell which, and pointed to the APC. The soldier who had just handcuffed them pushed them both forward with the barrel of his rifle. The meaning couldn't have been clearer. They were frog-marched to the rear of the APC and shoved inside. Bolan maintained his

balance as he was forced in, but Douglas fell face-
first on the metal floor. He gasped from the pain of
landing on his nose. One of the soldiers clambered in
and began kicking Douglas in the ribs, all the while
screaming at him.

Bolan turned, ready to kick back, but was prevented
from doing so by Xiblinti, who climbed in through
the side door, squeezing past the legs of the gunner
in the turret and pointing the Skorpion at Bolan. He
indicated with the barrel that Bolan should sit in the
rear on one of two wooden benches. Hissing something at the soldier beating Douglas, Xiblinti turned
and entered the driving cabin, pushing past a large
red leather chair.

The soldier kicking Douglas stopped. Bending forward he lifted Douglas by his handcuffs, forcing the
CIA man's arms high up behind his back. Douglas
screeched in pain, but it was lost as the APC engines
thundered and shook to life. The soldier pushed him
hard, over toward Bolan. Douglas straightened, banging his head on the metal roof. The soldier laughed,
grabbed the man by the shoulders, twisted him around
and forced him to sit on the wooden bench next to
Bolan. Douglas gasped as he slammed down onto the
bench, the back of his head impacting with the armored side of the APC.

Douglas cursed as he bent forward, his face almost
touching his knees. The soldier who had kicked him
sat opposite, a large grin plastered across his face,
clearly enjoying Douglas's discomfort. A second soldier climbed in, pulling the crew hatch closed behind
him. There was a moment of darkness before the interior cabin lights came on.

The Ratel lurched forward as the soldier sat down, facing Bolan, their knees touching. The soldier stared at him, unblinking, safe in the belief that the two Westerners were subdued. Bolan ignored the soldier, turning to take in Douglas's condition. The CIA agent raised himself so that his head was resting against the metal wall. Blood streamed down his face and onto his clothes. His nose was clearly out of alignment. The man's eyes were closed tight. He winced every time the APC lurched, which was every few seconds.

"Bet you wished you'd stayed behind now," Bolan said. The two soldiers didn't react to Bolan's statement. They either didn't understand English, or they just didn't care what was said; the prisoners couldn't do anything anyway.

"What, and be disemboweled along with Samar and his son? No, thanks. But I am going to kill that scarfaced bastard." Douglas spoke through red-stained gritted teeth. "I take it you have a plan for escape?"

Bolan didn't answer. He turned back to face the soldier and closed his eyes. He didn't plan on escaping, not yet. He was too curious about where they were going. Another piece of the puzzle had landed at Bolan's feet when Xiblinti mentioned "the General." The same general as the one the oil surveyors had reported to? He figured that it had to be. There couldn't be that many generals in so tiny a country. And they couldn't be so far from their destination, either. The Ratel was covering the ground far faster than their van could have done. But where did the army fit in? Did the thugs they had encountered back in Djibouti City belong to the same group that had ambushed them earlier in the day? Were they in the employ of the general or were they another group altogether? Bolan knew that he was failing to connect the dots, that he was missing a large part of the puzzle. He could only hope that when they arrived at their destination he would find more answers.

And not a firing squad.

CHAPTER SEVENTEEN

The Ratel jerked to a halt half an hour later. Xiblinti began issuing orders even as he shut down the engine. One soldier opened the hatch, the second soldier kept an eye on Bolan and Douglas. The soldier manning the turret gun lowered himself. Up until now, Bolan had seen only the man's legs. In reality he was a carbon copy of the other two. Xiblinti ordered something, and the two soldiers began herding and pushing Bolan and Douglas outside into the fading daylight.

Bolan allowed Douglas to lean on him; the CIA man was in a bad way. Bolan had no idea how hard Douglas had hit his head, but it had sounded awful at the time. Outside, the first soldier was joined by several more, all of whom kept their FAMAS rifles pointed at Bolan's and Douglas's faces. The Executioner glanced quickly around, taking in the surroundings.

The Ratel was parked in the middle of a military camp; desert-camouflaged tents surrounded them. The site was based at the foot of a hill. Other Djiboutian soldiers milled around, all eyes on the two captives. Another APC was parked nearby, this one a four-wheeler. Bolan didn't get chance to identify the make as he was pushed forward by a rifle butt in his back. Xiblinti appeared, leading the way to a large army tent where a guard was standing outside. Bolan and Douglas followed, prodded along by the soldiers. Xiblinti whispered something to the guard, who opened the tent flap slightly, coughed discreetly and muttered something to the occupant. A second later the guard turned and nodded at Xiblinti. The flap was held aside, and the two men were driven forward.

The interior was opulent. Tapestries hung from the canvas walls. To Bolan's left was a full-size bed, complete with duvets and cushions. Opposite was a broad oak desk, which would have cost several thousand dollars in America. A detailed map of Djibouti hung on the tent wall behind the desk. The only chair in the room was occupied by the largest man Bolan had seen in Africa in quite some time. The guy was huge in all directions; most of the bulk seemed to be made up of rolls of fat. The gargantuan man wore a parade military uniform, tailored to his girth, covered with medal ribbons. Adorning the man's bulbous head was a red beret the size of a dinner plate; a gold badge peaked above the man's left eye. Bolan knew he was looking at the general who had been mentioned so often in the past several days. Whoever he was, the man wasn't going hungry like the rest of his countrymen. The general didn't deign to look up from his desk, where he was pretending to study some paperwork.

"Bouh," Douglas muttered under his breath but not quietly enough. The general slowly looked up from the papers, staring at the two men brought before him. His lip curled back in disgust as he took in the CIA man's bloody condition. Douglas swayed slightly. The general looked down at the captive's feet, no doubt, Bolan thought, to make sure that no blood was dripping inside the tent. Douglas's nose had stopped bleeding a short while before.

Bouh snorted in contempt and turned his gaze to Bolan. The Executioner had no problem in returning the man's stare. Bouh refused to back down, safe in the knowledge that he had several dozen men waiting nearby. Bolan decided to look away, allowing the general to think that he had won this little pissing contest. The general smiled thinly. Finally he spoke, a deep voice matching his size, with an underlying English accent that likely meant Bouh had received officer training in Britain.

"So, Mr. Douglas of America's CIA, I see you remember me from that silly function at your embassy a few months ago. I am honored."

Xiblinti hissed gleefully at the general's mirth. Bouh raised a hand, a silent order to stop.

"Tell me, Mr. Douglas, what happened to your face? You do not look so well."

A bead of sweat dribbled down Douglas's face, leaving a stain through the accumulated dirt and grime. "I fell onto the gun Captain Xiblinti was holding. Then I fell onto my nose, then onto the boots of one of your soldiers. Then I banged my head and banged it again," Douglas said.

"Hmm, that was clumsy of you. Americans are clumsy people. But I see you have found a friend, a new friend after that unfortunate incident at the hotel. Terrible, terrible. Allow me to express my condolences at the death of your French compatriot. I am sure that the criminals responsible will be brought to justice soon."

"Are we your prisoners?" Douglas rasped. The dry

blood and equally dry mouth prevented Douglas from speaking naturally.

"Are you my prisoners? Mr. Douglas, you are amusing. You come here, dressed like soldiers, you carry all sorts of weaponry, you do deals with known smugglers and you shoot FRUD insurgents like it was—what is that irritating phrase?—oh, a walk in the park. I can only assume that you are spies. And I must say the uniform does not become you. You look uncomfortable in it. Whereas your very silent friend here does look very comfortable. Tell me, Mr. Blanski—yes, I know your name—tell me, what rank were you in your Army?"

Bolan thought for a moment. The best covers always closely skirted the truth.

"Sergeant," he answered truthfully.

"Really? So low? You possess extraordinary skills, I am told. Yet my friends in Camp Lemonnier can find out nothing about you. It is as if you do not exist, which leads me to conclude that you are some sort of Special Forces working for the CIA. You shoot up criminals in Djibouti City, you make amazing jumps onto speeding trains, you take out an ambush of nasty FRUD rebels, and you arrive in my country just after a piracy incident in our national waters. Really quite amazing, Sergeant."

"You didn't answer Peter's question, General," Bolan said. "Are we prisoners?"

"You are in no position to ask questions. However, we are going to keep you here. For your own protection. Safe, while we take care of those awful rebels that plague my country."

"And the American oilmen? Are they under your protection, as well?"

A dark cloud crossed Bouh's face for an instant, before the false jolliness returned. "Of course they are. Unfortunately Djibouti is a very dangerous country. The gentlemen from Mr. Trenchard are very safe. In fact, I was just working on a lease here to grant Trenchard exclusive oil rights in Djibouti. A deal that will be good for everybody."

"Including yourself."

"Mr. Blanski, you pain me. My only wish is to see Djibouti prosper, not to see its honest citizens die from thirst. And now you begin to bore me." Once more the fake humor left Bouh's face, only this time it stayed away. "So instead, let me tell you about your future. Do not worry. It will not be a long story. It seems that you were kidnapped by rebels, who then executed you as punishment for shooting their friends. Your bodies will be discovered by my men tomorrow. Of course, the rebels made you suffer first. You corpses will be found in the most appalling condition. Very hard to identify. Captain, take them to join the men they have spent so much time looking for. They can swap tales of woe that will make the Trenchard men even more compliant."

Xiblinti snapped to attention. "Outside!" he ordered Bolan and Douglas, while saluting the general. Bouh was inspecting the papers again, no longer interested in the two Americans.

They were ushered from the tent by Xiblinti. It was already dark; the air felt slightly cooler. Douglas stood, wavering. When the Djiboutian captain pushed him forward, Douglas staggered, gasping, but managed to keep his balance. Bolan turned to face Xiblinti.

"Do that again, and I'll kill you here in front of

your men, with my hands behind my back," he said in a graveyard voice. Xiblinti sneered but took a step backward. Instead of following up on the challenge, he waved four soldiers over, issuing them orders. Once finished, he stepped in close to Bolan, staring him in the eye, completely unafraid of the iced look Bolan was giving him.

"It is you who will do the dying, American. Very shortly. Very slowly."

One of the soldiers grabbed Bolan by his arm, leading him away. A second soldier stood back, rifle ready to fire. Douglas was given a similar treatment. They were led upward along a stony path, out of the camp, toward a dark hole in the side of the hill. A cave, Bolan realized. Two more soldiers stood by the opening, bookends for the darkness behind them.

Bolan began to feel more than a little concerned. In a cave they would be trapped with only one way out. If Xiblinti was competent, then more guards would be placed at the mouth. Then there was Douglas. The Agency man was groaning and wheezing a lot, which probably meant broken ribs and possible concussion from the beating that he had taken. There was no way Bolan could effect an escape with an injured man in tow. But he couldn't be left behind, either. And where would he escape to and how effective would he be? He had no idea how many Djiboutian soldiers were in the camp below, plus there were the two APCs that he had seen. Not to forget there was a helicopter gunship that could be called upon. And he currently had no idea what state the two oil prospectors would be in, though he was about to find out. The situation did not have a positive outlook to it.

Bolan was forced to bend at the cave mouth as his head scrapped the hard rough rock. Douglas was shorter than Bolan, and so managed to stagger in, helped by a shove from an unsmiling soldier. They were pushed several yards into the darkness before they both suddenly fell forward, almost in unison, kicked in the back of the knees by their armed escorts. The cave floor was sand, lessening the impact. Bolan quickly rolled over, struggling to sit upright, with his hands behind his back. Douglas just lay there, moaning. Bolan could just make out the shapes of the soldiers as they exited. Otherwise it was pitch-black. Douglas groaned again.

"Quiet," Bolan said. "Get your wits together. We need to get out of this mess."

"Who's there?" A voice spoke up from farther inside the cave, thin, weary. Bolan turned his head in that direction, even though there was nothing to see.

"My name's Mike. My friend on the floor is Peter. We're journalists. Are you the guys from Trenchard?"

There was a pair of yeses as another voice joined in. The second voice sounded. "Are they looking for us? Are we about to be rescued?"

Bolan paused, then decided to tell the men the truth. It would serve no purpose, lying to them, and he needed answers. General Bouh was involved in something, and he needed to know what.

"No, apart from us, nobody knows you are here. Sorry."

A disappointed silence fell, broken by Douglas's agonized coughing.

"Do you have any water?" Bolan asked. "I suspect that they broke his ribs."

"Yes," the first man replied. "I have it here. A little. It's all we've got. They don't allow us very much."

"They've got our families," the second man added.

"Twohig, we'll tell him in a minute." There was scrabbling in the darkness, then, "I can feel the back of this man's head. He needs to sit up."

"Peter," Bolan ordered, "sit up."

"I...I can't. My hands are cuffed" was the muted reply.

"Then stay there and die. It's your choice."

There was a long groan, followed by "I really am beginning to hate you," followed by more groaning.

Eventually Douglas had his back to the rugged wall. Fingers poked him in the face, found his mouth, pulled down on his chin. The rim of a cup was thrust clumsily into his mouth, and warm water was poured in. Douglas choked and coughed, and the cup was hastily pulled away. Once the spasm had stopped, the cup found his mouth again, and Douglas drank deeply. The cup was quickly emptied. Douglas put his head back against the stone, wincing when one of the many bruised lumps touched the cold side. He muttered a thank-you to the darkness.

The cup was somehow refilled, and Bolan found it at his lips. He, too, drank, knowing that it would revitalize him for the action that he had in mind. But first some answers were needed.

"What are your names?" he asked.

"I'm John Sanner," answered the man who had given him the water. "My colleague is Matt Twohig. He's in bad shape."

"What happened to him?"

"He tried to run, but that scar-faced asshole caught

him and beat him to within an inch of his life. He needs medical attention."

"Yeah, I've experienced Scarface's friendliness," Douglas said.

"How long have you been here?" Bolan asked .

"Well, I don't know. We've been kept in here for what seems like years. I don't know how much longer they'll keep us alive. Not long, I think. There has been lots of activity outside the last couple of days. Tell me what you know, then I may be able to fill you in."

Bolan leaned back against the cave wall and thought about what he knew for a fact and what he suspected. "I suspect that Bouh is trying to pull some sort of coup, but I'm not sure where you fit in. A Frenchman your company hired was assassinated."

"I didn't know that."

"And one of the two guides who brought you up here was also murdered."

"Oh, no."

"The other guide was still alive when we left him. We know you left the country, then came back. We know from the surviving guide that you communicated with General Bouh to inform him that there was no oil. Since the car bombing of the Waverley Hotel…"

"There was a car bomb?"

"Yeah, it was how they killed the Frenchman. Since the bombings, there have been several attempts to kill Peter and myself. Every time it seems like rebels are behind it, but I now think that Bouh has been prodding them into action. There have been unconfirmed reports that there is a group of mercenaries in the area, but we haven't seen anyone yet."

"They are about six miles to the north of here," Sanner interrupted.

"Right. But what role they play I don't know. Aid shipments are being intercepted by the rebels. Whether Bouh is using the food to feed his troops or just cause disruption, or both, I also don't know. In fact, there are a lot of gaps. So why don't you fill some of them in. Why are you here, and why did you leave and then return?"

"We never left," Twohig muttered in the darkness. "And what about my kids?"

"Let's start back a bit first," Sanner said. "Somehow Bouh got into contact with Trenchard. I don't know how. Something we have learned since we arrived is that Trenchard Oil Industries is going under. This is Trenchard's last grasp of the straws. He was led to believe that there was an untapped oil field here, a covert oil strike other companies had somehow missed. We were sent to assess it. We were told that we first had to report to General Bouh, on entering the country. So we came up here and found exactly nothing. We told him this via radio, and he wanted to meet us in person in Obcock for a report before we made contact with Trenchard. It is unusual, but we thought that this was just an African thing.

"So we left our guides in Obcock City and saw Bouh. He captured us, held us at gunpoint, told us unless we falsified our reports to America he would kill us, then kill our families. He showed us pictures of our kids going to school, our wives at the mall. He gave us all the materials we needed to fake a report, to tell Trenchard that there was an oil field, just ready and waiting for him. That Bouh was promising us we would have exclusive rights to it."

"Faking such a report can't be easy. Other experts would spot it, surely?" Bolan asked.

"Yeah, normally you would be right. But Robert Trenchard is desperate. He's been lying to everybody about his reserves, how much cash is in the bank. The authorities have no idea. Bouh told us this much."

"So what does Bouh get from a false report?"

"Money. Trenchard is backing him to the hilt. Borrowing heavily from other parties. Promises of building water desalination plants along the coast, of modernizing the harbor to take tankers, all that sort of thing. Trenchard thinks he is buying a country. Bouh and Trenchard hired the mercenaries. I have no idea what he is using them for, but I heard something about training Eritrean dogs, whatever that means. And he aims to drive America out of its base by the airport. The French would go, as well."

"Lemonnier," Bolan stated.

"Yeah, right!" Douglas added. "Like his ragtag soldiers and a gang of mercs could force out the US Marines. The US of A is keeping the current government afloat."

"Unless he intends to force them out some other way," Bolan said.

"How?"

"I'm not sure. He would first have to have the troops confined to barracks."

"They are already," Douglas said. "Since the city is so unsafe, they aren't allowed to have leave there. But it would take more than a few angry citizens to get Uncle Sam to pack up and leave. Bouh would need some sort of catalyst to drive the Marines and Navy away."

Bolan sat upright. "The Navy. And a catalyst. Is Bouh behind that, as well?"

"Who are you talking to now? Me?" Douglas queried.

"Yes. No. Let me think. Be quiet for a moment."

The cave fell silent, the quiet broken only by groans from Twohig and the occasional ones from Douglas. Bolan was lost in thought.

Eventually he broke the silence. "Sanner?"

"Yeah." The voice sounded nearby.

"Your hands aren't bound, are they?"

"No. We aren't considered much of a threat."

"Good. I want you to find my boots, untie them and pull them off."

"Okay." There was movement, hands touching his legs, then Bolan felt Sanner untying his laces, tugging his boots off.

"While you treat us all to your smelly socks," Douglas said, "would you mind informing us great unwashed what you have figured out? See if it differs from my views?"

"This thing is bigger than a mere coup. Bouh is planning to change the balance of power in the whole region. He's working with al Qaeda elements. That was what Zaid abu Qutaiba's suicide attack was all about. Sink or damage the USS *Ford*, drive the US troops back inside Lemonnier, have the base on lockdown. Stir up public opinion about the US presence. The French Legionnaires would also be locked down.

"The Eritreans that he's having trained would be used as cannon fodder to cause riots. Once the first gasoline bomb has been thrown against the army or police, then Bouh would move in. He would mount a coup against a weakened government, under the guise of restoring order. I bet that the mercenaries are US and European men. Bouh would then use them as scapegoats, claim that US forces were behind FRUD attacks and other atrocities.

"He could also point to Trenchard Oil Industries, saying, 'look at the greedy Americans, stealing our oil.' He could prove that Trenchard funded the mercenaries. This would enflame the public even more. It would be viewed as another Iraq. Lemonnier would no longer be viable. Bouh would order the US to leave, and we would lose our only sub-Saharan base. No more drone strikes in Yemen. Al Qaeda would move in. This is a Muslim country, remember, and from here they could push on to the rest of Africa. Bouh would be sitting here on the throne, supporting himself on the misery of his people, and the riches of various terror organizations and rogue countries."

"Jesus!" Douglas exclaimed. "How the hell do we tell anybody about this? And what the hell are you doing?"

Bolan was straining, stretching his arms, lying on his back with his knees pulled up almost to his face. He was working his cuffed hands down his legs. The metal chain was now by his ankles. He twisted more, pushing, pulling, his teeth clenched in effort. He wanted to get his hands around to his front. He labored against the unnatural position, forcing the chain down farther, hauling his feet up high. He could feel a cramp building in his muscles. The chain was under his heels now. His arms were stretched as far as they could go. By wriggling his arms he could walk the chain slowly down his feet. Now the chain was by his toes. He curled his toes upward, then pulled with his arms.

In an instant his hands were in front of him, almost hitting him in the face. He gasped and stretched out to relieve the ache in his muscles. After a few seconds he pushed himself back into a sitting position.

"Sanner?"

"Yeah?"

"Put my boots back on, would you? On the right feet."

"Okay," Douglas said, "so your hands are in front of you now. That helps, but I don't see how. What do we do now?"

"Not we. I was wondering how the mercenaries would like to know that they are being set up. And I can only get there alone."

"And my kids?" the forgotten Twohig said from the back of the cave.

"If I can get a message out, then there are people I know in the States who are more than capable of protecting them and neutralizing the threat. I can get help sent here. But I have to get to the mercs first. Six miles north?"

"Yeah, something like that," answered Sanner, who finished fitting Bolan's boots.

"Then I had better get a move on," the Executioner said as he began to tie his laces. Not an easy thing to do, he discovered, with his hands cuffed and in the pitch dark.

"How will you be able to escape?" Sanner asked. "You're a journalist, they're soldiers and…"

Sanner fell silent. There was a noise outside the

mouth of the cave. Talking. Footsteps. Then a flashlight snapped on, blinding three of the four prisoners. Bolan had quickly turned his head away upon hearing the sound of an object being withdrawn from a pocket. He screwed up his eyes, hoping to preserve as much of his night vision as possible. The flashlight shone around the cave, dancing over the men, before settling on Bolan.

"You. Stand."

Bolan slowly stood, still looking away from the flashlight, hoping that the soldiers would think he had been temporarily blinded. He ducked slightly, remembering in time that the cave had a low roof.

"Out. Now."

Bolan moved forward. He wondered if he could get close enough to attack the owner of the flashlight. The soldier holding it seemed to anticipate that and walked backward out of the cave as Bolan approached him. The lamp was turned off as Bolan exited the cave. Blinking he saw two soldiers standing before him, their FAMAS F1 rifles pointing at his chest. They were the same men who had the guard duty in the APC. The one holding the light was the one responsible for kicking Douglas half to death. Both men were smirking with delight.

"Follow," the lead soldier said. He turned, marching toward the camp. The second soldier pushed Bolan forward and fell in behind him.

And Mack Bolan realized that he was about to be tortured and killed.

CHAPTER EIGHTEEN

The Executioner quickly weighed up his options. The moon was full in the sky, illuminating the entire area in a blue-white glow. Xiblinti was standing outside a tent some forty yards ahead, slapping the blade of his machete into his left palm. Even from this distance it was clear that he was grinning in anticipation of what was to happen. So far neither of his guards had noticed that his hands were in front of his body instead of behind his back. If he was to tackle the two guards, then the two by the cave would come to their colleagues' aid. Also the alarm would immediately be raised by Xiblinti. On the other hand, once he reached the tent, escape would be impossible.

No choice, really.

Bolan made his move.

He kicked the lead soldier in the butt with his left foot, not hard enough to hurt, but enough to make the soldier spin in anger, which was exactly what the Executioner had anticipated.

Bolan's right foot shot up hard, impacting at high velocity with the soldier's groin. The guy squealed and automatically bent over. Bolan grabbed the barrel of the FAMAS rifle and wrenched it out of the soldier's hands. In the same movement he pivoted, holding the rifle like a baseball bat, slamming it against the head of the rear soldier. There was a sickening crack, and the surprised man dropped instantly to the ground. The first soldier was on his knees, clutching at his testicles. Bolan completed his spin by smashing the stock against the man's face, shattering the jawbone out of its sockets and sending the man's teeth flying in a spray of blood. The guy spun to the ground, either dead or unconscious, Bolan didn't care. Payback for kicking Douglas and enjoying it.

Now for the tricky bit. Shouts emanated from the cave and from the army camp. A quick check showed Xiblinti had dropped his machete and filled his fist with a sidearm. The two cave guards were unslinging their rifles. Bolan dropped to a crouch. He twisted the rifle around, grabbed the pistol grip. Awkwardly he moved the selector switch to semiautomatic. He rose, holding the bullpup rifle as he would a pistol. It was heavy, off-balance in his cuffed hands, but for the moment, accuracy was not an issue. Keeping the enemies' heads down was.

Bolan brought the weapon to bear on the two cave guards, who were just beginning to open fire. Metal hornets zipped past him as he squeezed the trigger. The FAMAS bucked hard in his hands, the recoil throwing the barrel upward. The bullets missed by a wide margin, but the effect was the same. Both soldiers fell to the ground, desperately scrambling for cover. Bolan twisted at the hips, bringing the muzzle to bear on the scarred killer, who was running toward him, his pistol banging out ineffective shots. Xiblinti saw the danger in time, dropping as Bolan opened fire. The soldier charging behind Xiblinti wasn't so lucky, catching at least one of the hot rounds. The man spun and fell.

Bolan used the brief lull to turn and run.

There was an outcropping not far from his position. He charged toward it, his feet slipping on the loose sand and stone. He could hear more shouting from the camp, followed by a lot more shooting. Some of the shots came close, kicking up the sand, forcing the Executioner to zigzag on the uneven ground.

He skidded several times before reaching cover. Bullets slammed against the black stone and ricocheted into the air. Bolan risked a quick look back at the camp. Men were running around, some partially dressed. Xiblinti had organized a party to advance on Bolan's position; some fired as they slowly approached. There was the roar of a diesel engine as one of the APCs was started. Bolan ducked back behind the rock as several shots came too close for comfort. He eyed the terrain in front of him, looking for a usable advantage. Thirty yards away was a shallow gully, a dried-up riverbed that led into the hills. Bolan got to his feet and ran toward it, ducking to use the rock formation as cover to hide his position.

He rolled down the slope of the gully. It was no more than four feet deep, enough to cover a crouching man. Bolan knew that the hills would offer the best escape and evasion possibilities. Bolan began to crouch-run along the gully.

Behind him came the thunder of a 30 mm machine gun from the armored personnel carrier, a barrage of bullets tearing the rock formation to pieces while providing cover to the advancing troops. It wouldn't take the soldiers long to discover the escapee's trail and mobilize a force to pursue him. The camp easily contained a hundred men, and General Bouh could call up reinforcements at a moment's notice. And somewhere was the helicopter gunship that had been used against them earlier. Bolan increased his pace, hoping to escape into the night.

"THEY'VE STOPPED SHOOTING," Sanner said. "They must have killed him."

Douglas snorted in derision.

"You think he's still alive?"

"I know he's still alive. You haven't seen my boy in action."

"Who is he, if not a journalist?"

"The Lone Ranger," Douglas replied enigmatically. "I guess that makes me Tonto."

BOLAN NEVER SAW his attacker.

The instant he felt the soldier's boots touch his back, Bolan realized his mistake. This was the Djiboutian military, French trained. Not some bunch of misfit amateurs. They were bound to have posted sentries around the perimeter of the camp, and this one possibly had a colleague covering him with his FAMAS rifle. Bolan threw out his bound hands to break his fall, dropping his rifle in the process. The breath was smashed from his body as he slammed into the dirt. He twisted quickly, hoping to throw the sentry from his back. A rifle butt thudded down hard, missing his head by inches. The sentry hurriedly stepped off Bolan, trying to regain the initiative and his balance.

Bolan wasn't in the mood for second chances.

Now flat on his back, he raised his legs, scissoring

them around his attacker. He twisted again, throwing the soldier to the ground. The man yelped and dropped his rifle as he landed on his side, but the guy was agile and scrambled back before Bolan could retaliate any further by kicking the sentry in the face.

The Executioner and the soldier sat up in the dust at the same moment. The sentry spotted Bolan's cuffed hands and grinned, clearly believing that he had the tactical advantage. He whipped out a knife from a scabbard on his belt and held it aloft for Bolan to see. Mack Bolan knew that he didn't have time for a prolonged fight. He could hear the rest of the search party firing odd shots as they approached. He began to push himself backward through the sand and stones of the riverbed, using the heels of his boots, hoping to put a little distance between himself and the sentry.

The African soldier was having none of it. The guy, grinning, launched himself upward and outward, aiming to land on top of Bolan and plunge the knife through his neck. It was a fatal mistake. The night once again came alive with the sound of autofire. A dozen bullets tore the man apart the moment he raised his body above the gully. The bullet-riddled corpse landed at Bolan's feet even as a cheer went up from the advancing soldiers, believing that they had killed their prey.

Bolan rolled over and pushed himself up into a crouch. He saw his rifle nearby and grabbed it, holding it by its barrel. It would have to do, as he didn't have the time to turn it around. He wanted to put as much space between him and the remains of the sentry as possible. It would be mere seconds before Bouh's soldiers realized their mistake and spread out to look for him. He had that long to disappear into the night.

XIBLINTI SIGNALED FOR a cease-fire as they approached the gully. Half a dozen men flanked him on either side. Behind him were another twenty, all with their rifles ready, all with itchy trigger fingers. Tentatively the thirteen men peered into the bottom of the riverbed, half expecting the enemy to still be alive. The mangled remains showed no sign of life, the blood dark against the dust. Xiblinti indicated to the soldier on his left to jump down and examine the corpse. The guy did so, then looked up at Xiblinti.

"It is Yahfa. Not the American."

Xiblinti cursed. The prey was skilled and cunning. If they waited too long, then the American would escape into the darkness of the hills. They had to find him before that happened.

"Send for Yam," he hissed.

BOLAN CONTINUED HIS upward scrabble. Holding the rifle in his cuffed hands had become more cumbersome the higher he climbed, as the slope became steeper. He stopped briefly to loop the rifle's strap around his neck. It wasn't comfortable, but it freed his hands, enabling him to ascend faster. Minutes later he halted to listen for pursuit. A cry had gone up from the soldiers below. Maybe they had found his trail. He pushed on, looking for a cave or hollow, somewhere he would be out of sight. Then he could set about removing the handcuffs. And that would be the most dangerous trick of all. He clambered higher, dislodging loose rocks and sand. Despite the moonlight, Bolan knew that he was hidden in shadows. If it had been daylight, he would have been completely exposed.

The rocks were warm beneath his hands, yet his breath was misting in front of his face. He wasn't clothed for the desert chill and could hope only that the temperature wouldn't plummet too low. He didn't want to freeze to death on the side of some unnamed hill, hiding from enemy search parties. He scrambled on, searching for cover. The rifle strap around his neck restricted his breathing. Stones and gravel slid under his boots. He reached what he thought was the peak of the hill, crossed the rise and sighed. The hill was much higher than he'd anticipated, another peak hidden behind the one on which he stood.

Bolan trudged on.

THE BUSHMAN WAS known only as Yam. The withered man was barely five feet tall, his grizzled black hair just reaching Xiblinti's chest. The bushman's history was unknown. The only thing Xiblinti did know was that the little man heralded from South Africa. How he had ended up in Djibouti was as much a mystery as his age. The general had somehow found the diminutive African and put him to good use in his army as an "external adviser." His real role was something else entirely.

The Bushman was a tracker, one of the best Xiblinti had ever seen. Yam could follow the spoor of any animal, no matter how small. He could identify individual beasts out of a herd. Once, to demonstrate his abilities, he'd led a small patrol out over the mountains into Eritrea, following the two-day-old trail of a herd of migrating Beira antelopes. Yam quickly had identified individual animals, pointing out characteristics and the hierarchy of the herd from the spoor alone. Xiblinti had been baffled by it all. Yam had showed him a particular track, identifying the antelope, and claimed that he could pick that particular animal out of the herd after only a brief observation. Xiblinti had called his bluff, claiming Yam could pick out any animal and say it was the same one. Yam had cackled and gone about proving Xiblinti wrong.

Yam had made sure that the patrol was upwind when they'd found the grazing herd. He'd climbed a withered old tree, taking his ancient Lee Enfield rifle with him, a rifle as long as he was tall. He'd observed the antelope for less than five minutes before sniggering and nodding to himself. He'd taken aim with his World War I relic and fired. The herd had scattered at the sound of the boom, kicking up a huge cloud of dust and earth. Yam, still chuckling, had clambered down from the tree. Xiblinti had accused him of shooting a random Beira. Yam had continued to chuckle. He'd led them over to the carcass and, taking a machete, cut off the animal's right hoof. Then he'd led them back up the trail, but not before Xiblinti had instructed some of his men to carry the antelope. They would eat well that evening. On the trail Yam had demonstrated how that particular antelope had been walking and why it had left such a trail. And explained how he had identified it out of such a large herd. Xiblinti's men had clapped and laughed with delight. Xiblinti stood in awe at the man's skill.

But now Yam was after much easier prey, a large American who left a massive trail. Yam was on point, leaping from rock to rock, with Xiblinti close behind. Another dozen men had spread out behind them, nervously eyeing the hill with all its nooks and crannies.

Rumors of the American's exploits had spread around the camp like wildfire. Many of the soldiers wondered if American movies involving action heroes were true, that such spies really could do the impossible.

Xiblinti did nothing to quash the rumors. When the American was found, Xiblinti would personally kill him. That way his reputation as a fearsome and ruthless warrior would be enhanced. Let the men worry like old women. The American was one man, armed with a stolen rifle with limited ammunition. His hands were cuffed, and he was lost in the desert at night. The advantages were all in Xiblinti's favor. Triumph would be his in no time.

Yam stopped and examined the ground. "He stop here," he said in a high singsong voice. "He put rifle around his neck. Now he use his two hands—one hand to climb. He go faster but leave big spoor. Bigger than elephant." Yam giggled at the thought of a white elephant man who had to use two hands as one. "He go higher. He have high ground but not enough. Not enough to hide from Yam. He was here five minutes ago."

"Five minutes head start already?" Xiblinti asked. "How is that possible?"

Yam giggled again. "He very fast, like gazelle. He run, but the Lion Yam will catch him. He cannot hide. Yam sees all."

Yam continued to climb nimbly up the side of the hill, the rest of the entourage trailing behind him.

BOLAN FINALLY FOUND what he had been looking for. The hill leveled out slightly, forming a miniplateau that was several yards wide. It was almost invisible from observation, as a wall of boulders and rocks surrounded it, creating a natural, defensible position. Bolan climbed over the boulders and dropped down, making sure that the rifle didn't clatter against the rocks. He stood behind the largest one, examining the hillside below. There was no sign of pursuit, but they were out there, Bolan was certain of it. It would be only a matter of time, maybe minutes, before they were in sight. And in those minutes he had to get out of his handcuffs and lay an ambush.

He removed the rifle from around his neck and placed it on the ground. Then he sat and unlaced his right boot. His sock quickly followed. What he was about to do required a sensitive touch.

Next followed the most dangerous part, and the trickiest.

The French FAMAS F1 rifle had been designed to work under all conditions, including the Arctic. To pull the trigger while wearing thick gloves required the removal of the trigger guard, and Bolan did just that. He pulled away the sheet-metal trigger guard by removing its retaining pin and twisted it around 180 degrees. He flicked the fire selector to single shot. Then he placed the rifle against the rocks so that it was standing on its butt, the trigger pointing toward him. Bolan took a deep breath and placed his hands on either side of the barrel, the handcuff chain across the muzzle. He knew that it was an incredibly dangerous stunt to pull. A thousand things could go wrong and he could easily be injured or killed. But for now there was no other way to remove the manacles.

He moved his bare foot in to operate the trigger and hit a snag. He couldn't get his foot in close enough while keeping the barrel pointing in the right direction. Bolan cursed. He was running out of time; he could feel the search party getting closer. He shuffled backward on his backside, taking the rifle with him. He would have to try a different position. Bolan twisted the rifle so that the trigger was pointing away from him. Moving into a lotus position, he wrapped his left leg around the butt to try to steady it. Once again he positioned his hands on either side of the barrel. But this time he would have to use his heel to depress the trigger. Bolan moved his bare right foot inward. He found the exposed trigger and placed his heel on top of it, taking up the slack of the trigger. He took a deep breath, closed his eyes and moved his head as far back as possible. The rifle remained steady.

He pushed down with his foot.

The resulting muzzle-blast was louder than Bolan had expected. The rifle butt kicked against his groin, bits of metal stung his face and the pressure between his hands was released. He rolled backward, the rifle dropping to the ground. The Executioner shook his head to clear it and opened his eyes. The first thing he felt was that his hands were free. He still had the cuffs on, but at least he could move his hands independently.

Bolan got to his feet and snatched up the rifle. He peered over the rocks but was unable to detect any movement below him. Using the few seconds that he had, he put his sock and boot back on before moving to the end of the tiny plateau. French FAMAS rifles had a bipod fitted out as standard, and this one was no different. Bolan flipped the two stubby legs down, resting the bipod on the lowest boulder that he could find. He would be firing downhill, while trying not

to be illuminated against the sky. Not an ideal sniping position, but he intended to fire only a few shots
before slipping away. The FAMAS's carrying handle
doubled as its sight. Bolan checked to make sure that
it was still set to single shot and waited for Bouh's men
to expose themselves.

THE BOOM ECHOED around the hills. Several of Xiblinti's men dropped to the ground, fearing that they
were under fire. Xiblinti tensed, ready to join them.
Only Yam seemed unaffected. The little man giggled
and danced.

"Oh, he is close. The antelope is close. The lion is
coming."

"What is he doing? Is he shooting at us?" Xiblinti
asked.

"No shoot us, no, no. He shoot at the moon. At the
moon." Yam laughed.

Shooting at the moon? Xiblinti wondered what the
American was doing. Maybe he'd slipped, and the rifle
had discharged. Xiblinti signaled his men to rise. He
would soon find out what the American was doing. It
was only a matter of time.

Then the satellite phone warbled in his pocket.

GENERAL BOUH ENTERED the cave with a small group
of bodyguards in tow. It had been a long, hard walk
for him, something that he was no longer used to, and
he fully intended to make the Americans pay for his
discomfort. At least the walk back would be downhill. Using a powerful flashlight, he surveyed the three
prisoners with a sneer. The Americans were huddled
together, showing how pathetic they were. And their

odor offended his nose. Even the CIA spy was cowed. The only man to show some initiative was on the run, soon to be hunted down and shot. For now, he would have to keep these prisoners alive, but not for much longer. The image of their corpses rotting under the desert sun pleased him.

"Where is your friend going?" the general growled at Douglas. The CIA agent shook his head and said nothing. Bouh nodded at two bodyguards, who stepped over and dragged Douglas to his feet. Bouh drew his service pistol out of its hip holster, a black Browning. Bouh showed it to Douglas, then lowered it to point at Douglas's left kneecap.

"One more time. Where is your friend going? Does he expect to find help? Not talking? Would you like me to shoot you in the knee? Then in the other one? And in both your elbows? Then you will be placed outside on the desert sand." Bouh smiled. "There are more creatures out there than most people would believe. Once they detect your blood, they will attack in droves. By morning, if you haven't already been eaten alive, then you will, as my British trainers once told me, be barking mad. And still you will be eaten alive. So, tell me, where he is going?"

Douglas raised his head slowly and stared Bouh in the eye. Bouh hoped for a moment that the spy would resist and was disappointed when he lowered his gaze.

"He…he's not going anywhere. He intends to lead your men into the hills, then double back and get us. Maybe steal a jeep or something."

Bouh's face lit up in amusement. "Unfortunately

your Mr. Blanski did not reckon on Yam. But do not worry, you will learn of his death shortly."

The guards simultaneously let go of Douglas as the general's arm shot up and around, pistol whipping Douglas to the floor. The CIA man collapsed in a heap. The Trenchard men recoiled in terror. Bouh smiled at their discomfort. "Oh, do not worry. I will not feed you to the desert creatures. Your deaths will be much slower if you lie to me. Did the spy speak the truth?"

Sanner and Twohig eyed each other nervously. Sanner looked up at the general, shielding his eyes from the glare of the flashlight. "Yes, General. The other man was planning on losing your men in the hills, then coming back for us."

"Good," Bouh said. "That makes it so much easier." The oversize army general replaced his pistol in its holster and withdrew a sat phone. He jabbed at a few buttons then waited for an answer.

"Captain, this is General Bouh. The American spy is planning on doubling back. If he does, then I will prepare a surprise for him here. And if he gets past you, then you need not return. Ever."

CHAPTER NINETEEN

Xiblinti snorted as he replaced the sat phone in its belt holster. The general's threat held no water. He had died before, and compared to that terrible day, nothing would scare him again. Certainly not the idle words of his overweight mentor.

The images of that day sprang unbidden to his mind. He'd been a child in Rwanda, there with his older brother and their parents. He no longer remembered why they'd been in that country, only that it was not where they'd lived, but he remembered when the mobs had come for them. Screaming, yelling, armed with machetes, with knives, with clubs. His parents had been torn apart. His brother hacked to pieces. He had been smaller and tried to hide. But they'd found him, dragged him out by his ankles and laid into him with their weapons. His age had been irrelevant to the hordes. They'd been in blood frenzy, mindless, incoherent, not caring who they killed. They'd chopped at his head, his throat. And then they'd disappeared and left him to die, lying with the bloody remains of his family.

A detachment of troops from the UNAMIR—United Nations Assistance Mission for Rwanda—task force, led by then Captain Bouh, had found him, barely alive. He had been rushed to a Red Cross hospital camp, where the doctors had only just been able to save him. For some reason Bouh had stayed in touch, eventually arranging for the young boy to be relocated to Djibouti with Bouh as his guardian. They never mentioned what had happened in Rwanda. Bouh had overseen his education and brought him into the army as his, what? Protégé? Attack dog? Bodyguard? Or a mix of all three? It didn't matter to Xiblinti. He had a task to perform and he intended to succeed.

He began to climb again, cresting a ridge, his men behind him, Yam up front, dancing from rock to rock like a mountain goat, sniffing the air and poking at the ground. Xiblinti was still bothered by Yam's statement. Shooting at the moon? Why would the American shoot at the moon? What could he achieve? A signal for help? Not suicide. The American was too strong willed for that. And his hands were still bound by handcuffs and… Xiblinti's eyes widened at the image of the American placing the handcuff chain across the muzzle and depressing the trigger.

"Down!" he rasped, even as he heard the first shot. He knew the order had come too late.

BOLAN WATCHED THE first shadowy figures cross the ridge. The second man was Xiblinti, of that he was sure. The third and fourth men were regular troopers. But it was the first figure who intrigued him. The character pranced and jumped around on the rocks. He wondered what part the diminutive man played in Bouh's army. The answer sprung to mind a second later. He was looking at a Bushman tracker, who was examining the rocks. The man stopped flouncing around and slowly raised his head to look straight at Bolan.

Their eyes met.

Bolan shifted the rifle barrel slightly, let out half a breath and squeezed the trigger.

YAM BARKED A warning a split second before the 5.56 mm bullet took his head apart. Yam's body stilled before collapsing as if his strings had been cut. Xiblinti was in the process of throwing himself to the ground when he saw the muzzle-flash and Yam die. Even as he impacted with the hard rocks he heard a second shot boom out. A man to his right fell backward without a sound. A third shot was fired before it dawned on his men that they had walked into an ambush. A man screamed, the third victim of the American's sniping. An element of fear wormed its way through Xiblinti. He could hardly believe that three men had died in two seconds. And the general would be very upset that his pet Bushman was among them.

One of his men crawled over. "Yam is dead. So are the two sons of Major Abdullah. The American has us pinned down. We cannot advance. We must return and get reinforcements."

Xiblinti would have backhanded the man if they had been standing. Instead he settled for a snarl and a glare that he hoped the other man could see in the darkness. Another shot rang out. Another man in the patrol screamed in agony. Xiblinti and his men pushed themselves even deeper into the ground.

"No! We will not retreat. Order the men to spread out and slowly work their way up to the American's position. You and I will provide covering fire."

The soldier hesitated for an instant, then nodded. He crawled backward, disappearing from Xiblinti's sight. The Rwandan smiled grimly. Soon they would outflank the American, and then he would find out what it was like to be cut a thousand times.

THE ONLY PROBLEM was that Bolan was no longer in the same position. After the fourth shot he had folded the bipod and quickly crept up the side of the hill, keeping to the shadows as much as possible. The FAMAS F1 rifle he carried held a standard magazine of twenty-five rounds. Assuming the magazine was full when he'd taken it, then he had maybe eleven bullets left. He reasoned that he had five minutes, probably less, before Xiblinti's men flanked the plateau and found that he had evaded them. Then they would have to cast around for a trail, and that would take longer since their tracker was dead.

Within minutes Bolan reached the summit of the hill, crouching to avoid being silhouetted against the night sky. A few miles to the north lay a camp. He was unable to estimate the number of occupants, but he counted a dozen campfires. It would take a couple of hours to reach its outskirts and an unknown amount of time to locate the leader of the mercenaries. Then there was the additional risk of confronting the soldiers of fortune.

Eleven bullets.

To his rear he heard two automatic rifles open up, spraying the hillside. Xiblinti would be laying down covering fire while his men performed a flanking maneuver. There wasn't any more time to lose. Bolan looped the rifle over his shoulder and began to work his way down the side of the steep hill. It was tough going. The descent was arduous, the rocks and sand loose and shifting under his weight. The dark didn't help, either; the moon was now hidden behind another peak. Bolan quickly ended up sliding, using his feet and left hand as a brake to arrest his acceleration. Stones rattled away, cascading down the hill. He knew that he was making too much noise, but there was no way to prevent it, short of stopping altogether. Again he had left a trail that anybody could follow.

In an instant the situation changed for the worse.

Bolan's left foot struck an unyielding rock at the wrong angle. A split second later Bolan was flat on his back, careening down the hillside, completely out of control. The stony ground tumbled down with him, causing a mini avalanche. The rifle dug painfully into his spine. He spread himself out into a star position, digging in his heels in an effort to halt his momentum. Skin was torn from his hands as he groped for a purchase, anything to grab hold of.

His fingers found a jagged piece of rock, sticking out of the ground. He snagged it, bringing his momentum to an arm-wrenching stop. Stones continued to cascade down the slope. He groaned. His whole body hurt: his legs, his buttocks and his back were battered and bruised. His left ankle was also sore but didn't feel twisted. He slowly sat up and removed the rifle to examine it and cursed. The magazine was gone, lost on the hillside having come loose during the slide. There would be one bullet in the chamber, but he could no longer count on the rifle's reliability.

The sound of the subsiding rubble died away as the mini avalanche came to a rest. It remained to be seen if anybody had heard the commotion.

From up above, several automatic rifles opened up, answering the question for him.

XIBLINTI CRESTED THE HILL, followed closely by some of his patrol. The soldiers were nervous. The shooting prowess of the American had clearly spooked them. Xiblinti snorted. The American had been lucky, nothing more, and he was clearly being lucky again—his hiding place was empty. The soldiers shuffled, agitated and afraid. One of the men approached, looking everywhere and nowhere, wondering if the American would appear out of the sky or if the next shot would be the fatal one. Xiblinti recognized him as the one that had suggested a retreat earlier. He bunched his fists, ready to strike if the man again suggested cowardice.

"The American has gone. Should we...should we wait until morning before continuing?"

Xiblinti allowed his fists to relax. The question was not unwarranted. It was even sensible. The American could not get far in the darkness. There was nothing around for miles, only their own military camp and...

Xiblinti smiled with elation as he realized where the spy was going. It was the only logical thing to do. Where else could he go in the middle of a wasteland? He spun on his heel, half running, half climbing to the top of the hill. A few miles down the valley burned the fires of the rebels. And the camp was full of American mercenaries. Would the spy seek refuge among his own kind? Would the mercenaries help? Or would he double back after all, wanting to rescue his friends? Xiblinti made a mental bet that the spy would run to the mercenaries. He heard his men approach from behind, wondering what their leader was thinking.

All of Xiblinti's questions were answered for him.

From several hundred feet below came the sound of a large rock fall. He grinned.

"It is the American. He has tripped over his feet. Open fire!"

BOLAN COUNTED EIGHT muzzle-blasts emanating from the top of the ridge. Almost all of the bullets went wide, the Djiboutian soldiers making the error of shooting at the sound of the avalanche rather than compensating for Bolan's movements. Several ricochets came close but not too close. Bolan slipped away into the darkness knowing that Xiblinti would not be far behind.

"WHAT DO YOU make of it, sir?"

Former Major Streib lowered his binoculars and considered Krulak's question. What indeed.

"Obviously they are hunting somebody or bodies who have upset them, and that somebody is heading in our direction. I would surmise it's Bouh's men doing the shooting, judging by the way they're waving their rifles around. The question is, who are they hunting?"

Streib raised his binoculars again. "I don't like this, Krulak. Not at all. Make sure the sentries are alert. Wake our men. We're moving out. And do it quietly. I don't want Bouh's ruffians to be spooked and turn against us."

Krulak turned away. Streib regarded the situation on the hill again. The muzzle-flashes had stopped, and he thought he could see movement on the slope, which indicated that Bouh's soldiers were advancing on their enemy. But who was their enemy? Streib felt a sinking sensation that he hadn't felt since Iraq. A sensation telling him everything was about to go to hell. It was definitely time to move out. The only real question was how much time did they have?

MACK BOLAN WAS a shadow among shadows, keeping to the base of the hill to make the most of the provided darkness. The moon had slowly emerged from behind the other hills, illuminating the surrounding desert. Glancing back, he could see Xiblinti's remaining men descending. They made no attempt at stealth. There wasn't much need, and the lunar light was like a second sun. Several slipped, sliding down in a similar fashion to Bolan. The Executioner moved away, the shadows his only ally. He had a ways to go before he reached the outer perimeter of the camp, and he didn't want to be observed by either the camp sentries or Xiblinti. Speed was of the essence. The night would last only so long.

XIBLINTI CURSED TO HIMSELF. There was no sign of the American, and his men seemed to be becoming more incompetent by the minute. Part was out of fear of what the spy had accomplished, part out of fear of reporting failure to General Bouh. Xiblinti observed the camp with interest, certain that the American was heading there. He was still uncertain if the mercenaries would offer aid. They probably would. Their contempt for him and the general had been thinly disguised. They deserved their fate. What Bouh had planned for them would be shown around the world.

The rebel trainees wouldn't lift a finger. They were as disloyal and temperamental as only Eritreans could be. Many would kill their own mothers—some probably had—so there would be no assistance for the spy there. But the mercenaries were a very different matter. He would have to reach the camp before the spy did. If that was possible. If not, and if the Americans decided to join together, then he would rouse the Eritreans. The Americans would quickly be overwhelmed. Bouh would not be pleased with that outcome, but plans could be changed. It was that or failure. Xiblinti made his decision.

"Follow me," he whispered. "We will advance on the camp and capture the spy there."

BOLAN OVERWHELMED THE first sentry easily. The African, dressed in shorts, T-shirt and what appeared to be flip-flops on his feet, was paying more attention to the raucous laughter in the camp than to what was happening around him. Not that he would have spotted his attacker anyway. The apparition that came from behind quickly rendered the man unconscious. Lowering the unfortunate guard to the ground, Bolan quickly relieved him of his FAMAS rifle and a spare magazine, leaving his defective one with the sleeping sentry. Another FAMAS F1. Bouh had to have had a stash hidden away somewhere. Bolan had the feeling that the whole operation had been in the planning for a very long time.

He checked his six, trying to spot Xiblinti and his troops. They were difficult to find, but they were there, in the distance. He wouldn't have much time before they arrived at the camp. The only thing delaying them was the fear that he might be hiding in the shadows, waiting to pick them off one by one.

Bolan turned his attention back to the camp. From his current angle it was impossible to tell where the mercenaries were. All he could see were rebels. He began to work his way around the perimeter, aware that the doomsday numbers were falling, that time was running out. At least he had more ammunition.

Bolan found the mercenaries five minutes later. The camp layout was pretty obvious. The rebels were at the southern end, partying or fighting among themselves; it was impossible to tell. At the northern end, separated by wide space, were the mercenary tents, laid out in a professional manner. This part of the camp should be better guarded but not impossible to penetrate. He had faced far more challenging infiltrations in the past. The jeering from the rebels would mask his approach.

Bolan watched as several mercenaries moved purposefully around the tents and the two APCs, parked farther back. He thought that he could make out more vehicles behind but wasn't sure. What intrigued him was that the men were loading kit bags into the back of the personnel carriers. It appeared that they were abandoning the camp, and the rebels knew nothing about it. And if they knew nothing about it, then Bouh would know nothing, either. A double cross? Did the mercs have their own agenda?

As Bolan watched, two of the mercenaries walked past a tent as a third man emerged. The two walkers began to snap a salute before stopping and quickly lowering their arms. Old habits died hard. These men were all ex-military and probably served together in the same unit. He needed to get into that former officer's tent as quickly as possible.

Rather than waste time and try to sneak in, Bolan decided to use role camouflage instead. It would be risky, but with Xiblinti about to arrive any minute,

Bolan didn't feel that he had much choice. During the Mafia Wars he had infiltrated the Mob a number of times, playing the role of a Black Ace assassin. He had walked among terrorists on numerous occasions, always playing the part that they expected. This one should be a piece of cake, despite his dirty appearance.

Bolan stood tall, slung the rifle over his shoulder and marched toward the officer's tent, looking as if he belonged there. He walked past one hurrying mercenary, who didn't even glance at him. Within moments he was at the tent. He make a quick check to make sure nobody was observing him, then he lifted the flap, slipping inside.

The tent contained a standard-issue military cot and a matching desk and chair. A kit bag lay on the bed, next to a pre–World War II, MAS 36 bolt-action rifle. The only illumination was from the glare of the moon, shining through the canvas. Bolan was about to examine the kit bag when he heard a noise outside the tent. He took a step to the side, slipping his rifle off his shoulder as he did so. A hand pulled back the canvas flap, and a man stepped inside.

STREIB KNEW THAT he wasn't alone the moment he stepped into the tent. The smell of sweat, gravel and cordite was unmistakable. The cold muzzle of a weapon pushed against his ear before he had time to react. He froze and waited.

"Don't try anything, and you might get to live," a man murmured in a voice as chilling as a grave. Streib didn't twitch. A dozen thoughts raced through his mind. Was this the man being hunted? It had to be. Could he overpower the intruder? Had anybody witnessed the intruder enter his tent? Was Krulak approaching? His presence had been requested. Streib had to have tensed because the muzzle pushed even harder into his ear.

"Don't even think about it. It won't get you anywhere." The voice was ice-cold.

"You think you can get away with this?" Streib whispered. "My men are former US Marines. You don't stand a chance."

"I've heard it all before. Sit on the bed, legs apart, hands on knees. Move."

Streib walked slowly to the military cot and sat. He had made no move toward his sidearm, and the intruder had made no mention of it. He was also sitting next to the loaded MAS 36 rifle. A sign of carelessness from the intruder? Streib wasn't sure, but he fully intended to take advantage of it.

"I let you keep your weapons. You may need them soon." The iced voice interrupted his thoughts.

"What are you? A fucking mind reader?"

"No, just experienced enough to know what you were probably thinking. Your men are moving out. Why?"

The intruder was a dark silhouette against the side of the tent, the FAMAS pointing between Streib's eyes. Streib could tell from the man's posture that he was a professional, that he could handle himself in a fight and that he was American, judging by his accent. Streib decided against action for the moment, wanting to know what the stranger was here for. Besides, Krulak would be arriving any second to find out what was keeping his commanding officer.

"And you are?" Streib asked.

"I asked first. You answer first. That's how it works. Your men are moving out. Why? And, who are you?"

Streib considered his options. It wouldn't hurt to humor the stranger. It would buy some time. Where the hell was Krulak?

"Major Victor Streib, one-time US Army. That's all you need to know."

"You know Bouh is about to betray you. That's why you are slipping away in the dark, isn't it?"

"Perhaps. It would take a foolish man to trust Bouh. And that man wouldn't live long."

"Yet I presume Trenchard paid you to stay the course."

Streib snorted. "Trenchard can keep his money, minus expenses. I'm not hanging around for..." Streib stopped, hoping that he had not said too much.

"Bouh has set up both you and Trenchard. There is no oil. It was a coup, pure and simple, and you have been designated to take the fall. Even as we speak Bouh's men are closing in on your position."

"So, who are you?" Streib still wanted to know.

"Mike Blanski. Journalist."

"Bullshit. You're no journalist. You're US Army, I can smell it. What are you now? CIA? Some other alphabet-soup guy? What are you here for? Me? Why?"

Streib watched as the stranger slung his FAMAS over his shoulder, took two steps to the side, reached down and grabbed hold of a dark object that was poking its way into the tent. A second later Krulak somersaulted into the middle of the floor, disarmed, landing at Streib's feet. Krulak jumped up ready to resume his attack, when his PAMAS G1 pistol, a French copy of the Beretta 92, landed at his feet. It was enough to give him pause. Streib had also drawn his pistol but hadn't yet had time to point it in Blanski's direction. He, too, stopped at the sudden reappearance of Krulak's handgun.

"Call your man off, Major," Bolan growled . "I'm not after your head. I wasn't joking about Bouh's men approaching, and I wasn't joking about you being double-crossed. Bouh has set you up to be the fall guys when his coup takes place. You'll be tried and publicly executed. I don't have time to explain any more. I need your help."

"Major?" Krulak was spoiling for a fight.

Streib hesitated for a second. "Stand down, Sergeant. Is Bouh approaching?"

"Yes, sir, at least his scarred bodyguard is just outside the camp, asking for you. I said I would see if you would speak to him. I don't think he noticed that we're packing up. What are your orders?"

Streib never got a chance to answer.

At that precise moment, shots were fired.

And all hell broke loose.

CHAPTER TWENTY

Xiblinti cursed his luck at not being able to catch up before the spy reached the camp. They had formed a skirmish line, once they had stopped sliding down the hill, in the belief that if the American was hiding then they would discover him. But no, the spy was gone, making for the camp. Xiblinti had his confirmation. They had discovered the unconscious sentry, his weapon missing, a broken rifle lying nearby. Xiblinti slipped a knife between the man's ribs, through the heart, as punishment for his slack guard duty.

Now the American was here, pleading and begging for aid and a hiding place. Even as the thought flashed through his mind, Xiblinti dismissed it. The spy would not plead and beg. He was too strong for that. No, he would appeal to the mercenaries' sense of patriotism, something that Americans wore on their sleeves. He doubted that the mercenaries would do anything to aid the spy. They were interested only in money. Xiblinti chuckled. Wouldn't they be shocked when they were captured, put on trial and executed all on the same day? That would show them what they could do with their patriotism.

They were challenged and stopped before they could get too close to the mercenary camp. The Eritrean Afar Adaemara part of the camp was loud and rowdy, undisciplined despite the training that the Americans had given them. They were the scum of the earth as far as Xiblinti was concerned. He spit in the general direction of the raucous rebels. Several of his men, those hailing from the Somali side of Djibouti, did the same. All of his men hated the Eritrean vermin and would gladly shoot the scum when the time came. And that time was fast approaching. Most of them would be dead within the next few days. Xiblinti looked forward to disemboweling a few himself.

He smiled at the thought, then turned his attention back to the sentry who had challenged them. One of the mercenary leaders was already approaching. Xiblinti struggled to remember the man's name. It was difficult; the word failed to spring to mind. Krulaa? Kruloo? He dismissed it. The man was Streib's dog and unimportant. He, too, would be dead soon, hanging from one of the large cranes in the harbor.

"What is it you want? Why are you here? Is General Bouh with you?" Streib's dog barked at Xiblinti in a disrespectful way. His men would not understand the English, but they would understand the tone.

Xiblinti felt anger rise but forced himself to remain calm. The general needed this man alive for another couple of days. Then he would take his machete to the dog. Typical Americans. Insolent, bullying, demanding and arrogant, believing that they owned the world and the world owed them a favor. Gutting the mutt would be extremely enjoyable.

"Major Streib. Now," Xiblinti rasped.

"And just what is your business with the major?" the dog demanded to know.

"Major Streib. Now. Please." Xiblinti riled at having to be polite, but maybe the dog would show some obedience.

The American paused, studied Xiblinti hard for several seconds before finally nodding. "I'll go and see if the major is available. Wait here. Please." The American turned and marched away before Xiblinti could respond.

A soldier in his patrol coughed and said, "Captain?"

Xiblinti turned to look. They were gathering an audience. The Eritreans had noticed them standing, waiting, had seen the confrontation between him and the American dog. Like sharks, they could smell blood. The majority seemed to be high on khat or something similar. Either that or they were drunk. Or both. It didn't matter. They didn't appear to have firearms, but their sheer numbers made them dangerous. His men shifted uneasily. They had started out with thirteen in the patrol. Now they were down to nine. Nine against the more than hundred here in the camp. The sentry who had challenged them backed away, disappearing into the shadows.

Some of the Eritrean Afars took several steps closer. Maybe twenty meters separated the two groups. Their eyes shone yellow in the moonlight; the hate for the Djiboutian Issa soldiers was written on their faces. Xiblinti could feel the fear of his men, could feel them getting nervous, knew their fingers were tightening on triggers. They were here for the American spy. These animals would be dead within a few days. His men could take as many potshots as they wanted. But not yet. The general had plans.

"Don't fire at them," Xiblinti ordered.

He then called out to the Eritrean Afars. "You men,

go back to your camp. Soon you will be rewarded for your hard work. Go back."

The Afars paid no attention to his words. Or they were beyond hearing his rasp. Several were beginning to smile, yellow teeth and yellow eyes. There was going to be bloodshed. He needed to extract himself from it.

"You, with me," Xiblinti ordered to the man on his left, the one that he had almost thumped earlier on. "The rest of you, stand ready. If the…Eritreans advance, then defend yourselves. I will get the American mercenaries, a show of strength. Then these… people will listen."

The men shuffled nervously at Xiblinti's words. Their captain was abandoning them? Was he running? Would he be back?

The captain and the one soldier skirted the Eritrean camp, heading straight for the mercenary tents. But what he saw brought him up short. The Americans were loading boxes into the back of the personnel carriers that General Bouh had given them. They were running. Treachery was everywhere, and the general's plan was falling apart.

Xiblinti was in the process of flicking his rifle's selector switch to triburst when the first shots were fired. Xiblinti spun. A mob roar went up, followed by the chatter of automatic fire as his troops retaliated against the Eritreans. For a few seconds, his troops seemed to be holding their own, but then the gunfire died away as his men exhausted their magazines within three seconds, foolishly firing on full-auto. After that they didn't stand a chance. The mob fell upon them, impervious to bullet and knife wounds, high on khat. He was unable to tell his men's dying screams from the hysterics of the Eritreans. The butchers and the butchered merged as one.

The last remaining soldier grabbed his arm. "What do we do now? We must run!"

But Xiblinti was unable to run. He saw the mob, heard the same animal noises. They were hacking his parents apart. His brother! He had to hide! No, they had him! He screamed a long and terrible scream as the first club came down, followed by the machete. Knives. Pain. The sound of his parents dying was horrendous; his brother had stopped screaming. He was dying...

The soldier shook his arm again, bringing him out of his paralysis. "Sir, Captain! We must run. We must."

Xiblinti turned toward the mercenary camp, gasping hard. They were grabbing weapons, running around, organizing themselves. It was too late to find the American spy now. The mob would overrun him. The sound of an APC thundered to life, followed by another. The Americans had several vehicles, including the French jeep-type vehicles.

He saw a way out.

The only problem was in reporting the failure to General Bouh. The general had a lot riding on his plan; he had a lot of backers. The general would not be pleased. But that would come later. For now, escape was the most pressing problem. The mercenaries could sort out the Afar hordes.

"Follow me. Run!"

BOLAN STEPPED OVER and grabbed the MAS 36 rifle. Streib was on feet, pistol drawn. The three men exited the tent.

"Report!" Krulak bellowed at a passing merc.

"Sir, the rebels are attacking the Djiboutian patrol. They are all high on khat."

Streib cursed. He had left the Eritreans alone, as long as they didn't interfere with his men. He didn't care what they got up to at night. And khat was perfectly legal in Djibouti. But now they were enflamed and likely to turn on the Americans, as well.

"Sergeant, get the men formed up here, ready to repel an attack. I think they will try their chances."

"Also get the APCs in a position where they can supply covering fire," Bolan said.

Both Streib and Krulak gave him a look, but Streib nodded. "Do it, Sergeant."

"How many men do you have, Major?" Bolan asked.

"Twenty."

"And how many of them?"

"Never counted. It fluctuated daily as some ran off back home. Some stragglers joined up. Some died from heat, drugs, whatever. But I guess one hundred."

"Then we definitely need those APCs. Come on." Bolan started to move toward the rear of the camp where the APCs were idling. He didn't get that far. Bullets whizzed over his head. He threw himself into a roll, dropping the old French rifle and coming up with the more modern FAMAS F1 in his hands. Streib had likewise dropped prone. A handful of Africans were charging toward them, intent on chaos, screaming wildly. Bolan flicked the selector to single shot and squeezed the trigger three times. Three targets fell. The fourth was put down by pistol fire from Streib. But not all were dead. High on drugs, two staggered back to their feet, unable to feel the pain. Bolan fired again. Two head shots. Drugs or no drugs, they were not getting up again.

"Some journalist!" Streib yelled over the mayhem.

The mercenaries were running over, forming up and ready to fight. Krulak was yelling at them to make a defensive line, ready in the event that more of the Afars attacked. A quick head count revealed all to be present, apart from two men in the APCs.

"Get those APCs over here, Krulak," Streib bellowed. "I want a wall of steel at our backs." Krulak hurried off to comply.

Bolan saw that two of the men had brought RPG-7s with them, probably to keep them away from rebel hands. Some of the mercenaries had noticed him and were giving him looks. Who was this stranger in their midst, covered in dust and dried blood? Bolan couldn't care less; there was too much going on. He kept his rifle up and ready. It seemed that the Afars had turned on themselves. Not all had been under the influence of khat. Those who had tried to stop the massacre were now being pursued through the camp. Was Xiblinti dead? Bolan didn't know, but it seemed likely. His entire patrol would have been torn apart in seconds.

Streib had formed his men into two rows of nine. There was no cover out here, nothing to hide behind. The formation reminded Bolan of films where British soldiers of old would create skirmish lines or squares to fight the French or the Zulus. One would fire while the other was reloading. Sound tactics against the murderous horde. His men were well drilled. They couldn't have been out of the military too long. Streib had to have bagged them the moment they left the Marine Corps.

There was a thundering behind them as one of the Renault personnel carriers rolled up. Its turret 7.62 mm machine gun swung, pointing into the camp. Krulak jumped out of the rear.

"Only this one, sir. The other won't start," he reported.

"Damn. Very well, Sergeant. Let's hope it's enough."

"Sweet Jesus!" Bolan heard one of the former Marines say. Tents in the camp were catching fire, going up quickly. A figure ran out, screaming, aflame. Arms waving, the burning man plunged into another tent before Bolan could line up a mercy shot. More shots rang out from the camp.

"Where the hell did they get weapons from?" Krulak wanted to know.

"From the dead Djiboutian patrol. And smuggled in," Bolan replied.

"Shit!" growled Krulak.

"Here they come," another ex-Marine stated.

Wild men ran toward them, at least fifty, brandishing clubs, poles, knives and guns, screaming unintelligibly. One stopped to take aim at the Americans.

"Put them down," Streib ordered.

The front row of the former Marines opened fire in disciplined three-round bursts. The approaching enemy fell, cut to ribbons by the wall of lead. The turret gun of the APC joined in, scything left to right. Bolan had picked up the MAS 36, chambered a round and aimed it at an enemy farther back, one who was returning ragged fire from a stolen FAMAS. Bullets rattled ineffectively against the side of the Renault APC. Bolan aimed, compensated for the heat from the burning tents and fired. The man flew backward, weapon falling from lifeless fingers.

The second line of mercenaries was now engaged, the front row busy reloading and giving their rifles a chance to cool. The APC's turret gun blasted away, shell casings clattering to the ground. More of the Afars fell.

Then it was over. The remaining survivors turned and fled, dropping their weapons, running for the open desert or through the remains of the camp.

"Cease fire!" Streib yelled. "Who is in the armor? Lanier, give pursuit. Drive through their tents, drive through the mock-up, drive them away. Fire only if fired upon. Let them run."

Bolan couldn't see the man called Lanier from his angle, but the APC belched smoke and rolled away, past the line of mercenaries and into the rebel camp. It drove through a burning tent, then through one that was on the verge of catching fire. Sparks flew into the night sky.

"Show-off," Bolan heard one of the men mutter.

"Any casualties? No? You four, check the rebels for wounded. We'll offer them aid if needed," Streib ordered.

XIBLINTI CLAMBERED INTO the back of the ACMAT truck. He motioned his last surviving soldier—he couldn't remember the man's name and didn't want to ask—into the driver's seat.

"The keys are in the ignition," the man whispered.

Xiblinti nodded. The vehicle was equipped with a .50-caliber Browning machine gun, mounted in a pintle, but Xiblinti wasn't interested in it for the moment.

Cut and run was the name of the game. He crouched
in the rear of the truck, looking for enemies. The mercenaries were fully engaged with the scum who had
murdered his men. Good. Maybe they would kill one
another. He was waiting for the right moment to leave,
his comrade looking at him, fear written across his
face. The gunfire faded, and he heard the APC move
off. This was their moment. If the transport couldn't
pursue them, then they would get clean away.

"Go!" he ordered.

The soldier turned the key and gunned the engine.
They shot away, heading for the open desert, past the
milling mercenaries. Xiblinti quickly looked for the
spy as he passed but didn't have time to identify him.

"XIBLINTI," BOLAN SAID as the ACMAT rumbled past.

"That scar-faced bastard," Krulak added.

Bolan ran to the spot where the ACMAT had driven
by. The 4x4 was now fifty yards away, rapidly increasing the distance and throwing up a trail of dust behind
it. Xiblinti was obscured, having ducked, but Bolan
could make out the head and shoulders of the driver in
the moonlight. In one smooth motion he brought up the
old rifle, adopted a rifleman's stance, aimed and fired.

His aim was slightly off due to his unfamiliarity
with the MAS 36. The bullet dropped. Instead of hitting the driver through the head, it went clean through
his neck and out the windshield. The driver coughed
and died, his foot no longer on the accelerator, his
hands no longer on the wheel. The steering wheel
spun, and the ACMAT slalomed to the left. It hit a
large rock with its leading tire, catapulting the vehicle
onto its side where the momentum carried it another

dozen yards before it came to a rest, its underside exposed to the mercenaries.

"Nice shot," Streib said.

"Sir?" One of the mercenaries had an RPG-7 in his hands. Streib looked at it then at Bolan. "Do you want to see if he's alive?"

Bolan considered it for a moment, then thought of the smuggler Samar and his son. There had been no reason to disembowel them other than sadistic pleasure. Who knew how many people Xiblinti had tortured to death over the years.

"No," the Executioner said.

"Light him up," Streib ordered the man.

"Sir." The ex-Marine jogged to a clear spot where no one would be caught up in the rocket's back blast. He sighted and fired.

XIBLINTI CRAWLED, GASPING. One of his legs was broken. He had to get away from the vehicle, and quickly. He had to hide. He turned and looked back. The ACMAT was only four yards away. Four yards! He felt he had been crawling a lifetime. He had to continue. He had to report in. He began to drag himself again. Through the pain of his shattered leg, he barely felt the flames that engulfed him.

THE ROCKET WHIZZED downrange toward the ACMAT. The 4x4 detonated in a fireball, the impact of the rocket and force of the explosion cartwheeling the vehicle over the desert sand before it came to a rest upside down, burning brightly and lighting up the surrounding area. If Xiblinti had still been alive and hiding behind the vehicle or had been crawling away, then he would surely be dead by now. Bolan didn't feel like checking the 4x4 for corpses.

"Whoa," Krulak said, shielding his eyes from the heat. "That cooked his goose."

Bolan turned to Streib. "I still need your help," he said.

"Still? We've given it and then some. We're out of here. As soon as the personnel carrier is back, we're leaving. Krulak, take some guys and figure out why the other one didn't start."

"Sir!"

"The job's not done," Bolan said.

"For us, it is. We cut our losses and run. In case you didn't notice, we just fired on members of the Djiboutian military, one of which was an aide to General Bouh. That won't make him happy, and he'll call in his army to mow us down. We have a rendezvous with a freighter that will get us away. No, we're done, Mr. Whoever-you-are."

"No, not yet. Bouh is holding three hostages in a cave by his camp. Two are Trenchard people, the other is CIA. All are in bad shape. I need to get them out and to do it I need your help."

"Why should we? What's in it for us?"

"You get to leave unmolested. You keep the money that Trenchard paid. He'll no longer be needing it. You meet your ride and leave Djibouti. When you return stateside, you won't face questions from any agency."

That brought Streib up cold. "And how are you going to arrange all that? You'll have a word with the President, will you?"

"If need be. It won't be the first time. And I have

a friend who has words with the President on a daily basis. It can all be arranged."

"No comebacks?"

"None."

"You guarantee it?"

"Yes."

"All right. What do you want us to do?"

CHAPTER TWENTY-ONE

General Bouh surveyed his troops packing up and moving out. He swelled with pride. His men were extremely efficient and well trained. In the few hours since Captain Xiblinti had left, the camp had been almost cleared. Now they would return to barracks outside Obcock, reorganize and move out. He would lead the military convoy to the outskirts of Djibouti City, waiting in the desert for the signal that the civil unrest had begun. Then he would move in, end the uprising and kill the president and his lackey ministers, making it look as if the rebels had done it. He would have no choice but to declare martial law and assume power. Of course, he would promise the people that there would be new elections, but those elections would never come. No, he intended to be president for life.

But the captain still hadn't reported in, and that was worrying. It was out of character. Something had gone wrong. Had the spy escaped? Had he evaded the patrol? No, that was impossible. Yam was there and nothing escaped Yam. Xiblinti was just being slack. Or he hadn't caught the spy yet and didn't want to inform him of failure.

But he still felt uneasy. Something wasn't right. His instincts told him to get back to base. It was part of the plan anyway, so showing up early wouldn't raise suspicion with his fellow generals.

Then there was the problem of the prisoners. He had intended to make an example out of all of them, along with the mercenaries. Representatives of American oil and members of the CIA hanging side by side after a show trial. But they were not vital or even necessary, and he had decided to do away with them. He'd have one of the guards at the cave throw a grenade in. The Americans were in no state to survive it, and even if they did, there was no medical attention to be found out here. They would die, no matter what.

Bouh decided to give the order himself. The walk up to the cave would do him good. He had become too lazy at a time when his men needed to see a fit and healthy leader. Too indulgent. He felt rather than saw his men sniggering behind his back at his size. General Elephant! No, that would have to change. He waddled away from what was left of the camp, heading up toward the cave. As he did, an aide ran over to him and saluted.

"Sir! Shall we bring your Ratel closer?"

Bouh considered. If the Ratel was closer, then he could leave so much quicker. Yes, have the Ratel wait for him at the foot of the path. Not so far to walk then.

"Yes, soldier. Have it parked just over there, ready to leave at once."

The soldier saluted and hurried off. Smiling, Bouh continued his upward trek. He stopped, breathing hard. Yes, he definitely needed more exercise.

Something made him turn to his left. Six lights flared on a nearby ridge from a neighboring hill. Six flaming contrails flew down toward his camp.

Rockets!

Bouh turned and began to hurry as best as he could down the path. It was clear now. Xiblinti had failed. The spy had survived. He had found support and was now here to rescue his friend. His APC was beginning to back into place as the rocket-propelled grenades struck their targets. Several trucks exploded in huge fireballs, throwing the machines into the air. His helicopter at the far end of the camp went up in a massive show of light and flame. Another rocket hit a large pile of boxes that contained ammunition.

The result was both spectacular and terrifying.

The shock wave threw Bouh onto his backside. The fireball rose high into the sky, turning the remains of the night into day. Bouh clamped his hands to his ears and screamed. The sound of the explosion engulfed everything. It was incredible. Hell on Earth. Men, his men, hurtled through the air like grains of sand. Already dead. The blast would have killed them outright. The few remaining tents, including his command tent, had been flattened and torn away.

His APC was still there. He had to reach its sanctuary. Even as he struggled to his feet he saw a rocket strike the rear and detonate. The vehicle was wreathed in flame for an instant. Was it still intact? Could he escape? The rear hatch swung open. The driver poked his head out, looked around and saw Bouh, waving him over. Yes, the machine still worked!

Bouh tottered toward it.

BOLAN SILENTLY CURSED the mercenaries for opening fire too early. If they had waited a minute more he would have had Bouh. The fat man was now wobbling toward his armored carrier, which meant that Bolan would have to catch up later. But first he had to deal with the two sentries guarding the cave.

Streib had communication gear with him, unsecured but workable. A battered laptop was hooked up to a portable satellite terminal, a white-colored device not much larger than a touch-screen tablet. The internet speed was not impressive, but Bolan managed to send an email to Stony Man Farm, a quick rundown on the situation and a request for an evac for him and the three hostages. Once he had entered the GPS coordinates of Bouh's camp and sent the message, he broke the connection without waiting for a response. The Farm would make all the arrangements and time was precious. The State Department could warn the Djiboutian government of an impending coup, leaving them to batten down the hatches.

While Bolan was busy with his email, Streib organized his forces. Fourteen of his men would take the now-working APC and a couple of the ACMATs to the rendezvous point where the dinghies were hidden. He and Krulak, together with six other men, would accompany Bolan to Bouh's camp. Streib had stressed that he didn't want to fully engage Bouh in a war, and Bolan understood. But a distraction was needed. Streib had twelve rockets and six launchers.

A plan was quickly formulated in which Streib's men would fire two rockets each, destroy as many vehicles as possible, then withdraw to the rendezvous, leaving Bolan on his own. It would be enough. Bolan would eliminate the cave's guards and get the three men to safety. Nobody would notice them missing for a while. And by that time, some sort of evacuation should have been organized. "Should have been" being the operative phrase.

The two sentries were standing, slack jawed, staring at the carnage of the camp. A solitary rocket whizzed away from the brow of the neighboring hill, detonating against a burning APC. One of the sentries pointed to the launch site of the rocket-propelled grenade. Bolan drew a bead on him and squeezed the FAMAS's trigger, sending three rounds downrange. The sentry staggered under the impact, falling sidewise. His fellow soldier turned toward the sound of the shots, unlimbering his rifle. Too late. Another three bullets caught him in the chest, throwing him backward.

Bolan approached the cave in a crouched position, weapon up, ready to fire on another target. A quick scan of the camp showed a few remaining soldiers staggering around in confusion, unsure where to begin with damage control. Bouh was climbing into the Ratel. Bolan crept past one of the corpses and entered the blackness of the cave.

"Who's that?" The voice was weak, watery.

"Me," Bolan replied.

"You sure took your time," Douglas said.

"Still alive? I was waiting for you to croak before I mounted a rescue."

"Yeah, well, your timing sucks. I figured you were back when things began to go boom. Your calling card. So what happens now? Is Bouh dead?"

"Not yet. First we have to get you out of the cave and onto the hill. There should be some sort of extraction soon, but I'm not sure when. Failing that, we have to find a working vehicle and get to Lemonnier, or extract with the mercs."

"Sounds like a piss-poor plan. You know our hands are still cuffed? Tried doing that thing you did, but it hurt too much." Douglas was struggling to his feet. Bolan could sense Sanner and Twohig leaning against the cave wall, doing their best to stay upright.

"I'm going out now. Walk forward slowly," Bolan directed.

He led the three prisoners out of the cave, into the night, which now glowed orange from burning fires. And straight into somebody's gun sights.

Bolan reacted instantly, dropping to his knees, bringing his rifle around. He held off as the other figure lowered his weapon.

Streib.

"Figured you could use some help," the major said. Krulak and a couple of others stood to one side. "Bouh is making off in his APC. Do you want to go after him?"

"Yeah."

"Thought so. There's an untouched ACMAT down there with what looks like a .50 cal. Some of my guys have been sniping off anybody who shows an interest in it. You interested?"

Bolan considered for a moment. A nighttime pursuit against an armored vehicle that could reach up to sixty miles an hour and armed with what? A .50 caliber? A 7.62 mm? A 20 mm cannon? It would be extremely risky. On the other hand, allowing Bouh to escape back to his barracks and make excuses, cause an international incident by claiming that US troops had murdered his men, was not an option. Bolan's considerations lasted less than a heartbeat.

"Let's do it."

Streib nodded. "Sergeant, get these men back to the Renault and give them aid. Wait for me. I'll be accompanying... I don't even know your name."

"It's irrelevant."

"Mr. Irrelevant to capture or kill Bouh."

"Sorry, Major, but no." Krulak stepped up close. "You're the CEO of the company and are responsible for the men's paychecks, and you're the only one who can access the money. You should stay. I should go."

"Dammit, Krulak, I..."

"Krulak goes," Bolan ordered, taking charge. "Major, get my friends some medical attention. Sergeant, with me."

Bolan left with Krulak in tow, leaving a stunned Streib to organize the evac.

The Executioner and the former sergeant had their weapons ready as they crossed the remains of the camp, heading toward the untouched all-terrain vehicle. They passed burning tents and stepped around corpses. A couple of surviving Djiboutians were creeping toward the French ACMAT, hoping to avoid the attention of the snipers in the hills. A small pile of bodies lay around the vehicle, testimony to the mercenaries' accuracy. Bolan put one soldier down with a triburst from his automatic rifle. Krulak fired twice, filling his target with six rounds of lead. The two men encountered no resistance as they reached the ACMAT. They scanned the remains of the camp to make sure. No interest in them at all.

"You drive," Bolan said as he reloaded and shouldered his rifle. He climbed into the bed of the truck and examined the .50-caliber Browning M2 machine gun that was mounted on the rear. It was fully loaded and ready to go. Bolan pulled back the lever to arm the "Ma Deuce." The powerful machine gun was capable of firing 450 rounds per minute. Would it be enough to stop Bouh's APC?

"You ready?" Krulak started the big engine.

"Yeah," Bolan replied.

TWENTY MINUTES LATER they caught up with the Ratel. They bounced across the desert without headlights, not wanting to give away their position. Now there was enough light in the sky to see by. Dawn was breaking and ahead of them was a rooster's tail of dust, kicked up by the speeding APC. Krulak increased the speed of their captured truck.

"How do you want to play this?" Krulak yelled over the roar of the engine. "That vehicle's also armed with a .50 cal."

"Not sure," Bolan yelled back. "Get us in close, right behind them."

In a race, on a flat surface, the two vehicles would have been equally matched. As it was, Bouh's Ratel was moving fast but not at top speed. The personnel carrier was one hundred yards ahead when Krulak pulled in directly behind it. If there was a gunner in the turret, then he hadn't spotted them yet.

"You see that?" Bolan shouted.

"What?"

"The rear hatch is damaged. It isn't closed."

The rear hatch was swinging open a foot or two, then slamming shut again as the APC bounced over the rough terrain. Bolan recalled that it had been hit by an RPG.

"I have an idea. Get us right in close, almost to the door. I want us there before we go up that slope."

"Roger." Krulak's foot was flat against the floor. The ACMAT drew closer and closer. Still the gunner hadn't seen them.

Closer. Closer.

Bolan was choking on the dust kicked up by the six fat tires of the armored carrier. His eyes were narrowed to slits. Krulak shouted something, but it was lost over the cacophony of the two engines. He waited.

They were a mere three yards behind.

The APC slowed slightly as it ascended the rise. Krulak dropped back a little.

The rear hatch swung open, pulled agape by gravity.

Bolan could see a little way inside.

It was more than enough.

The Executioner depressed the twin button triggers with his thumbs, and the Ma Deuce bellowed to life. He held the triggers down for a full two seconds, pouring at least twenty heavy rounds into the vehicle before the hatch swung shut again. He hadn't seen a living target to shoot at, but he didn't need to. The heavily armored floor plates of the carrier would cause the bullets to ricochet, bounce around like peas in a tin can. And hopefully hit something.

At least that was the idea.

BOUH CLASPED BOTH hands over his ears. He was screaming. The soldier in the turret was screaming. The driver was screaming. The attack had been completely unexpected. The gunner's right leg lay severed on the floor. Bouncing with the APC. Blood was

squirting everywhere. The man was held in place by
straps. He couldn't fall out of the turret, even though
he wanted to.

"Shut up!" Bouh shouted. "Shut up! Stop screaming. I order you." Bouh could not stand it. The man
continued his high-pitched wail, oblivious to everything except pain. With shaking hands the general
drew his automatic pistol and shot the dying soldier
twice in the back. The man shuddered and died.

"Drive! Drive faster!" Bouh's voice was hoarse,
shrill. He didn't know if the driver heard him or not.
He glanced over his shoulder, eyes wide as the broken
rear hatch swung open again.

He ducked back as his enemy once again opened
fire. The driver jerked and shuddered as the rounds
penetrated his chair, tearing him to pieces. His now-
dead foot fell from the accelerator, the Ratel instantly
losing speed. The shooting stopped as the enemy drove
around the Ratel, barely missing it.

Bouh had to get away. He had to. Run. Hide. His
enemies may yet overlook him.

He fumbled with his restraining harness, cursing,
his fingers barely responding. There was a click as the
belt was released. The APC stalled and rolled to a stop.
Bouh staggered out of the blood-splattered chair and
hobbled to the rear hatch. The open rear hatch. He still
had his pistol gripped in his hand. He could still fight
back. He was a soldier. Trembling slightly, he climbed
out into the early-morning light. And took a step.

Then another one.

After four steps he looked around—right at the escaped spy, who was manning a machine gun. One of
his own machine guns. The driver was one of the mer-

cenaries. Bouh didn't see any others. Only two men. Then he stood a chance. If he could shoot fast enough.

He brought his right arm up.

MACK BOLAN DIDN'T give the renegade general a chance. As the arm came up, Bolan depressed the two trigger buttons, sending a stream of metal into the general.

Bouh literally came apart. Disintegrated.

The three-second burst was overkill. When Bolan released the triggers and the gun smoke cleared, little remained of the ambitious Bouh. Most of him was completely unidentifiable, spread over the desert sands.

THEY MADE IT back to the rendezvous, Bolan riding in the shotgun seat. Douglas and the two Trenchard employees were sitting in the rear of the Renault VAB. Bolan realized this was the first time that he had seen Sanner and Twohig. He had never spoken to them except in the pitch black of the cave.

"You look like a sand monster. You're covered in it. And?" Douglas asked, clutching a half-full bottle of water.

"It's done," Bolan replied. "Now, give me some of that water." He poured some of the water over his face, washing the grime away. The rest he drank.

Streib was listening to Krulak, nodding. Then he strode over to Bolan.

"You want a ride with us?" he asked.

Bolan shook his head. "No, I think you'll find that's our ride." He pointed to the west where a shape was slowly materializing in the sky, accompanied by a familiar racket.

"A Navy Seahawk," Streib said. "I think it's time for us to be on our way."

"What ship are you sneaking out on? I'll ask the Navy to give it wide berth."

"The MV *Cape Faith*. It's a rust bucket. What?" Mack Bolan had started to laugh.

EPILOGUE

Dallas, Texas

"Lesley! Lesley! Where are you? Damn that woman!" Robert Trenchard slammed his briefcase onto his secretary's desk. He felt both furious and scared. Furious because his personal secretary was not behind her desk, furious because he was the first in the office. He had to switch on his own lights! He had no idea where everybody was. But they would be sorry when they did roll in.

Deep down he knew something was wrong. The elevator had been empty. There had been nobody manning the main reception desk.

There had been no word from General Bouh for two days.

No word from Djibouti at all. Trenchard cursed himself for entering into an alliance with that fat African general. Cursed himself for trusting the man to keep to his end of the bargain. He had borrowed heavily, investing in the promised oil of Djibouti.

No news was bad news.

He all but kicked open his door, flicked on the lights and stopped. Sitting behind his oak desk in his high backed leather chair was a man he had never seen before. A man dressed in a black polo who held a pistol pointed directly between his eyes.

"Who...who...?" His voice shook. Trenchard blinked and cursed that weakness, as well.

He noticed that the man's eyes were ice blue. Cold. Chilling.

"I'm Djibouti." The voice was frozen.

Trenchard felt his knees buckle. It was over. He knew that now. Something had gone catastrophically wrong. His company, the company his great-grandfather had begun, was about to collapse. He would be declared bankrupt and have to face all sorts of questions. He'd be the laughingstock of the oil world.

"Sit down," the man commanded. Trenchard considered resisting, saying no. He could still bluff his way out of this mess. There had to be something to salvage.

The sound of the pistol being cocked was the loudest sound he had ever heard in his life.

On wobbling knees he crossed the floor and sat in one of his guest chairs. He had never sat in one before. The opposite side of the desk was his.

The pistol never wavered.

"Listen," he said, "listen. It was General Bouh. It was Bouh. He made me..."

"Bouh's dead."

Trenchard rubbed his eyes.

"Are you going to shoot me?" he asked.

"I should. You're a traitor to the United States."

"I am not!" Trenchard shouted.

"Bouh was using your money to fund an al Qaeda–backed coup. Your money. Do you know how many people have died because of your greed? Do you know how many would have died if the attack on the USS *Ford* had been successful?"

"I...I have no knowledge of those things. Bouh..."

"Planted bombs and attempted to kill two CIA agents. As it was, the ground floor of the hotel was devastated. Twenty-six people died."

"I had nothing to do with it!"

"You have everything to do with it. Without you Bouh would not have had his funding. I'm sure some other greedy businessman would have stepped up, but it was you. A friend of mine wants to make an example of you. You're going to be put on trial. Your staff has been sequestered in a room downstairs. They're being questioned by the Justice Department as we speak. You're locked out of your computers. Your bank accounts have been frozen. The telephones are blocked. Your home is being searched. Your wife and daughter are being held for their own safety at a secure facility. It's over, Trenchard."

"The CIA men?"

"What about them?"

"What happened to them?"

"One was evacuated to the USS *Ford*, along with your two employees Bouh was holding hostage. From there they were taken out to the military base before being flown out to Ramstein in Germany for medical attention. Bouh had a private detective watching the families of your employees. That man has been brought in for questioning."

"So what happens now?"

"We wait."

"For what?"

They heard the elevator down the corridor ping in the silence of the office.

"That."

Mack Bolan stood and holstered his weapon. Without looking at Trenchard he walked away, out of the office.

Trenchard didn't watch him leave. It was all over. He was going to need a good lawyer.

He looked for his briefcase, which contained his cell phone. He didn't see it. He had to have left it on Lesley's desk. He stood and turned, just as a man with an unlit cigar stuck in a corner of his mouth entered the office accompanied by two uniformed police officers and several men in suits. The man held up his credentials.

"Robert Trenchard? Justice Department. You're under arrest."

* * * * *

COMING SOON FROM

GOLD EAGLE®

Available May 5, 2015

THE EXECUTIONER® #438
THE CARTEL HIT – *Don Pendleton*

Facing off against a Mexican cartel,
the Executioner races to secure the lone
witness to a brutal double murder.

DEATHLANDS® #122
FORBIDDEN TRESPASS – *James Axler*

While Ryan and the companions take on a
horde of hungry cannibals, something far
more sinister—and ravenous—lurks beneath
their feet…

OUTLANDERS® #73
HELL'S MAW – *James Axler*

The Cerberus warriors must confront an alien
goddess who can control men's minds. But are
they strong enough to eliminate this evil interloper
bent on global domination?

ROGUE ANGEL™ #54
DAY OF ATONEMENT – *Alex Archer*

A vengeful fanatic named Cauchon plans to
single-handedly resurrect the violence of the
Inquisition to put Annja and Roux on trial…
and a guilty verdict could mean death.

Bolan heard the clink of metal on metal as the *a la muerte* soldier took another step closer, his equipment giving him away.

The guy was muttering to himself as he edged around the twisted roots of the tree and moved along its length. He stepped into Bolan's field of vision, and when he tilted his weapon, Bolan caught the dull gleam of light as it rippled along the barrel. That gave him his target, and Bolan intended to make use of it.

In one swift motion, the Executioner sprang from his hiding spot, grasping the guy's throat with his left hand as he rose to his full height, his right striking hard at the midsection of the exposed torso. The Tanto's cold blade sliced through clothing and sank in up to the hilt.

He felt the man shudder as he slid the penetrating blade left to right to extend the wound. A harsh groan burst from the Mexican's lips. Bolan slid his left hand around to the back of the guy's neck, yanking him forward, pulling his body in closer to the cutting blade. He felt warm blood oozing from the stab site.

Bolan pulled the weakening man in against the log, leaning on him hard, feeling the tremors that followed the damage done by the knife. The guy let out a long, ragged sigh as he began to slip to the ground. Bolan kept up the pressure until all movement and sound ceased. He pulled out the knife and cleaned the steel blade against the man's shirt, then sheathed it.

He could hear faint noises coming from the headset the man was wearing. Bolan slipped the comset from the body, held the earpiece close and listened to the transmission. He identified two voices. One ordered the other to silence, then spoke in swift Spanish.

"Enrico, what is going on? Talk to me. Where are you?"

"I found him," Bolan said, keeping his voice low. "You want to come and see?"

There was a brief silence.

"You are not Enrico… Who are you?"

"The one you cannot find. The one who is going to send you to Hell."

Don't miss
THE CARTEL HIT by Don Pendleton,
available May 2015 wherever
Gold Eagle® books and ebooks are sold.

JAMES AXLER
DEATHLANDS

The top of the food chain has never seemed so high...

Read on for a sneak preview of
FORBIDDEN TRESPASS
by **James Axler**

Ryan wanted the enemy to run, and preferably not stop until he and his companions had escaped.

He saw J.B. coolly step into the road and fire a medium burst from his Uzi. A man to Ryan's left screamed and clutched his paunch as a line of red dots was stitched across it. He fell howling and kicking to the ground.

Ryan shifted targets and fired. Another man fell.

The chill joined at least a dozen others fallen in the roadway. At the rear of the mob, which had lost momentum and had begun to mill about, Ryan saw a tall woman, just visible before the bend. She had raven-black hair and creamy skin. She looked shocked, and her eyes were wide.

It was Wymie, the woman responsible for all their problems—including the fact they were now fighting for their lives against what seemed like half the population of the ville.

"Fireblast," he said, and lowered his aim to shoot a young man trying to point some kind of flintlock at them.

"Why didn't you chill her, lover?" Krysty called from the cover of the nettles across the road.

"She's the leader," he called back. "She's beat. She'll spread her exhaustion to the rest once we chill or drive off the hard core."

Even as he said that, he saw it start to happen. The initial volley of blasterfire from his team, crouched in cover to either side of the thoroughfare, had dropped so many of the attackers they formed a living roadblock. Those behind, mad-eyed and baying for blood a heartbeat before, now faltered. This mob had clearly let self-preservation reassert itself in the face of their waning bloodlust.

They were done. It was all over but for the fleeing.

Then, from the corner of his lone eye, Ryan saw a skinny old man, standing by the side of the road, leveling a single-action Peacemaker at Ryan's head.

He already knew he was nuked, even as his brain sent his body the impulse to dive aside.

The ancient blaster and its ancient shooter alike vanished in a giant yellow muzzle-flash. It instantly echoed in a blinding red flash inside Ryan's skull.

Then blackness. Then nothing.

Don't miss
FORBIDDEN TRESPASS by James Axler,
available May 2015 wherever
Gold Eagle® books and ebooks are sold.